READERS LOVE *THE BABY DRAGON BOOKSHOP*

'A cozy, magical and bookish delight that left me smiling long after I finished.'

'*The Baby Dragon Bookshop* is pure joy from beginning to end.'

'This was my most anticipated book of the year and I absolutely loved it.'

'If you want a cozy, charming read (with added baby dragons) I definitely recommend this one.'

'This story was honestly so sweet and cozy. Cuteness overload with just a hint of chaos.'

'I absolutely adoreeeeeeed this book!'

'This book completely stole my heart. I loved how the story mixed bookshop coziness with gentle magic. It felt like stepping into a world that smells of paper, tea, and a hint of smoke.'

'This book was so fun and sweet.'

'This is like being wrapped in a cozy blanket and eating comfort snacks near a warm fire.'

'The world building was whimsical, the dragons stole every scene, and the ending wrapped things up in that warm, fuzzy way that makes you smile.'

'Completely adorable and had me smiling from start to finish.'

'Such a cute, cozy story.

'The perfect cozy romantasy if you're looking for a lighthearted and happy read.'

'A delightful, lighthearted romantasy that blends small-town charm, adorable baby dragons and the enemies-to-lovers trope.'

'I think this is my favourite Baby Dragon book!'

'I love these books so much! They're so cute and cozy.'

'These are cute romance movies in book form (with adorable baby dragons!)'

'Yet another fantastic lighthearted book in The Baby Dragon series.'

'A new, sweet and romantic addition to my favourite series!'

'I highly recommend reading this book. I cannot wait to read the next book in this series.'

'The third book in The Baby Dragon series did not disappoint! It was just as charming, lighthearted, romantic, and full of baby dragons as the rest of the series.'

'Omg these books. Absolutely too cute to handle.'

A. T. Qureshi is a Pakistani, Muslim American who adores words. She is the author of the Baby Dragon series and the upcoming Dragon Racer series.

Aamna grew up on Long Island, New York, in a very loud household, surrounded by English (for school), Urdu (for conversation), and Punjabi (for emotion). Much of her childhood was spent being grounded for reading past her bedtime, writing stories in the backs of her notebooks, and being scolded by teachers for passing chapters under the tables. Through her writing, she wishes to inspire a love for the beautiful country and rich culture that informed much of her identity.

When she's not writing, she loves to travel to new places where she can explore different cultures or to Pakistan where she can revitalize her roots. She also loves baking complicated desserts, drinking fancy teas and coffees, watching sappy rom-coms, and going for walks about the estate (her backyard). She currently lives in New York.

By the same author:

Young Adult:
The Lady or the Lion
The Man or the Monster
When a Brown Girl Flees
My Big, Fat, Desi Wedding
A Witch's Guide to Love and Poison

Adult:
If I Loved You Less
The Baby Dragon Cafe
The Baby Dragon Bakery

The BABY DRAGON BOOKSHOP

A. T. QURESHI

avon.

Published by AVON
A division of HarperCollins*Publishers* Ltd
1 London Bridge Street
London SE1 9GF

www.harpercollins.co.uk

HarperCollins*Publishers*
Macken House, 39/40 Mayor Street Upper
Dublin 1, D01 C9W8, Ireland

A Paperback Original 2026
26 27 28 29 30 LBC 8 7 6 5 4

A catalogue record for this book is available from the British Library.

ISBN: 978-0-00-874296-6

Set in Birka by HarperCollins*Publishers* India

Printed and Bound in the United States of America

For Isra,
my dearest.

CHAPTER 1

Snow fell from the sky in thick clumps, blanketing the hills of Starshine Valley. Emmeline Sterling watched from the window as the snowflakes fluttered down, a steady stream of white against the cold and dark night.

Winter was always her favorite season, but there was no time to appreciate the season's beauty now. Taking a deep breath, she returned to her task: she needed to find a needle and thread.

"Aha!" she spoke aloud in the empty bedroom, spotting what she was looking for in the dresser drawer. "There you are." She grabbed the needle and thread, shutting the drawer with a snap.

Her heels clicked on the marble floors as she exited the bedroom, joining the sounds of the party raging below: the clinking of champagne flutes, the quick bursts of melody, the laughter and chatter, and, of course, baby dragons playing (or fighting) together. Wind whistled outside the great Sterling estate, home of Emmeline's only paternal uncle and favorite cousins.

Today, she was here for her youngest cousin, Genevieve, who was turning twenty-two. Ginny was throwing a joint birthday party for her and her baby dragon, Fang, who had just turned one. Only the most enthusiastic threw parties for their baby dragons, and Ginny was very enthusiastic indeed.

Emmeline walked down the stairs, back to the party, where Ginny and Fang were attached at the hip. Fang never strayed more than half a foot away from Ginny, his black scales glimmering under the lights, his purple eyes adoring as he looked over at his rider. Dressed in a black velvet jumpsuit, her dark hair pulled back in a neat fishtail braid, Ginny looked at her baby dragon with equal affection. A few baby dragons played outside in the snow, while a handful were on the dancefloor, bouncing to the music beneath the lights.

The party was in the ballroom, which was used in the winter months, when it was too cold to have parties outside on the grounds. As Emmeline searched for her aunt, she was stopped by cousins who wanted to say hello and ask her advice, and she paused to ruffle nieces' and nephews' hair.

She petted baby dragons and evaded uncles' questions, before finally, *finally* making it to the other end of the ballroom, where her aunt was seated at one of the tables, her mood twice as sour as the citrus soufflé served for dessert.

"I'm back!" Emmeline said, sitting down on the empty chair beside Auntie Marie, the eldest of the Sterling siblings. She wore a sleeveless navy blue sheath dress with an embroidered shawl around her shoulders, her dark hair pulled up in a neat twist to reveal the pearls on her ears and necklace.

"Darling, you took your time," Marie said, clutching her shawl around her arms tighter. She leaned in close, dropping her voice. "Did you find it?"

"Yes, Auntie," Emmeline replied. She held up the needle and thread, and Marie released an exhale. She dropped her shawl from one shoulder, revealing a slight tear in the seam on the dress's shoulder. Emmeline quickly threaded the needle and got to work.

"I will be having *words* with my tailor," Marie fussed, brows crinkled with distress. "I cannot imagine how such a thing could have occurred."

"Don't worry," Emmeline coaxed, fingers moving quickly. "Just a moment and you'll be back on the dancefloor with Grandad."

Emmeline winked, and Marie finally smiled.

"Your grandad needs to share his secrets with the rest of us," Marie said, shaking her head. "I have no idea how his knees haven't given out!"

"All done!" Emmeline said, finishing off the stitch. She pulled a compact mirror from her purse, then opened it for Marie to see.

"Excellent," Marie said. Emmeline stood, offering her aunt her hand.

"Can I get you anything else?" Emmeline asked.

"A coffee would be splendid, dear," Marie said. "All that tension has given me a headache."

"Of course." Emmeline set off, finding a waiter on the sidelines to bring Marie her coffee. "Decaf, with two creams," she instructed. If Marie had caffeine this late at night, she'd never be able to fall asleep.

The waiter nodded, heading off to complete the order and, after kissing her aunt goodbye, Emmeline scanned the room, catching sight of a table full of discarded dishes. She tsked, then stalked over to another member of the staff.

"Can you please pick up the dishes from that table?" she asked, pointing it out.

Then, there was a spilled drink, and Emmeline had to make sure that got cleaned up before somebody slipped. All night, she'd been keeping her eyes peeled, and little things kept popping up.

Releasing a sigh, Emmeline rubbed her temples. Luckily, the party was almost over, and with it, the tension of the last few weeks would be over, as well.

When Ginny had asked Emmeline to help with throwing the joint birthday party, of course Emmeline had said yes, even though Ginny's mother, Cecilia, was well-versed in throwing such parties.

"I can't ask my mom because you know she will just do too much," Ginny had explained.

"Don't worry," Emmeline had replied. "I'll handle it."

She had spent the last few weeks organizing it all, and the party had gone off without a hitch, which was to be expected. Emmeline Sterling never failed. Things always went flawlessly according to plan, and everyone had complimented her all evening for a job so well done.

She was used to the praise, but still it warmed her, and she tried to hold onto that now as her head pounded. Eyes scanning the ballroom, she looked around at her expansive family, taking in the sight of laughing children and couples holding hands, cousins jesting and aunts scheming, along with some tiny baby dragons asleep in bassinets, while other baby dragons played with one another.

Emmeline smiled to herself. The Sterling clan was big; her father was the youngest of five, and she had many, many cousins, who were divided into two sections: the older ones in their late thirties and early forties who were married with children, and then the younger ones who were all in their mid- to late twenties and early thirties.

In the younger section, Aiden was the oldest, then Emmeline, but Aiden was not that involved, so it was Emmeline who took care of everyone and everything. While she did love being there for people, she was growing tired.

She thought of stealing away for a moment but, just as she turned, she caught two of her nephews arguing, both of their little faces turning red. With a sigh, she walked over to them, crouching down to grab hold of both their shoulders.

"Hey, you two," she said, and the five- and six-year-olds turned to her.

"He won't play with me!" the younger of the two complained, lip wobbling.

"You keep cheating!" the older one told Emmeline.

It was well past their bedtimes.

"Why don't you both go find your mothers, hm?" Emmeline suggested. "I think there's hot chocolate."

Both little boys forgot their argument. "With marshmallows?" the younger one asked.

"With marshmallows," Emmeline confirmed, standing up straight again.

"Race you!" the six-year-old said, and then they were off.

Emmeline watched as they ran into the crowd, past a familiar face.

"Emmy!" Saphira called, spotting her. She waved, and Emmeline went to where Saphira stood with Aiden. Saphira was one of the newest additions to the Sterling clan, as the massive engagement ring stacked with a diamond wedding band on her hand would attest to.

The sweet owner of the Baby Dragon Cafe was dressed in a flowy midi dress in a deep pink color, her wavy black hair done up in a complicated updo—which must have been courtesy of her mother-in-law. Ginny had always been boyish, and Cecilia had long since yearned for a daughter-in-law who would allow Cecilia to dress her up. Saphira had a girly and romantic style and thus happily obliged.

Her dress was accessorized with a stack of gold bangles and a simple nose-pin, both of which she always wore, as well as heels that had long since been kicked off. Her husband was beside her, and Emmeline's cousin Aiden smiled as she walked over to them.

"I feel like I haven't seen you all night!" Saphira said. One of her arms was around Aiden's waist as she was tucked into his side, but with her free hand, she reached for Emmeline.

"Oh, you know me," Emmeline replied, pulling Saphira out of Aiden's arms and twirling her. Saphira laughed.

"Hey, don't steal my dance partner," Aiden objected, wrapping his arms around his wife from behind. She giggled, leaning back against his chest as she held his forearm. The sleeves of his white dress shirt were rolled up.

Without heels, Saphira was average height, considerably

shorter than Emmeline, but she fit adorably in Aiden's arms. Emmeline wrinkled her nose at them fondly. "You two are too cute."

Aiden smiled, while Saphira giggled.

"We're just missing Millie tonight," Saphira said. Emmeline felt a slight stab in her chest at the mention of her little sister.

"I miss her so much," Emmeline replied.

She didn't have many close friends—she had never needed any, not with a family as large as hers. She had always had a built-in partner-in-crime in her sister, Millicent, who was a year younger than her. Unfortunately, Millie had gotten married a few years ago and moved hours away.

With two children and another on the way, she didn't visit more than a few times a year, and Emmeline sorely missed her, though she was used to the ache of it, now. Sometimes, it almost felt as if this was how it always was, and she was surprised to recall her memories in which Millie lived in Starshine Valley. It was strange how when you got used to things changing, it almost felt as if the way things were hadn't happened at all.

Emmeline could barely recall a time in which she didn't know Saphira—the bright soul had quickly become like a close cousin to Emmeline. After all, Aiden was Emmeline's favorite cousin, his rank only increasing ever since he had gotten together with Saphira, who Emmeline had technically known first, as Saphira sourced her coffee for the Baby Dragon from Emmeline's dragon-roasted coffee company, Inferno.

"She's due any day now, isn't she?" Aiden asked.

"Her babies are *so* cute!" Saphira said. Millie's son, Noah, was four while her daughter, Ira, was two.

"They take after me," Emmeline said proudly, lifting her chin. She and Millie often got confused as twins, and Millie's kids definitely took after their mother.

"You get all the credit, then?" Aiden teased.

"Of course!" Emmeline replied. "I'm the one who told her, I said, 'Millie, you *must* marry a man with weak genes because if *my* nieces and nephews don't look like me, I will riot.' And then she did just that."

Saphira and Aiden both laughed. "I guess we need to find a man with weak genes for you," Saphira said.

Emmeline waved a hand. "Don't worry about me."

"Why are we worrying about Emmeline?" a familiar voice asked.

Emmeline turned to see Lavinia Williams join them. She was wearing a forest green dress that hugged her curves, along with platform heels that added a few inches to her short height. A delicate gold necklace hung from her neck; in the center was a small letter T.

The inspiration for the letter stood beside her: her boyfriend, Theo Noon. Tall and lanky, in slim black trousers and a sage green button-down shirt. They were holding mugs of hot chocolate in opposite hands while their other hands were clasped together, fingers entwined.

The pair were childhood best friends but had only started dating last year. Lavinia used to work at the Baby Dragon, and Theo worked there as Saphira's business manager, as well as the manager of the Baby Dragon Bakery, the bakery section of the cafe.

"We're not," Emmeline replied, shifting the focus away from how single she was. "We're more focused on how cute these two are."

"They're still in their honeymoon phase," Lavinia said.

"They've pretty much been in their honeymoon phase since they met," Emmeline replied, earning laughter from the rest of them. Aiden and Saphira didn't even attempt to disagree; they only looked at one another with stars in their eyes, lips turned up into smiles.

"*We* could be in our honeymoon phase, too, you know," Theo said, pinching Lavinia's side. She squealed.

"Stop trying to propose to me!" Lavinia hit his chest. "Not until I graduate in May!"

What a problem to have, Emmeline thought wryly, a painful twang reverberating in her chest. Lavinia and Saphira were both younger than her, and it was Ginny's twenty-second birthday, which made Emmeline feel positively *ancient* at twenty-nine, not at all helped by the fact that she was turning thirty in January with no possibility of a grand romance in sight.

She had only had one serious relationship post-university. Since then, she'd had her flirtations and her fun, but there didn't seem to be anybody who could pierce her very soul.

Shaking her head, Emmeline pushed the thought away before it sent her into a spiral. She focused on the conversation at hand.

"How's the ring hunt going?" Saphira asked Lavinia, who made a pensive sound.

"It's going," she said. "They're all just so pretty! I can't narrow down the shape."

Aiden and Theo exchanged a fondly amused glance over the girls' heads. Then the song changed; the chords made Saphira's eyes light up. Emmeline grinned. It was one they both adored.

"Sorry, Aiden," Emmeline said, taking Saphira's hand, "but your girl is mine for this one."

She stole Saphira away, and Saphira grabbed Lavinia as she went, the girls walking over to the crowd of dancing partygoers. Two baby dragons were already bouncing on the dancefloor, jumping up to try and catch the colorful strobe lights.

Across the dancefloor, the birthday girl caught sight of them. Her mouth fell open, and she ran over. "Wait for me!" Ginny cried.

The girls opened their little circle, pulling Ginny in as they danced together, laughing and having fun.

Until Emmeline caught the sight of flames in the corner of her eye.

"Uh oh," Lavinia said, slowing.

Emmeline narrowed her eyes. "Don't worry," she told the girls, catching Ginny's gaze. "I've got it."

With a squeeze of Ginny's hand, Emmeline was off, grabbing two members of the staff as she went. At the scene of the crime was Motu, her brother's baby dragon, who had lit a tablecloth on fire and was now watching the flames with shocked purple eyes.

"Motu!" Emmeline scolded, and the baby dragon immediately looked chagrined, hiding his face behind his wings. She tsked at him. As the staff members put out the fire, Emmeline knew it wasn't the baby who was at fault, but his rider.

She scanned the crowd for Haris.

When she spotted him, he was laughing with their cousin Oliver and Emmeline's other brother, Naveed. Both her brothers looked like her, though their skin was a lighter shade of brown.

Oliver caught Emmeline's gaze first, and he immediately stopped talking, elbowing Haris apprehensively. Emmeline crossed her arms against her chest as her younger brother followed Oliver's gaze, then swallowed. He slowly walked toward her.

"Uh . . . Everything okay, Emmy?" Haris asked, giving her a small smile. His dimples made an appearance. He was trying to be cute. She glared.

"You tell me," she said, voice sharp. Motu walked over to Haris, then, the chubby little dragon's head hanging low. Haris was twenty-four and in medical school; he was not doing the best job training his baby dragon, and Emmeline ended up babysitting half the time anyway.

She had told him on a number of occasions not to hatch his egg while still in medical school, but had he listened? No. Sometimes, she really hated being right.

Haris had the decency to look embarrassed as he scooped Motu into his arms. Emmeline looked over at the burnt tablecloth the staff members were replacing.

"Look at Fang!" Emmeline scolded, gesturing to Ginny's well-behaved baby dragon calmly bobbing his head to the music as he flapped his wings.

Even though Motu and Fang were a month apart—with Motu being older—Fang was much better-trained. While Ginny devoted her time to Fang after graduating from university last May, accelerating Fang's training until he had his first flight at just seven months, Motu had only had his first flight last month, and was still a bit rough around the edges due to Haris being too busy with medical school.

"Sorry," Haris said, sheepish. Emmeline gave him a dirty look. She didn't even need to say anything; the look was enough for her brother to understand how disappointed she was. He winced.

She took Motu from him, and the baby dragon came to her willingly, despite how she had scolded his rider. The little dragon knew their family dynamics.

Taking Motu, she went upstairs, away from the crowded party in the ballroom to a much quieter section of the mansion. As she passed by the living room, Motu touched a paw to her cheek, looking up at her with big purple eyes.

Her heart softened.

"Your rider needs to be more responsible," she whispered to Motu, smushing his face with her free hand. Motu flapped his wings. She laughed. "Come on."

She rang for a dragon caretaker to come look after the baby dragon, and a few moments later, one arrived, taking Motu from her. The caretaker left with Motu, and Emmeline was alone. In the quiet, she sighed and, as she turned, she caught sight of herself in a gilded framed mirror.

She was wearing an off-the-shoulder dress with dramatic bell sleeves, the gown floor-length but with a slit going up one thigh to reveal her strappy jeweled heels. While the outfit was still perfectly in place, her hair was coming undone. She pulled the jade hairpin out, and her hair cascaded down, falling to her hips. It was glossy and pitch-black, cut in long layers.

She shook her hair out, meeting her gaze in the reflection. Her kajal was a little smudged and her blood-red lipstick had faded, but she still looked picture-perfect. Rolling her shoulders, she adjusted her elaborate gold nose-ring, her only jewelry, then headed back towards the party.

And that was where she saw him. With deep brown skin and a clean-shaven face that showed off his defined facial features, he was easy to recognize, and heat spread through her as she took in the long, lean shape of his muscular body.

Luke Hayward.

Her enemy.

Emmeline stopped in her tracks before the living room, her heartbeat jumping violently. He was the only one up here, though he hadn't seemed to notice her just yet. Leaning against the wall, he was entranced with the view from the wide windows, watching the snow fall.

He was dressed in an all-black suit, sans tie, his black dress shirt open at the collar to reveal the chains around his neck. It wasn't the only jewelry he wore; rings covered almost every finger, and there was an earring looping in one ear. His signature look.

For a moment, Emmeline thought she was hallucinating. She really must have been tired. She took a step forward, looking closer. There was no way he was here.

At the sound of her heels, he turned. His gaze fell upon her. The devilish tilt of his lips sent sparks down her spine, informing her that he was in fact very much real.

"Hayward," she snapped, stalking over. He lifted off the wall easily, straightening. Emmeline had always been tall, and she was used to being one of the tallest in the room, especially with her high heels, but he was still taller, easily clearing six foot two. Another reason to hate him.

"Sterling," he said easily, eyes lighting with amusement.

Irritation burst through her as she stood before him. She didn't understand—what was he doing here? She had sent out the invites; she knew for certain he wasn't invited. He was not part of any of the Drakkon circles. He was a chimera owner and lived in Bayview, down by the lake. Starshine Valley was divided into hamlets, and everyone tended to stay in their own corner.

Except for him. He was always trying to poach her business. While her coffee was dragon-roasted, his was chimera-roasted. His business, Tempest, rivaled hers. She had started her business straight out of university seven years ago, and he had started his business about two years later, all but stealing her idea, though he applied it to chimeras.

He was a ruthless businessman—successful, gorgeous, heartless.

She knew he was trouble from the first time she had heard about him, when she was a senior in college and Millie was a junior claiming to be in love.

"What are you doing here?" she asked him now.

"Maybe the birthday girl invited me," Luke replied, running a hand through his long black hair. That made her vision turn red as a fierce feeling of protectiveness came over her.

Bridging the space between them, she poked his chest with a finger.

"Stay away from her," she snapped. "You've already broken one little sister's heart."

He cocked his head to the side, regarding her. His dark eyes were like coals, simmering with heat just beneath the surface, and his gaze pierced through her. "You got your revenge for that, if I recall."

She felt a stab of guilt at that—though there was no reason for her to. Emmeline was not the kind of person who had regrets.

Luke's gaze dropped down to where her finger was still on his chest. He made as if to bite it and, horrified, she snatched her hand away.

He looked up and met her aghast expression with a wolfish smile. Her pulse quickened, blood pounding through her veins like the beating of a drum.

She was about to do something drastic when she heard a voice say, "Ah, Luke, there you are."

CHAPTER 2

Luke Hayward didn't know what he was doing at Genevieve Sterling's birthday party, but he had come for two major reasons. The first was to speak to Emmeline, and that goal had come true.

She was as formidable and dangerous as any dragon and just as beautiful and thrilling. She was a ruthless businesswoman—successful, gorgeous, heartless. He didn't care that she had broken his heart all those years ago.

He had seen her earlier—she was impossible not to notice, though she hadn't noticed him. She was too busy running around, managing everything with efficiency.

He'd followed her upstairs to try and get her attention but then lost her, so he'd stopped to watch the snowfall before he'd heard the sound of heels clicking.

When he'd turned, there she had been, face blazing. She was stunning. It had taken him a moment to collect himself; even then, he'd done so with difficulty. She looked like she belonged in the pages of a magazine, or on a movie screen.

He couldn't believe she was real until she was stalking over, and he inhaled the scent of jasmine from her skin, at once familiar and foreign.

He had said something to rile her—he loved the look on her face when he pissed her off. It felt like watching a lightning strike, and he didn't care about how close he was to the danger.

Then he recalled the second reason he was here.

"Ah, Luke, there you are."

Simultaneously, he and Emmeline turned to see an old lady approach them both, her wrinkled hand clasping an ornately carved cane. It was Anh, the eighty-year-old matriarch of the Trang family, the representative family for the azura breed of dragons on the Dragon Council.

While Luke didn't know much about Drakkon politics, he did know that there were four members of the Dragon Council, one for each breed. Anh's nephew was the representative for the azuras, while Emmeline's uncle was the representative for the basaltas. The opala breed was represented by a Cartwright, and the garneta breed was represented by a Kiani.

Anh Trang was one of the richest women in Starshine Valley. She had a magic touch when it came to business, which was why Luke was interested in her.

He had been trying to get Anh to invest in his coffee-roasting company, Tempest, for *months*. She had finally gotten back to him, but not to set up a meeting. Instead, she had asked if he would be her plus-one to a birthday party of a family friend, and he had agreed immediately, figuring he could at least get her to warm up to him. The birthday party being a Sterling's was an added bonus, because he knew Emmeline would be here.

They had arrived late to the party, and he had spent most of the night trying to get on Anh's good side to secure an investment for Tempest. Unfortunately, his business wasn't doing well, but he had plans that could fix it. He just needed a chance.

It looked as if Anh had her own ideas, though.

"Anh!" Emmeline said, immediately straightening, her expression softening. She took a step back from Luke, holding a hand out for the old lady, who took it with a fond smile.

"Lovely to see you, darling," Anh said, as Emmeline and she kissed cheeks. Anh was almost a foot shorter than Emmeline, but still she stood tall, her back straight and chin lifted.

"I haven't seen you all night," Emmeline said, still holding Anh's hand. "Come, sit." She led Anh to a couch, helping Anh get comfortable on a sofa.

Luke watched with curiosity, the way he had throughout the night. Emmeline took care of everyone. He wondered if there was anyone who took care of her. He hoped so.

But then the image of her having a lover to take care of her entered his mind, and he frowned.

Starshine Valley was small; he'd surely know if she was in a serious relationship. He knew that she had her flirtations, that she was considered a bit of a heartbreaker. Men got involved at their own risk.

A risk he wouldn't mind taking, even if he had already been burned once before.

"Luke, dear, come join us," Anh said, voice soft.

Mentally scolding himself, Luke focused on the situation at hand. With a nod, he went over and sat down on an armchair across from the sofa. Emmeline sat on an identical armchair.

Anh looked at both of them and smiled. "It has been some time since I have attended such a party," she said, still holding her ornate cane in front of her. "I thought about killing two birds with one stone. My time is very precious, as you know."

Intrigue was clear on Emmeline's face, and Luke felt the same emotion spark through him. He listened intently as Anh continued.

"I wished to meet the both of you together, which is why I brought Luke here as my date," Anh said, looking pleased with herself.

"An opportunity I am truly grateful for," Luke replied, giving Anh a charming smile. Emmeline gave him an icy look but sobered at what Anh said next:

"I have been monitoring both of your businesses for some time," she said, folding her other hand on top of her cane. "I keep track of all the businesses in Starshine Valley, particularly those run by young blood. You have both been vying for me to invest in your companies."

Luke wasn't surprised Emmeline was striving for Anh to invest in her business, too: she had smart instincts; she always had.

"I am ready to invest," Anh said.

A thrill shot through him. *Finally*. After months of effort, things were moving forward. Tempest would be saved; he could continue to pay for his mother's medical bills.

Everything would be alright.

Luke smiled. "That is incredible news," he started, only for Anh to cut him off.

"I wasn't finished, darling," she said. "I have a proposal of my own."

Luke's heartbeat quickened. He could feel the unease radiating off Emmeline; she seemed to be bracing herself.

"The two of you should consolidate your businesses into one," Anh said. "Your products are similar enough, and such a step would surely increase profit margins."

The idea made Luke's heart beat even faster, though not with dread—with excitement. Despite their history, he would be open to such an idea.

Until Emmeline's sharp voice snapped out, "Absolutely not."

CHAPTER 3

Working with Luke was out of the question for Emmeline.

She had been trying to get Anh to invest in Inferno for months. Business was doing well, and she wanted to expand, but she needed investment money to take such a big step. Even if it was the only way, working with Luke was out of the question.

"Absolutely not," Emmeline said, voice leaving no room for negotiation. "Tempest is leagues behind Inferno. While consolidating would be to his company's advantage, it makes no sense for mine. I have no desire to move backwards."

Luke barked out a laugh at that. "We're not so far behind."

Emmeline bristled. In reality, she did know that what Luke said was true, but she couldn't tell Anh the real reason she refused to merge with Luke was because she couldn't stand him. Ordinarily, Emmeline could be relied upon for her professionalism, but Luke Hayward had an uncanny knack of making her behave in ways she otherwise wouldn't.

Around him, she felt entirely out of control—unhinged. And she preferred being hinged, thank you very much.

From her position on the couch, Anh looked from Emmeline to Luke, then back at Emmeline, her eyes assessing. For a moment, Emmeline considered ceding, but she refrained. She knew she couldn't trust Luke Hayward, of all people.

Releasing a sigh, Anh let out a thoughtful noise. "I am only going to invest in one company," Anh said. "Are you sure?"

Neither Emmeline nor Luke wasted a moment; they both immediately began talking over one another, leaning forward on their lounge chairs as they pitched their businesses.

"Tempest is a stronger candidate—"

"Inferno is the company to go with—"

"Our numbers—"

"Our distribution—"

"The reliability of the dragons—"

"The chimeras' work ethic—"

Frowning, Anh held up a hand, quieting both of them. "Don't give me a headache," she ordered, and both business-owners were immediately chagrined. Emmeline felt the urge to hang her head like a scolded child; she hated to disappoint.

"I did, of course, consider the possibility that you would be averse to consolidating," Anh said, looking at both of them carefully. As Anh assessed them, Emmeline straightened her already straight back, keeping her hands folded neatly on her lap.

She had never shied away from scrutiny; she knew she wasn't lacking. She made sure of it. Even so—there was something about the way Anh looked at her and Luke that made Emmeline nervous.

Her nerves only doubled when Anh's lips curled into a pleased smile. "I am sure you've both heard of the Tales & Tails Bookshop?" Anh asked, clasping her wrinkly hands together.

At the name, Emmeline's heart stopped entirely. Before she could stop herself, her gaze flicked over to Luke, just as he turned to her. His lips parted, and an expression she couldn't understand flitted across his face.

The Tales & Tails Bookshop was where they had first met all those years ago.

A memory entered her mind unbidden: the taste of tea sharp and bitter on her tongue, her back flush against a bookshelf as she snatched him closer.

It was such a vivid memory, even now. Her skin burned.

Snapping out of it, Emmeline focused on Anh, on the present: the party going on downstairs, the snow falling outside the big windows around her, and the businesswoman in front of her.

Beside her, Luke cleared his throat. From the corner of her eyes, she saw Luke flex his hand. *Did he remember it, too?* she wondered.

"Tales & Tails belongs to my younger brother, Minh," Anh said. "He's been after me to expand his bookshop with the addition of a coffee shop—he isn't very business-minded himself. The success of the bookshop can be credited entirely to me, so of course, now he wishes for me to tackle this undertaking, as well."

Anh rolled her eyes; Emmeline understood how she felt. Younger brothers could be quite vexing.

"Little brothers," Luke said fondly. As Anh smiled, Emmeline tried not to frown; she was going to say that.

"To the point: coffee is your forte," Anh continued. "Why don't you both get me proposals for how to include a coffee shop in the bookshop? Whichever proposal I prefer will secure the investment in their company. Plus, I'll add a stake in the bookshop as a bonus."

A buzz went through Emmeline. Along with the investment, a stake in the bookshop would be lucrative.

"Yes," Emmeline agreed immediately, her mind already whirring with ideas. The bookshop was a thriving slice of Starshine Valley and a flourishing community space; a coffee shop would do splendidly there.

"That does sound fun," Luke said. Emmeline didn't need to turn to know there would be a glint in his eyes.

"Splendid!" Anh said. "We'll need a deadline, of course. It's early December now, so how about the middle of January? Six weeks should be enough time."

"More than enough time," Emmeline replied. She turned to Luke. "Unless you would need more? I am happy to accommodate."

Her attempt to rile him only amused him further, which she detested sorely. "Oh, I know just how accommodating you can be," he said to her. The words made sparks skitter across her skin as Luke turned to Anh. "Six weeks is perfect." He flashed his teeth.

"Wonderful. That's settled then." Anh stood, holding onto her ornate cane. "I think it's time for me to have some cake."

Emmeline and Luke stood as well. "I'll take you,"

Emmeline said, stepping forward. Luke mirrored her, the both of them reaching out for Anh, who ignored them.

"I can manage on my own," Anh replied.

"Really I—" Emmeline began.

"Don't try and fuss over me, dear," Anh said, making Emmeline feel silly.

After Anh took her leave, Emmeline turned to Luke. He stood with his hands in his trouser pockets, making the open collar of his black shirt stretch open. Her gaze flicked over the two chains on his bare chest.

Emmeline made an irritated noise, giving him her best withering glare, which was quite withering indeed. Luke twitched, though he only doubled down on the arrogant posture.

"You might as well bow out now," she told him, putting her hands on her hips. "You do know everyone calls Tales & Tails the Baby Dragon Bookshop, don't you?" She raised a brow. "The last time I checked, you don't have a dragon. Best for you to stay on your side of the valley."

Where most people were easily scared off by Emmeline, Luke only smirked. He cocked his head to the side as he regarded her. "So threatened that you're already trying to deter me?" She narrowed her eyes as he continued: "From what I recall, you like a challenge."

Irritation flashed through her like a crack of lightning. "You don't know me."

"I did," he said, his gaze intense. "Once."

A shiver ran down her spine, making her feel unsettled.

"That wasn't real," she said, but her heart hammered all the same. "It was just pretend."

As Luke took a step toward her, Emmeline's breathing hitched. She inhaled the scent of his cologne. He smelled like winter: cypress and spruce and a biting chill.

"Pretend," he repeated, voice low. "Are you sure about that?"

The warmth of his body invaded her senses, and she clenched her jaw, feeling slightly weak in the knees. He still looked self-assured, but there was something else in his voice, as if the question was genuine.

But as soon as the flicker of emotion was there, it was gone. Emmeline must have imagined it. Luke was heartless, she reminded herself.

"Yes," Emmeline snapped. "Do what you want; I couldn't care less."

As she turned on her heels and stalked away, Emmeline was more determined than ever to secure the investment.

Seeing her company succeed was one thing—but beating Luke would be its own prize.

There was no way she could lose to Luke Hayward.

CHAPTER 4

Emmeline spent all of Sunday recovering from Ginny's party.

She was meant to be doing things like laundry and meal prep and a seven-step skincare routine—which she absolutely did do—but she was a multitasker at heart, so she was also mulling over ideas for the Tales & Tails coffee shop expansion.

The ideas stayed in her mind the next day, on Monday, when she was back to work. Currently, she was at Inferno's roasting plant, overseeing the day-to-day business of her company. The plant was where the green coffee beans arrived processed from the farm and were stored until it was time to roast, which was when her dragons came in.

Taking a sip of her karak chai, Emmeline walked out of her office on the second floor, which held the other offices and storage rooms. There were balconies looking down to the main floor, which was beneath a retractable roof of window panels, allowing natural light to flow in from above.

The main floor was where the roasting happened, and

where her dragons were now. Emmeline had three dragons who worked on roasting; each roast took about twenty minutes, before being cooled, then they were packaged and sent out for deliveries.

Going down the steps, Emmeline went to check on the dragons, though she was stopped along the way by an employee.

"Can you sign off on this delivery slip?" A clipboard was presented to her, and Emmeline quickly dashed along her signature.

She made it a few steps before she was stopped by another employee. "Is the Starshine Valley Diner the franchise, or is that the Starshine Diner?"

"The Starshine Diner is the franchise," Emmeline replied. "The Starshine Valley Diner is singular." While she supplied coffee to cafes, she also supplied to diners and a variety of restaurants and bistros. She was slowly but surely trying to take over the coffee supply of the entire valley.

Emmeline finally made it down to the roasting floor, where her dragon, Torch immediately perked up at the sight of her. Torch walked over—the building was far too small to fly in for a full-sized dragon—and nuzzled against Emmeline's side.

"Hiya, girl," Emmeline cooed, patting Torch's cheek.

Together, they walked back to the main area, where the other two dragons were. Each were basalta dragons; the breed was the largest and as such had the strongest fire.

Emmeline had started the business straight out of university when she was twenty-two, and in the beginning years, she used to borrow her father's dragon because Torch was still a baby. At the time, one dragon was enough, but as the business grew, so did her needs.

"Hi, Midnight," Emmeline said, leaving Torch's side to go to her eldest dragon, Midnight, who used to belong to Emmeline's grandmother. When she passed away, Emmeline took Midnight in, since the dragon was only in her sixties, with some good years left before retirement.

Dragons lived for about a hundred years and were very active in their first quarter-century, when they were classified as "young." Young dragons actually grew depressed if their riders neglected them. Then in middle age, from around age twenty-five to seventy-five, they became less needy, and in elder age, they grew tired of domestication entirely.

That was when dragons took their last flight and lived up high in the mountains for the last quarter of their life. Elder dragons who lost their riders usually retired early, which is what Midnight could have done, if Emmeline hadn't had use for her.

"How are you doing, old girl?" Emmeline asked Midnight, stroking her black-scaled neck. Midnight leaned into Emmeline's touch. After a few moments, Emmeline went to her third dragon, Char, who was her father's dragon and middle-aged.

Char blew a ring of smoke her way, and she wrinkled her nose as it passed over her. "Hey, old boy," she said, going over to pet the dragon, who nudged his nose against her chest.

"Whose turn is it?" Emmeline asked, looking at the three of her dragons. The floor manager, Kareem, was in charge of the roasting schedule, and came forward then.

"It's Midnight's turn," Kareem replied. He was from a

Drakkon family and could handle dragons well; he brought Midnight to the next batch of coffee beans that needed roasting. As Kareem tended to Midnight, Torch and Char butted heads, fooling around on the side.

"Hey," Emmeline said, voice stern. "Behave."

They liked playing together, especially when Kareem's attention was on Midnight's roasting. Torch and Char bowed their heads, acquiescing, but once Emmeline shifted her focus to Midnight, she heard them wrestling with one another. They knew better than to wreak havoc, so she let them be.

As Midnight worked on the next batch, Emmeline washed her hands and went to check on the batches from earlier today, which had already cooled down. They were in steel drums, and she peered into the drum at the end.

The green beans were now a deep brown, so dark they were almost black, and had two cracks. The first crack appeared when the bean was beginning to develop during the roast, while the second appeared a few minutes later.

Emmeline always checked the batches of beans to ensure the quality was up to her standard. After inspecting the color and cracks, she closed her eyes and inhaled the smell—the roast had a very particular smell: charred and strong, with a hint of dragon smoke. She was well-practiced now and could immediately tell if a batch had been under- or over-roasted.

Once it had passed the smell-test, she touched her hand to the beans; they were meant to be slightly oily, which this batch was. Emmeline knew exactly how the coffee beans should look, smell, and feel.

While she was a coffee fanatic, and always had been, she

didn't taste each batch—she had enough caffeine daily as it was, but she knew how the coffee would taste once brewed: sweet and rich, full of body and texture.

By the time Emmeline was done checking the cooled-down batches, Midnight was done with the next batch, and Kareem moved the drum to the side to cool down, after which it would be packaged and ready for delivery.

Emmeline returned to her office to check over invoices, return missed phone calls and oversee all the other aspects of the business. Very soon, it was time to break for lunch. After drinking some soup to stave off the winter cold, Emmeline went down to check on the dragons again.

While Kareem could manage the roasting schedule, the dragons were still Emmeline's; she needed to be there to ensure things were running smoothly.

And she was responsible for taking them out for rides. She saddled Midnight up, then pressed the button for the roof to open. The panels slid aside, letting in frigid midday air. Inhaling a deep breath, Emmeline mounted Midnight.

"Come on, old girl," Emmeline said, holding on. With a happy sound, Midnight kicked off.

They flew out of the building, soaring into the sky. Exhilaration bounded through her as they sailed through the clear sky. Their elevation increased quickly, and soon, a snow-covered Starshine Valley came into view.

It was freezing out, but the dragon was like a furnace beneath her. Emmeline loved winter as well as the contrast of the cold wind whipping against her face with the warm animal beneath her.

After a refreshing ride, Emmeline made her way back to

the roasting plant, where Torch was flying above the building, stretching her wings. Upon seeing Emmeline and Midnight, Torch flew inside with them, where Char was resting on the floor.

Emmeline settled the dragons, closing the retractable roof, then went to check on the coffee bean supply. Harvesting took place from March to September, so it was the off-season now, but she had enough stored to fulfill the orders until March. Her supplier, Liam, would have his hands full then.

After a long day of work, Emmeline sent Char and Midnight home to her family's estate, where the dragon caretakers would look after them. Then, she went over to Tales & Tails Bookshop, flying on Torch, who dropped her off on Elderberry Lane in the Hills, the hamlet of Starshine Valley where the dragons and their riders resided. Elderberry Lane was off Main Street, the busier road in town with the larger establishments.

She needed to brainstorm ideas and get started on her proposal. While she had already started a bit yesterday, being on site would be instrumental to her plans.

"See you later," Emmeline said, touching Torch's face.

Torch flew overhead; there wasn't exactly parking for dragons in their small town, and the dragons preferred to fly above. If Emmeline called or whistled, Torch would return; dragons had keen hearing and could hear their rider's call from miles away.

The sun set early these days, and while the sky was dark, the town was well-lit with lights and festive decor for the winter. The storefronts were adorned with wreaths and thick red ribbons in bows. Snowflake lights twinkled over the lane, while small fir trees stood by every door, strung up with golden fairy lights and dusted over with snow.

Luckily, the street and sidewalk had been cleaned of the snow, but there was still six inches of snow on either side as Emmeline trudged up the slope; the Tales & Tails Bookshop was at the top of the lane, in a narrow crevice.

A strong gust of wind blew against Emmeline, and she reached up to hold her black fur hat in place. It matched her fur coat, which she wore above a satin mini dress, fleece-lined stockings, and knee-high heeled boots.

Rushing through the cold, she made it to the bookshop, pausing by the front to take in the warm lights and exterior, the window display full of books and the shop's logo: an open book with a dragon tail. She could see the inside was busy as ever.

While the bookshop was officially named the Tales & Tails Bookshop, many locals called it the Baby Dragon Bookshop, because baby dragons had always been welcome inside—even if a store full of very flammable paper wasn't exactly the optimal location for mischievous fire-breathing baby animals.

After many singed bookshelves and burned-up books, the baby dragons learned to behave. Saphira and the Baby Dragon Cafe had had a similar problem in the beginning, until—like in the bookshop—the baby dragons got accustomed to the place and learned to act accordingly.

Emmeline entered through the front door, relishing the warmth inside the shop and the regular buzz of the busy bookshop. She spotted two baby dragons immediately: a tiny white-scaled opala who must have been a few months old, snuggled in a basket by the roaring fire, sound asleep; and a one-year-old red-scaled garneta, bouncing after its owners, a young couple with a toddler who was smaller than the baby dragon.

The bookshop spanned three stories, and she saw a steady stream of people going up and down the stairs. The event space was on the top floor, and a sign by the stairs told her there was a meeting of the Baby Dragon Book Club currently taking place. She quickly snapped a photograph and sent it to Ginny and Haris for them to attend with Fang and Motu.

Smiling to herself, Emmeline inhaled the clean scent of ink and paper, watching as a bookseller recommended something to an old lady, who peered at the back copy from atop massive reading glasses, looking intrigued. Emmeline's heart warmed.

She had missed this place. Too busy with work, she hadn't been here in a while. A sudden wave of nostalgia hit her—while at university, she used to come here often to get new books for class (she had been an English major along with Business). Being a student felt like it was forever ago, but at the same time also like it was just yesterday.

Her gaze went to the front counter, where the store manager checked out customers. Beside her was a familiar old man sitting on a chair reading a book. Emmeline went over to say hello, and when she did, Minh Trang looked up from his book, pleasantly surprised.

"Ah, Emmeline Sterling! My sister told me you might be popping by," Minh said, his wrinkled face turning into a smile. His hair was a soft tuft of gray-white, parted to one side. He set his book down and rose to his feet to give her a hug.

"I'm so happy to see you," Emmeline said. "Though I am cross you didn't come to Ginny's party!"

"Ah, the site of all Anh's scheming," Minh teased.

She laughed. "Well, if we don't scheme, who will?"

Chuckling, he waved a finger at her, sitting back down in his chair. It was effectively his throne, from which he looked out at his kingdom. "Do what you must," he said, picking up his book again. "And you can ask Ola here if you need anything." He gestured to the store manager, and Emmeline shook her hand, introducing herself.

"I'll leave you to your reading," she told Minh.

With that, she left him and went to scope out the bookshop, though she knew it well. A contented feeling spread through her as she ambled towards the shelves. She was glad for Anh's competition if it meant she would be spending more time here.

That is, until she saw Luke inside.

CHAPTER 5

Luke went to the Tails & Tales Bookshop after work at his roasting plant, and the moment he entered, he was hit with a wave of memories.

He hadn't been to the shop in some time since it was on the other side of the valley, but he had been here practically every week during university to buy books for class (he was an English major along with Business).

Unable to stop himself, Luke remembered that winter night all those years ago: Emmeline's hands twisted in his hair as he bit her lower lip and she gasped against his mouth. Heat bolted through him, and he was promptly reminded of *why* he didn't come here that often.

After the initial (nauseating) wave of memories subsided, he introduced himself to Minh, who introduced him to the store manager, Ola, as the point person if he needed anything. Then, Luke grabbed a small leather notebook and a pen from his coat's inner pocket and began looking around, taking notes as he went up the three floors.

The top floor was for children's and young adult books,

as well as for the event space. At the moment, there was a meeting of the Baby Dragon Book Club, in which he saw riders with their baby dragons, reading from a picture book about a dragon's adventures in trying to become a baker.

Half the baby dragons were riveted, while the other half were trying their best to either eat their books or light them aflame while their harassed riders looked on.

Luke wondered if the third floor would be best for the coffee shop; it was well situated in terms of the event space, but he didn't know if the coffee shop's proximity would disturb the events or create too much of a rush. The third floor was also a bit out of the way, so there would be less natural foot traffic.

He checked out the second floor, which housed nonfiction and literary novels; this was by far the quietest floor, with the least traffic. While there was ample space for it, a coffee shop on this floor might disturb the patrons, who mostly seemed to be older or browsing alone, enjoying the peace.

Jotting down a note, Luke made it back to the first floor, which housed the most popular fiction and was the busiest. It seemed like the best option, but he'd need to work out where the best location would be.

Another thing he'd need to consider was the fact that they were just a street away from the Baby Dragon Cafe, which was a roaring success, so they would need to ensure their coffee shop was different. In Luke's opinion there could never be too many cafes, and the coffee shop extension could be beneficial to him, personally, if he could source the coffee.

He desperately needed to up his number of clients, among other things. Tempest was, to put it lightly, drowning.

About nine months ago, the owner of his roasting plant had sold the property to another corporation and, rather than keeping Luke's rent on the place fixed, the new owner had doubled it. Luke had been saving for a new packaging system that would save time and increase profit margins, but since the rent had doubled, all of his money had been funneled towards that bill.

Things were getting pretty dire. Which was why he needed Anh's investment. With it, he could buy the new packaging system, and things would fall into place on their own.

Running a hand through his hair, Luke perused the first floor, passing by a fireplace with a roaring, crackling fire. He inhaled the scent of paper, smiling to himself as he watched patrons pulling books from the shelves. There was a magical quality to books; they were endless keepers of stories: the author's, the book's, the reader's, each different and distinct.

Luke recalled now why he had loved coming here so much in university. While the bookshop was far away from where he lived in Bayview, it was close to the university and had always been a sanctuary.

But that serene feeling vanished as he turned out of a row of bookshelves and spotted an obnoxious fur coat with a matching hat. The energy that jolted through him was better than any espresso shot.

"Ugh." Emmeline rolled her eyes when she spotted him, as if she thought he was tedious. She shrugged her coat off, revealing a tiny dress that made her long legs seem as if they went on forever. All the ideas from the last hour emptied out of his head.

Luke mentally scolded himself, reminding himself to focus.

She was his competition. He needed to beat her. The investment was an opportunity he couldn't afford to lose; if he didn't get it, he knew what the projections looked like.

Tempest would have to permanently close.

All those years, all that energy, and all the money he had given to his business would go to waste, and he couldn't let that happen. Besides, it wasn't only about him—he needed a profitable business to pay for his mother's medical bills.

Luke walked past Emmeline. As he did, she turned her nose up at him, irritated, though the vexed expression did nothing to take away from her beauty. She slung her coat over one arm, sticking her ridiculous hat (that only she could pull off) into one of the pockets before shaking her long hair out.

For a moment, Luke was mesmerized.

"What?" Emmeline snapped, catching him looking.

Embarrassment shot through him, but he gave her an easy smile. "You have fur in your hair."

"No I don't." Still, she touched a hand to the crown of her head.

Luke snorted, and she rolled her eyes at him before stalking off, disappearing from sight. Once she was gone, he felt like he could think again. He went over to the small table against the wall in the back of the shop, where there was a cart with complimentary tea and coffee.

Turning on the kettle, he made himself a cup of tea. When he took the first sip, he wrinkled his nose. This stuff really was terrible. But it was hot, and gave him something to hold, so he continued sipping from the disposable cup.

Nursing his tea, he walked around the shop, trying to see where the best position for the coffee shop on this floor was. Once he had a location locked down, he could work through the logistics.

As he analyzed, he caught a glimpse of Emmeline walking toward a bookshelf. Luke turned his attention to his notebook but lasted a second before he glanced up again, eyes searching for her. She had disappeared between the stacks, and he took a step back, craning his neck to catch a glimpse.

She was scanning the shelves, a painted fingernail tapping against one of the spines.

The image reminded him of that evening years ago, when they had first met in this very store.

Despite the busy bookshop, Luke had noticed her immediately. It was hard not to, and he wasn't the only one; more than one head turned when she entered a room. A fact she seemed used to. Unperturbed, she had headed for the bookshelves, and he had watched as she searched for a title.

She had tilted her head to better read the spines, and her dark hair was pushed back, revealing the slant of her throat. His gaze had traveled down the slope to her collar; he'd stopped his eyes from wandering before they went lower, desire spreading through him.

Enraptured, he had watched as she strode over to the lounge chair Minh was sitting on, holding a book in one hand and a mug of tea in another.

"Minh, do you have *Letters to Milena*?" she had asked. "I can't find it."

His heart had kicked as he looked down at the book in his hands. *Fate*. He had picked up the last copy.

He'd walked up to her, offering her the book and his heart on a silver platter. She'd taken care of the book, he was sure, but she hadn't handled his heart with the same delicacy.

A fact he reminded himself of often. Behind that beautiful exterior was a heartless woman. She had used and discarded him.

He should have hated her.

Unfortunately, he didn't. She had gotten under his skin all those years ago and never left. All he wanted was to do the same, to drive her as insane as she drove him.

She walked past him to the back, pausing to pet a blue-scaled baby dragon who was trying to (incorrectly) reshelve a book.

Unable to stop himself, he tossed his empty teacup and headed in the same direction. Pretending to look around, he stole glances her way, indulging himself even as he knew he shouldn't.

It was impossible not to look at her, like being out in the cold on a winter night for a bonfire: everyone circled around the warmth, watching the flames. No matter how far into the darkness you went, your gaze was still directed to the light.

Emmeline glanced back, and he immediately turned his attention to a random book in front of him, pretending to have been looking at it the whole time. When she turned around again, he shifted his focus back to her, wondering what ideas she was thinking of for the bookshop.

She was brilliant and clever—a fact he needed to *not*

admire at the moment when those very qualities would lead to his downfall.

Emmeline whipped around, catching him looking. "Are you following me?" she snapped.

He absolutely was, but he looked at her like she was absurd. "Not at all," he said. He pointed to the table behind her. "Just getting more tea."

She narrowed her eyes at him as he strode toward her. "You hate that stuff."

The words were spoken as if they had slipped out; her dark eyes immediately widened. He slowed his steps, stopping right in front of her.

His lips parted with surprise. *She remembered that*. Why would she remember that?

Could it be that she thought of that time together as often as he did?

He took a step toward her, looking closer. Before he could dissect her expression, she went to walk past him, turning her cheek.

She made it two steps before a red-scaled baby dragon shot across the bookshop, right into her path. And for the first time, Luke saw Emmeline falter.

In trying to avoid stepping on the baby dragon, she lost her balance. Arms flailing, she dropped her coat and stumbled forward. Luke stepped toward her, easily catching her as she landed straight into his arms.

Her hands clutched the front of his shirt, the fabric bunching between her fingers. He inhaled the sweet scent of jasmine on her skin. His blood quickened, roaring in his ears as he touched her bare elbows, holding her up.

Her sharp intake of breath filled his ears. She brought her gaze up to his, and he found himself drowning in her kajal-lined eyes. Her lips parted.

Suddenly, they weren't business rivals with a complicated history—they were just two university students, their eyes big and bright.

CHAPTER 6

Emmeline's pulse quickened.

Luke's arms were strong as he held her upright. His gaze lowered to her mouth, scorching through her. Her hands tightened, and his eyes dropped to where the fabric of his shirt was bunched in her hands, her fingers brushing against his bare chest and the chains lying there.

She felt wholly disarmed, and the moment stretched between them.

Until he seemed to recall something, and his expression shifted. Dark eyes glinting, he gave her an amused tilt of his lips. He leaned closer, and her heart pounded painfully as he brought his lips close to her ears. Inadvertently, she clutched him closer.

"You don't have to throw yourself at me, you know," he said, voice husky.

Indignation burned through her.

"You wish," she snapped. Pushing him away, she righted herself. Grabbing her coat off the floor, she stalked away, hoping he didn't notice her warmed cheeks.

She couldn't risk him having the satisfaction.

The only reason she felt hot to begin with was because they had known each other intimately; this was a natural bodily reaction, she reasoned with herself. Plus, he was objectively good-looking, there was no point in trying to deny that.

But neither of those things meant *anything.*

Emmeline gathered her hair together, twisting it up and holding it in place with one hand to get some cool air on the back of her neck. Her curtain bangs fell forward immediately, over her eyes, and she blew out her cheeks, trying to remember what she was doing.

She had been scoping out a location for the coffee shop. Just as Emmeline was retracing her train of thought, her phone rang in her purse. She dropped her hair, letting it swoosh down her back, and answered. It was her mom, Samreen.

"Hi, Ammi," Emmeline said, picking up.

"Where are you?" Samreen asked. "It's loud."

"Just doing something for work."

"Tch, always working," Samreen said, voice displeased. If Samreen had her way, Emmeline's full-time job would be solely to be her mother's daughter.

"I like working," Emmeline replied. She liked it much better when she didn't need to cross paths with an insufferable chimera owner, but that was neither here nor there.

"And I like being a grandmother," Samreen replied. "Maybe think about that."

"Ammi, please." Emmeline snorted. "Besides, Millie is dutifully seeing to that task."

"And she's younger than you!" Samreen tsked. "Have some shame."

"Ammi! You can't say things like that. It's considered *rude*."

"Acha, acha. Millie is why I called—the baby is coming, so I'm flying down."

"What?" Surprise pricked her. Usually Millie told Emmeline things first; the sisters were always united.

Emmeline removed her phone from her ear to check her notifications; she saw four missed calls from Millie, as well as a text from her brother-in-law, Liam.

So Millie *had* tried telling her. Emmeline had just been too distracted to realize. She snuck a glance behind her to look at the distraction in question: Luke was at the tea table, pouring out boiled water.

She shot him a dirty look, then turned her attention back to her mother.

"I'm flying down to be with her," Samreen was saying. "I've already told them at work, and then the winter holidays begin next week, so I'll be at Millie's for the next three weeks until school begins again." Samreen was a school librarian.

"Okay, Ammi," Emmeline replied. "Should I fly down now as well?"

Stress bounded through her; did Millie need her? How fast could Emmeline fly down? She'd need to close the roasting plant for a day or two because it was a two-hour flight away.

"Ugh, I wish Millie lived closer," she complained, not for the first time.

"That *is* your fault, you know," Samreen reminded her.

Emmeline frowned. This was the response she got from any of her family members when she complained how far away Millie had moved after getting married, because it was Emmeline who had introduced Millie and Liam.

Liam owned coffee farms. Years ago, when Emmeline was starting out with her business, she'd brought Millie along with her to a variety of farms to see who she wanted to source her beans from.

Coffee had always been Emmeline and Millie's thing; they both loved cafe-hopping and being baristas at home, so when Emmeline needed to decide where to get her coffee beans from, of course she brought Millie along as her partner-in-crime.

Coffee farms were down south in the warmer, tropical climate: a two-hour dragon ride or a four-hour car ride. Back then, Torch wasn't old enough to be ridden, and Millie hadn't hatched an egg yet. They could have borrowed their father's dragon, but they didn't mind making a whole day out of it, driving down together and talking the entire way over.

When they got to Liam's farm, it was an instant connection between Millie and Liam. Millie always fell in love easily, but with Liam, it was different. A year later, they were married, and two years after that, she gave birth to her first son, then a daughter two years later, and now the third was coming.

"The doctors say it'll be another day," Samreen said. "I'm going early to watch the children. Check in on your father and brothers and come down tomorrow."

"Okay, got it," Emmeline said. She chatted with her mother for a few minutes more. After hanging up with her mother, Emmeline dialed her sister. It rang twice before the call went through, but instead of Millie answering, it was Liam.

"Hey, Emmy, Mills just fell asleep," Liam said. Emmeline

could hear her niece in the background demanding juice. "Ira, one second!" Liam said. "Sorry, it's a madhouse in here."

"As per usual," Emmeline replied with a laugh. "But don't worry—Ammi will be there soon, and I'll come tomorrow. Do you need anything? Millie? The kids?"

Anxiety shot through Emmeline as she thought of her very pregnant sister about to go into delivery. Millie had done it before twice, but still. Emmeline knew she couldn't relax until both her sister and new niece were safe.

"We're okay—but actually, Noah has been remembering your cookies, if you could bake some?" Liam asked.

"Of course." Emmeline froze large batches of cookie dough for this precise reason (and because she needed an emotional support sweet treat every other day).

"You're the best," Liam said. Ira shrieked in the background. "Okay, see you soon."

"Bye!"

Putting her phone away, Emmeline released a long breath. Unbidden, a pang of jealousy went through her; she wanted what her sister had, a little family of her own.

The Sterling family was huge, but it didn't feel like any of those people were just for her. And while Emmeline was really close with different people, they all had lives of their own—their partners. Aiden and Saphira. Millie and Liam. Even her parents; even her two younger brothers, who were a unit on their own.

Most of the time, Emmeline enjoyed her independence, but sometimes, she felt so lonely.

Emmeline looked up and caught Luke watching her. His expression was soft and curious, and for some reason she felt exposed, as if he'd read her mind. She glared, and he only raised his brows before turning his attention back to his notebook.

He was surely making astute notes for his proposal—something she needed to be doing as well. While Emmeline was happy for her sister, the timing wasn't the best. Flying down and back would take all day, and she needed to get to her parents' place now to check on the men of her family.

Putting on her hat and jacket, she headed out into the cold. She called for Torch, and a few moments later, the dragon swooped down.

"Let's go visit Dad," she told Torch, mounting. Torch took off, and Emmeline relished the cold wind against her cheeks as they flew to her parents' estate, on the land neighboring her uncle Edmund's estate.

After dismounting, she walked to the front door, while Torch headed for the dragons' stables where the dragon caretakers would be. Torch knew the drill, and so did Emmeline. She punched in the code for the front door and entered, inhaling the familiar scent of cardamom and cloves.

"Hello!" she called, taking off her shoes, but there was no answer. Finally, a fat little creature came into sight. "Hiya, Motu."

Her brother's one-year-old baby dragon bounced over to her, and she smiled, crouching down to hug him hello. Motu flapped his wings happily. She knew half of his delight came from the fact that where Emmeline was, Torch was. Motu was one of Torch's eggs.

"Come on," she said, scooping Motu up. He was heavy in

her arms as she opened the front door and called out Torch's name.

Torch peeked her head out from the stables at Emmeline's call, and when she saw who Emmeline carried in her arms, Torch immediately flew over. Motu bounced in her arms.

"Go on," she told the baby dragon, as Torch came to collect him. Motu jumped out of her arms, flying toward Torch, who picked him up in her paw and flew back to the stables.

Emmeline headed back inside, turning in the direction of her father's office, where she found Charles at his desk.

"Hi, Dad," she said, entering. At her voice, her dad looked up from above his glasses. Surprise lit his face.

"Oh, hello, darling," he said, standing. She went over to give him a hug, and he kissed her cheek. "How's Char doing? Not giving you trouble at the plant, is he?"

"He's wonderful, as always," she said.

"Splendid." Charles nodded. "It does the old boy good to have something to do. And how are you?"

"I'm well, too, thank you," she said. "Just came by to check in since Ammi's gone."

"Ah, well, thank you, but we're all fine, really," he said. "We can order in for dinner. Nothing to fret over."

"It's alright," Emmeline replied. "I can make something." She knew her father and brothers were fussy about eating out, so she went to the kitchen, poking around the fridge and cabinet to see what was in store.

There were some measly leftovers, so Emmeline pulled out ingredients to make a mixed vegetable curry. At least there was dough for roti, and when the curry was done, she made roti to go alongside it. She rarely made roti for herself; there was something kind of depressing about making a singular roti and eating it all alone in her home. So though she was tired, she didn't mind making dinner if she got to eat it with everyone together.

At the smell of food cooking, both of her brothers made their way into the kitchen.

"Hey, Emmy, when did you get here?" Haris asked.

"A little while ago," she replied, flipping the roti on the flame. "Did Ammi tell you about Millie?"

"Yeah, she texted us," Naveed said, entering behind Haris. Her brothers were a year apart at twenty-four and twenty-three and could pass for twins if not for Naveed's longer hair.

Emmeline pinched Naveed's cheek, bothering him on purpose as she left a streak of aata on his face. He swatted her hand away, and she smiled, returning to her roti.

"No meat?" Naveed asked with a pout, pulling the lid off the pot to check the curry. He poked it with a spoon, moving the potatoes and cauliflower around.

"No," Emmeline said, voice turning stern. "And don't complain—set the table. Dinner's almost ready."

They all sat down together to eat, chatting about random things: Dragon Council politics and Naveed's job in finance.

"Hey, where's Motu?" Haris asked, reaching for a second roti.

Emmeline gave him an arch glance. "You just noticed your baby dragon is missing?" Haris winced. "He's outside with Torch."

"Thanks." Haris gave her an easy smile, and she rolled her eyes, continuing to eat.

"I'm going to fly down on Torch tomorrow, but you all drive in," she said. "I'm making Mills chicken corn soup and cardamom buns, so bring those with you; I don't want the soup to spill on the flight."

As she spoke, she remembered the cookies for Noah, but the cookie dough was at her place. Mentally adjusting, she planned to make a new batch here for the boys to bring everything together.

"Why doesn't Ammi just make soup for Millie there?" Haris asked.

"Because Millie likes my soup," Emmeline replied. "I made the soup and buns when she had the last two babies, too. A fact you'd recall if you had any sort of memory."

"God help his patients," Naveed snorted.

"I cannot even imagine him being a real doctor," Emmeline said with a shudder. Before Haris could respond with a retort, one of the dragon caretakers appeared with Motu.

"He's getting fussy," the caretaker told them, looking at Haris.

"Here, I'll take him," Emmeline said, standing. She had already finished eating, so she took Motu from the caretaker. At a year old, Motu was quite big, but she could still carry him, though he entirely filled her arms.

He scratched at his face, fussing, and she made a soothing sound. "Oho," she said, rubbing her nose against him. "It's okay."

Baby dragons needed love and attention from their family the same way human babies did. Nannies could only do so much. After the caretaker left, Emmeline took Motu to the living room, setting him down on the couch and sitting beside him.

"Hey, um, so speaking of Motu," Haris said, wiping his hands with a napkin. He looked nervous as he came over to Emmeline and sat down next to her, wrapping an arm around her shoulder. "You know you're my favorite sister, right?"

"It's not much of a competition with Millie four hours away," Naveed said from the table. By then, Charles had finished eating as well and had retreated back to his office.

Ignoring Naveed's comment, Emmeline gave Haris an unimpressed look. "What do you want?"

Haris pretended to be offended. "I can't appreciate my caring and kind sister without wanting something?"

"Precedent says no," Emmeline replied.

"Don't use big words around the bechara." Naveed snorted.

Haris gave him a dirty look. "I know what precedent means, you asshole." His voice sweetened as he spoke to Emmeline again. She could tell there was something he wanted to say that he had been building up the courage to mention.

"What is it?" she asked.

"You're so good with Motu," Haris said. "I was wondering if you could watch him for a few weeks."

"What?" she asked. "Why?"

He looked embarrassed then. "I kind of failed one of my university courses," he told her.

"*What?*" she snapped. Haris cringed, and even Motu hid behind his wings.

"It's okay!" he added quickly. "I can take it again during the winter and it won't affect my graduation timeline."

"I can't believe you failed one of your courses! I told you

to stop going out so much and focus on your studies, but do you ever listen? No!"

Haris winced. "I know, you're right. I'll focus on my studies now, promise, but do you think you can watch Motu while I do?"

As if she didn't have enough on her plate! Motu was a little over a year old and hardly trained, though he was more lazy than mischievous. Even so—it would be extra work, and she already had her business and the bookshop proposal for Anh plus Millie's baby.

"Haris . . ." she said, drawing out his name, but he knew she wouldn't refuse him. She never did. The problem with Emmeline was that she couldn't say no to her family. She had been taking care of everyone and everything for so long that they all relied on her.

"Come on, please!" he said. "You're the one who says I need to focus, and if I don't pass the retake, then my whole timeline will be screwed."

She couldn't let that happen.

"And I'd leave him with the caretakers, but you see how he is," Haris said, reaching over to pet Motu. The baby dragon closed his eyes, happily leaning into Haris's touch. "He needs one of us, and he already likes you better than me!" Emmeline took a deep breath. "Plus, he's Torch's egg. It's only for a few weeks, a month tops! Just until my winter course is over."

Glancing at the baby dragon, Emmeline knew that if she didn't look after Motu, he would be left to the caretakers and suffer for it. There was no one else Haris would ask, and there was no one else Emmeline trusted with such a matter.

Releasing a long breath, she looked back at her brother, and a grin lit his face.

"Fine," she agreed, drawing the word out to express her irritation. "But after we get back from Millie's."

"Of course . . . You're the best!" Haris hugged her, kissing her cheek.

She let him, saying, "You owe me."

"My life," he agreed. "I owe you my life."

As annoyed as she got with her siblings, she was still fond of them in the way only an eldest sister could be.

Emmeline went to the kitchen to get started on the soup for Millie, running through a to-do list for the rest of the evening and tomorrow. She rubbed her temples.

She really wouldn't be getting any sleep for the next six weeks, would she?

CHAPTER 7

Emmeline was up late making the soup, buns, and cookie dough. Then, she slept for a few hours and did a half-day at Tempest before flying down to Millie's on Torch.

It was a two-hour flight but she loved being in the air. It was one of the few places where she could stop working and thinking and just be. Up here, there was nothing she had to do, and nothing she could do, since she had to hold onto her handlebars. It was liberating.

Looking down at the vast world below, Emmeline watched as the snow-covered Starshine Valley gave way to uncovered earth as they went farther south, the air around her getting less frigid the longer they flew.

They arrived at Liam's farm two hours later. In the summer, the farm was lush, the fields bright and green, with a constant flurry of workers on the land; in the winter, it was empty and quiet. Torch landed in front of Millie's large gray farmhouse, and while her dragon was hardly winded, when Emmeline dismounted, she stretched her muscles.

Millie and Liam didn't have dragons—Liam wasn't from

a Drakkon family, and Millie had her hands full with her kids—but they did have a small stable for the dragons to rest in when the Sterlings came to visit, and Torch headed there now. It was beside the farmhouse, and Samreen's dragon, Sholay, was already there on the rocks, a huge pile of fish beside him, along with a water basin.

The dragons rubbed their faces along each other's necks in greeting, and Emmeline climbed up the three steps to the front door, pulling her phone out from her crossbody purse to check her father's location. They had left an hour before her and his location showed that he and her brothers were still an hour away.

Emmeline punched in the key code for the front door. She had hardly made a step into the house when she heard a shriek from within.

"Khala!" four-year-old Noah cried, running down the hall toward her. Emmeline glimpsed two-year-old Ira hanging off Samreen, then Noah launched himself into her arms. She caught her nephew, spinning him around as he screamed with delight and she smothered him with kisses.

"I missed you!" she told him, setting him down. Noah grinned up at her, and Emmeline saw Millie on his face, a sight that made her heart warm.

"You're finally here!" Noah replied, jumping up and down.

"Let me look at you," she said, putting her hands on his shoulders. She inspected him, then said, "Noah, why do you get bigger every time I see you, huh? I need to tell your mama to stop feeding you so many vegetables. You have to stay my little baby forever!"

He giggled, then looked over Emmeline's shoulder, out the window of the storm door. "Did you come on Torch?" he asked, trying to run past her. She grabbed him before he could.

"Hey! Where are your shoes? And your jacket? It's cold!" He pouted. "We can say hi to Torch in a second. Come on."

Emmeline closed the front door, then went to kiss her mother and niece hello. Ira reached for Emmeline, and Emmeline scooped her into her arms, twirling her around. Ira giggled.

"Okay, now you watch them while I clean up and cook," Samreen said, straightening the front of her top, which was navy blue and part of a matching set. Her dark hair was clipped back in a knot, and she redid it now.

"I made soup," Emmeline said. Ira reached for Emmeline's nose-ring, and Emmeline scrunched her nose, blocking Ira's hand. "Dad's bringing it with the boys."

"Is there enough for everyone?" Samreen asked, picking up toys and throwing them into the basket. Emmeline never knew how things would be when she saw her mother, and the complicated nature of their relationship made her nervous.

Sometimes her mother could be her best friend, but sometimes, her mother could be so harsh. Emmeline loved her, and knew her mother loved her as well but, as the eldest, there was a lot expected of Emmeline. That pressure often pushed her to succeed and surely had a part to play in her success, but sometimes, it felt like too much.

"Yes, there's enough," Emmeline said.

"Good." Samreen nodded in approval. "I'll make some

sooji ka halwa, then. Millie's in labor and Liam is with her. The baby should be here soon."

Emmeline hoped the labor didn't last too long; she had told Millie to do her pelvic floor exercises, but she wondered if Millie actually had.

As Samreen cleaned up the house, Emmeline distracted her niece and nephew, both of whom were fighting for her undivided attention. She loved them to bits, but they were a handful, and she wasn't running on much sleep, so she was glad when, an hour later, her father and brothers arrived with Motu.

Then it was an absolute madhouse, but fun, too. They baked the cookies, and while her family could be tiresome at times, she did love having everyone together. Finally, Liam called her to let them know they could come to the hospital; the baby was here.

"How's Mills?" Emmeline asked.

"She's good," Liam replied. "Tired, but good."

Before Emmeline could respond, she heard her sister in the background: "*Where* are my chocolate-covered pretzels, Liam?"

"Uh . . ." Liam trailed off.

"Don't worry," Emmeline told her brother-in-law. "I'll bring them."

"You're a lifesaver."

"*Liam?*" Millie asked again.

"Come quick," Liam whispered, before the line went dead.

With a snort, Emmeline went up to their bedroom and found them in the bedside table drawer, knowing her sister's favorite snack would be there instead of in the pantry.

Bringing the pretzels down, Emmeline packed them with the rest of the food as her brothers attempted getting the kids into their jackets and shoes. You would think that between four adults, they could handle two toddlers, but the toddlers gave them a run for their money.

Finally, everyone was ready, and they went out. Haris left Motu with Sholay, and they all went to the car, while Emmeline went to Torch. Noah followed Emmeline, and Ira's gaze strayed to the two of them, immediately sniffing out plans she wasn't being included in.

"Distract her," Emmeline told her brothers, and when Ira was looking the other way, Emmeline turned to Noah. "Quick, before Ira sees!"

Noah grinned and Emmeline took his hand, both of them running over to Torch. Her dragon perked upon seeing Noah and blew air into the kid's face, making Noah laugh. Then, they mounted and took off, Torch flying slowly with the child on board.

When they got to the hospital, Torch went back to Millie's; Starshine Valley was particular in that it was a haven for dragons, so it had the necessary infrastructure, but most other places, like where Liam and Millie lived, did not.

At the hospital, Liam met them in the lobby, earning congratulations from each of them before they went up to meet Millie and the baby.

"What name did you settle on?" Samreen asked Liam, as they exited out of the elevator. Emmeline already knew.

"Eve," Liam replied.

They all went into the hospital room, arms filled with the food and flowers and balloons.

"Mama!" Ira cried, rushing to Millie's side.

"Hi baby," Millie replied tiredly, reaching a hand out for Ira.

Emmeline looked over at Millie, and it suddenly felt as if she hadn't seen her sister in so long.

"How are you faring?" Emmeline asked in a low voice, as the others crowded around Liam and the baby. Ira ran off as well, leaving the sisters on their own for a moment.

"I keep forgetting how painful childbirth is," Millie replied, eyes wide, though there was a soft smile on her lips, as well.

"It's the hormones," Emmeline told her, squeezing her hand. "That's how you got tricked into it again."

Millie laughed, squeezing Emmeline's hand back. Emmeline felt a pang in her chest. She wished her sister lived closer, that they could see each other more often.

If Liam wasn't so wonderful, Emmeline would surely be more bitter about it, but how could she be when her sister was so happy?

Still, Emmeline missed her all the time.

"Go check out Eve," Millie said with a smile. "You'll be happy."

Emmeline glanced over at the little bundle, her lips immediately spreading into a smile as she saw the brown skin and dark hair.

"Yes," Emmeline said proudly. "Three for three; she looks just like me."

Liam snorted. "You always say that."

"Yeah, but she's right," Millie said, as the baby passed into Emmeline's arms. Emmeline and Millie looked very similar, and those same genes went down to Millie's kids.

"No complaints from me if our kids get the more good-looking half of the gene pool," Liam said, kissing Millie's temple; she smiled. Emmeline bopped the little baby's nose.

They all hung out for a bit, until Millie nestled deeper into her bed. "Okay, now everyone leave me alone, I'm tired," she said, yawning. Everyone got up to leave, including Emmeline, until her sister said, "Emmy, not you, obviously."

Emmeline's heart warmed. She sat back down with her sister, until it was just the two of them left. Then, she pulled out a cardamom bun and handed it to her sister, who immediately began unraveling it. She took a bite, sighing.

"Amazing, as always," she said. Emmeline smiled, taking a bun out for herself as well. They had come out well, though she wished they had risen a bit more.

"This would be so good with coffee," Millie said, pouting. "I miss coffee." Her pregnancies always made her hate caffeine.

"Speaking of," she started. "There's a situation I need to update you on."

"I love a situation," Millie said, perking up. "Tell me."

"If you're finally done being pregnant and giving birth, I can," Emmeline said.

"Yes, yes, I am done—tell me!"

Feeling nervous then, Emmeline warned, "It's possibly dramatic."

"Even better!" Millie replied, ripping off another piece of cardamom bun and popping it in her mouth. "The drama in my life at the moment is trying to stop my children from killing each other."

"Stop, they aren't so bad," Emmeline said, going to her niece and nephew's defense.

"Mhm." Millie didn't look convinced. "You know the other day Noah proudly came over and told me that he gave Ira a bath."

"Oh god. How did he reach the sink?

"He didn't."

Emmeline cringed. "Do I want to know?"

"I'm telling you either way—he used my favorite coffee mug and toilet water."

"Nooooo!" Emmeline cried, covering her face with her hands.

They both shook their heads, laughing.

"It's okay; he's cute so it makes up for it," Emmeline said.

Millie laughed. "Okay, now tell me!"

"Oh, right." It was so easy to lose track of what they were talking about when she was with her sister; conversation kept shooting off in a million directions. "Well, remember how I've been trying to get Anh Trang to invest in Inferno?" Emmeline started.

"Yes," Millie replied.

"She came to Ginny's birthday—we all missed you, by the way."

"Ohmygod, I saw the pictures, everyone looked so good. I can't believe Ginny isn't a baby anymore."

"Absolutely. *Anyway*. Anh was there, and she wants to add a coffee shop to Tales & Tails."

"The bookshop? I haven't been there in forever!"

"Yes. If I can get her a good proposal, she'll give me a stake in the shop, plus invest in Inferno."

Millie's mouth dropped open. "That would be amazing!" she said. "You've been wanting to get her investment forever and this is the perfect opportunity to impress her." She paused, confused. "Where's the drama in that? You can definitely do it."

"Um . . . well . . ." She trailed off, wondering how her sister would take the next bit of news. "Anh made the same offer to someone else, as well, and she's only going to pick one of us."

"Ooh, a competition. Slightly more saucy." Millie finished off her cardamom bun, thinking. "But not really, since there's no one you can't beat."

"That's not what I'm worried about," Emmeline said. "My rival—it's Luke Hayward."

"Oooooh." Millie drew the word out for a good thirty seconds, eyes growing wider and wider, her mouth open. "Now *that* is dramatic."

Emmeline looked at her sister closely, but Millie's expression was unreadable. Luke was, after all, the guy who had broken Millie's heart.

In university, Emmeline and Millie were a year apart, and when Emmeline was a senior, she had to spend an entire semester hearing Millie crush on Luke Hayward, notorious man-whore.

"It's a bad idea, Mills," Emmeline warned, over and over, but Millie was undeterred. She was a girl with a crush. Eventually, Millie succeeded in going out with Luke and, one date later, she claimed she was in love.

Until two dates later, after they had slept together, Luke callously broke Millie's heart.

"I'm not interested, and I never will be," he had said, blunt and unfeeling.

Emmeline could not leave such behavior unpunished. He needed a taste of his own medicine, so Emmeline did what he had done to Millie: she'd made him interested in her, slept with him, and then been cruel. She had told him exactly what he had told Millie when he had broken it off with her, and it was then that he finally realized the ruse.

She would never forget how he'd blinked, jaw slack with shock. "This was all for revenge," he said, dumbfounded.

Guilt had prickled through her, but she had finished what she'd started. Emmeline barked out a laugh. "Did you really think I don't already own a copy of *Letters to Milena*?"

His face flashed with pain, but it was so quick she must have been imagining it because, not even a second later, he'd laughed out loud. His teeth shone as he'd flashed her a wolfish grin.

"I am just gutted," he had replied with mock disappointment, holding a hand over his heart. "Here I was thinking it was *fate*."

Sarcasm had dripped off his words, and for some reason, his tone had made her bristle. Her cheeks felt hot. He was letting her know it didn't mean anything to him—and why had she been surprised? Nothing ever did, as his reputation would confirm.

She couldn't really hurt him.

Then, he'd looked at her carefully, something turning in his mind.

"I must say, I'm impressed," he said, stepping closer. "You really are like me."

Her heart sank at that. She wasn't like him—she *couldn't* be. She'd left him without another word, avoiding him entirely until they graduated that spring. Later that year, she opened Tempest, and two years after, he opened Inferno, making them business rivals.

Emmeline might have gotten her revenge, but she had never forgiven Luke for breaking Millie's heart. Millie had cried for a week! It had been horrible to witness her little sister so sad because of a stupid boy. Just the thought of it now made Emmeline upset.

"Em," Millie said, voice confident. "You'll win the investment. I know you will."

Luke was her match, which would make beating him difficult, but Millie was right.

There was no one Emmeline couldn't beat, and that included Luke Hayward.

CHAPTER 8

Seeing Emmeline again so frequently was not good for Luke. At all.

It was opening up the floodgates of his memories: the ones he had kept safely locked away all these years, for the sake of his own sanity. As he sat in his office at Tempest, he took a sip of black coffee, trying to focus on the financial spreadsheet on the computer in front of him.

His thoughts strayed for the hundredth time that day, and he released a sigh, leaning back in his desk chair. Perhaps if he allowed himself to indulge, it would finally help him focus again.

Luke closed his eyes, going back to that time. Twenty-two years old, which had felt so grown-up when he was there but, looking back now, he had still been so young. The night he met Emmeline at the bookshop, he had imagined it was a chance encounter, a stroke of fate.

They had spent a perfect evening together, then a perfect night, and morning. All before she had torn his heart out of his chest when he realized she had orchestrated the entire thing in order to get back at him.

It had gutted him, but of course, he hadn't shown it. Instead, he'd laughed, trying to find some way to salvage his pride. "You really are like me," he had said, and he would never forget how her face had fallen, as if there was no worse insult he could have given her.

The entire situation had messed him up—no, *she* had messed him up. Luke had genuinely liked her. They had hit it off immediately, in a way he never had with anyone else, but it wasn't real.

Or was it? He still wasn't sure how much of that time was fiction. It had certainly felt real, but, in the end, what did it matter? She had only been trying to hurt him, and she had succeeded.

She was ruthless.

Though, a part of him did understand. She had done it to protect her younger sister.

He hadn't known Millie was Emmeline's sister, which was his own fault. He should have realized because the sisters looked so alike, but there was just something so different about Emmeline: her mannerisms, her style. The way she carried herself.

During those twenty-four hours together, he had memorized every detail, paying much more attention to Emmeline than he had during the week he had seen Millie, which was why he hadn't been able to connect the dots.

When he hadn't hit it off with Millie in the way he had hoped to, he wanted to be clear. He could see she really liked him, and he didn't want her to hold out for a future that he knew could never exist.

"I'm not interested, and I never will be," he had told her,

precise and to the point. He knew he was being an asshole about it, but it was always easier if the girl could hate him, and he didn't mind being the villain if it meant there was no room for misunderstanding.

He just didn't realize how much those words could feel like a knife to the gut until he heard them from Emmeline's lips.

Except, whereas he had successfully ensured that Millie would never be interested in him again, Emmeline had failed. No matter how many years had passed, a small part of Luke returned to her, again and again.

With a sigh, Luke rubbed a hand over his face. That was more than enough memories to make him sick. He needed to get back to work.

Standing, he went down to check on the chimeras. "Hey, Sharptooth," he said to his chimera. She lowered her head, nudging him with her horns, and he petted her goat head as her snake tail slithered. "How's it going, girl?"

Sharptooth was on break while his other chimera, Nightfire, was doing a session. Nightfire was his mother's chimera but, since her health had declined, Luke had been looking after him with his younger brother Farhan.

Chimeras' flames weren't as intense as dragons', so he imagined it took the chimeras longer to roast the coffee beans than it did Emmeline's dragons, but his business was smaller than Emmeline's anyway. His coffee was just as good—he knew because he had tried hers. They both had distinct flavor profiles.

Her business was flourishing, while his was struggling. The hills of Starshine Valley were the most popular and populated. Plus, her business started two years before his, so she had the first chance to sink her teeth into the market. But he didn't have a rich family to just hand him the investment money. He had to fight for it, which took time.

Luke thought back to what Anh had said at Genevieve Sterling's birthday, how both companies should consolidate. It would make sense for the sake of lucrative business, and he wouldn't mind working with Emmeline. But her and her pride—it should have been *him* who was angry with *her.*

With a sigh, he finished up his work at Tempest. He flew home on Sharptooth, Nightfire behind them. Chimeras were much smaller than dragons.

Chimeras had the body of a lion, but their wings were skin, muscle, and bone, without scales like dragons or feathers like griffins. Although chimeras did not fly very high or very fast, Luke was still chilly in the evening winter air as he made his way home, even in his neck scarf and coat. Emmeline must have kept warm in that ridiculous fur hat of hers, he thought to himself.

He and Sharptooth flew home to Bayview, the part of Starshine Valley that was all around the bay which opened into the lake. It was always colder and windier by the water, but chimeras loved the water, and most homes were walking distance to the lake. His neighborhood was no different, and they landed in his snow-covered backyard, Nightfire landing a moment later.

Nightfire went straight into the barn to rest, while Sharptooth played in the snow. Luke entered his family home, a mid-sized house that had always been comfortable for his family of four, though his brother had moved out ages ago, while Luke had stayed to look after their mom.

She had been sick since he was in university with a chronic illness; there wasn't much they could do, but she still had regular doctor appointments, medications, and treatments to help mitigate the pain. While Luke's father had a decent job, Luke and his brother Farhan still contributed. Though Farhan could only do so much as a teacher at Bayview Middle School with his own bills to pay.

Besides, Luke was older. Only by two years, but still. He felt it was more his responsibility, and his business had been doing well—until the rent on his plant doubled. If he didn't win Anh's investment, soon keeping Tempest open wouldn't be feasible, and he'd need to pivot to do something else. He couldn't afford to not be making a good income.

Coming in from the cold, Luke went through the house, turning on the lamps and lights now that the sun had set. His mother was asleep in the living room, two blankets over her legs and knitting needles and pink yarn in her lap. Two baby chimeras were asleep at her feet, and he smiled at the twins.

Picking up an empty mug and bowl from the table beside his mom, he took them to the kitchen, putting them in the dishwasher. As he did, he heard his mother's voice.

"Luke? Is that you?"

He washed his hands then went over, kissing her hello. "Hiya, Mama."

"Hello, darling," she said, giving him a slow smile. She tucked a strand of hair behind her ear; her hair was almost all gray now, very little black left, and it was cut in a short bob, easy to manage.

"How are you feeling?" he asked. "Have you eaten?"

"Yes, don't worry," she replied. "Ayman came by a little while ago and we had chai together, and before that, Farhan popped by during his lunch break."

While Luke hated leaving his mother alone at home during the workday, it was only for a few hours. They had all worked out a schedule: his dad left for work around midday, then Farhan would check in during his lunch break, and after that, someone from the neighboring Din family checked in until Luke got home from work. Ayman and Rhea were best friends, and Ayman's eldest, Basim, was Farhan's best friend. Ayman's three daughters also visited often.

"How was your day?" Luke asked. "How's the knitting going?"

Rhea smiled at that. "I'm almost done with the sweater for Butternut," she said. "Then they'll finally be able to match."

Luke reached down to pet Butternut and Squash with both of his hands, and the twin baby chimeras woke up. At the sight of him, they perked with excitement, jumping onto him. He laughed.

"Hey, guys," he said, scratching the cubs' fur coats. Their tiny wings flapped, and they jumped off him, heading for the backdoor. They knew that when Luke was home, so was Sharptooth, their mother.

"Alright, alright," he said, going to open the door. They ran out, and he watched as they made it to the barn before going back to his mom.

"Do you need anything?" Luke asked.

Rhea shook her head. "Come sit with me," she said. "I feel like you've been very busy this week."

Releasing a breath, he went and sat beside her on the couch, sinking into the cushions. "I'm sorry," he said. "There's a new project I'm working on."

"Oh? What is it?"

He had been coming home late the last few days and hadn't spoken to her properly. He hadn't told her about the bookshop proposal, but he told her about it now.

"I'm sure you'll come up with something wonderful," Rhea said, voice confident.

Luke let out a breath. "It needs to be exemplary," he said. "Especially since I need to beat my opponent, too."

"Who's your opponent?" Rhea asked, and his heartbeat quickened just at the thought of her.

"The owner of Inferno." He paused. "Emmeline Sterling."

"Emmeline?" Rhea thought about it for a moment. Recognition flashed across her face, and she opened her mouth. "Ah, that girl you used to like in university?"

Embarrassment flushed through him. "How do you even remember that?" he asked. "I don't recall even mentioning her." That was a bald-faced lie, but he had to salvage some shred of his dignity.

A task his mother would not aid him in, apparently. Rhea snorted. "You only went on and on about her for weeks," she said. "You always mention her, even now."

Luke scowled. "I do not."

"It's always *Inferno this* and *Inferno that*."

She looked amused, poking his side. He scowled. "Well,

I'm not a schoolboy with a crush, Mama," he said. "She is my *rival*. I need to *beat* her, or Tempest fails."

"Okay, jaani," Rhea said, touching his face. "Don't work too hard, though."

She went back to her knitting, and he looked at his mother, how tired she looked, how tired she always looked.

He *had* to work hard. For her, he had to.

He had to win.

CHAPTER 9

After the chaos of visiting Millie, Emmeline was happy to return home to her routine and work, though things were slightly thrown into disarray with the addition of one fat baby dragon.

She was babysitting Motu for the next few weeks, which Torch was happy about, but Emmeline had her hands full with the curious baby dragon, especially at the roasting plant. While he was mostly trained, he wasn't nearly as disciplined as Torch had been at that age.

Which meant that Emmeline was currently chasing Motu around instead of getting any work done.

"Motu!" she cried, running down the stairs. The baby dragon had managed to slip out when her manager had opened her office door to ask her something.

By the time Emmeline reached the baby dragon, he was watching Char roast a batch of coffee beans, his purple eyes alight. Torch and Midnight were on the side. Midnight was lying down, eyes closed, while Torch was sitting watching Char.

Motu hopped and flew over and tried to join Char, puffing out a little fireball.

"Uff, Motu, no!" Emmeline scolded, reaching to pull him from the air.

She didn't want the baby so close to Charr's fire, and Char didn't seem too happy about it, either. Without pausing his flames, Char batted a wing out, pushing Motu away, though the baby dragon was hardly deterred.

Motu went around Char, trying to join him on the other side, and Emmeline let out a groan. "Motu, stop it."

Seeing Emmeline was upset, Torch scowled at Motu, hissing. That had the desired effect.

Chagrined, Motu drooped down to the floor. Dragging his feet, he waddled over to the side, head hanging low before he hid his face behind his wings. Emmeline's heart broke.

"Okay, I'm sorry!" she said, going over to him.

Even though he was heavy, she scooped him up into her arms, and he moved his wings to the side so she could cuddle with him. He pressed his little paws against her chest, then nuzzled against her, no longer upset at all.

Emmeline narrowed her eyes. Had she just been played by a baby dragon?

"You have to behave, okay?" she told him, voice warning. Motu jumped from her arms, bouncing on the ground as if he hadn't heard her. "Motu! I mean it." She pointed a finger at him and he kept jumping happily. Midnight lifted her head, unamused.

The older dragon roared at Motu, and he jolted, settling down. While Torch thought Motu's shenanigans were cute,

Midnight was too old and easily irritated to be won over by the baby dragon.

Luckily, Motu was afraid of the old girl and obediently sat in place.

"Thanks, Midnight," Emmeline said, as Midnight set her head back down to rest.

Emmeline was just about to go back to her office when her phone rang; she picked up.

"Hiya, Dad," she said.

"Hello," Charles replied. "How are you? Are you coming for dinner tonight?"

"No, but there should be leftovers from yesterday for you guys to eat," she replied quickly, wanting to get back to work.

"Oh, I wasn't asking because of dinner," he said. "You know we can manage on our own."

They really couldn't. "Yes, Dad, I know you can."

"It's just nice to see you, that's all."

Emmeline pinched the bridge of her nose, thumb brushing against her nose-ring. Her father was just as bad as a baby dragon with his need for attention. Going to the side, Emmeline slowed down. "How has your day been?" she asked. "What are you up to?"

Her father was a retired engineer and usually spent his time golfing, but in the winter, he truly didn't know what to do with himself. Even more so with Samreen down at Millie's.

Emmeline would suggest he go down to Millie's as well, but she knew the man would only drive everyone there absolutely insane. Charles was fastidious—that was where Emmeline got it from—a quality not needed in a home with two toddlers and a newborn.

"Oh, not much," Charles replied. "I was just doing today's crossword puzzle. Can you guess what I got stumped on?"

No matter how old or busy Emmeline got, her parents always assumed that if they were free, she would be also. Never mind that it was the middle of the weekday, a time universally reserved for work.

Still, Emmeline indulged her father, and after chatting with him for a bit, she grabbed Motu and finally went back to her office, where she went over her ideas for the coffee shop. But she needed to spend more time at the bookshop before she could really get down to the details.

Luckily, Anh had already told her to come by the bookshop today so she could show her the office with all the files and relevant information. Emmeline was heading over straight after work. She was on a tight schedule and spread thin, but she had planned things out meticulously so it would be fine.

After work, Emmeline mounted Torch, who scooped Motu up in her claws, and they took off, flying to the bookshop. Motu couldn't fly long distances yet since he was only a year old, and she didn't trust the little menace on his own. It was typical auntie behavior of her, but she couldn't help but compare Motu with Ginny's Fang, who was so well-trained.

They arrived at the Tales & Tails Bookshop soon, at the exact same time Luke arrived on his chimera. Chimeras and dragons didn't get along very well, and Emmeline didn't help matters by immediately tensing at the sight of Luke. Torch growled, baring her teeth, and Luke's chimera replied in kind.

"Easy, Sharptooth," Luke said, petting his chimera before dismounting. Emmeline dismounted as well, and

Torch released Motu, who had also begun growling, blindly following Torch's behavior.

Luke glanced from the dragons to Emmeline, as if waiting for her to chide them. Emmeline didn't bother, and Luke raised a brow, gaze going to Motu.

"New baby?" he asked.

"My brother's," she replied.

"Haris's or Naveed's?" he asked, and she narrowed her eyes at him. Why did he remember her brothers' names?

More importantly, what was he even doing here? Then she realized Anh must have invited him, too, for the same reason. *Ugh*.

"Haris's," she replied, voice curt as she headed for the door. He took a large step forward, getting there first, where he placed his hand over hers on the door frame. She retracted her hand and he held the door open.

"After you," he said with a smile. He was making a show of being gentlemanly, probably to annoy and/or distract her.

Emmeline glanced back at Torch, who had a protective wing around Motu and was looking sternly at Sharptooth.

"Torch," Emmeline said, voice steady. "Relax."

Her dragon settled, and Emmeline called Motu, who came flying over, landing in her arms. Emmeline nodded at Torch to go on. Torch flew off, but Emmeline swore she saw the dragon give Luke a dirty look.

Sharptooth looked unhappy but Luke nodded at her, and the chimera took off as well, heading in the opposite direction. Still holding the door open for Emmeline, Luke gave her an easy smile.

With Motu in her arms, Emmeline strode inside, Luke

following behind her. The bookshop was toasty warm, filled with patrons and light. She spotted a newborn opala dragon wrapped in blankets, sound asleep in its basket. A year-old red-scaled garneta crept close, trying to take a look at the tiny newborn.

Emmeline set Motu down, and he held onto one of her legs with his paw, looking around the bookshop. He grew excited when he saw the other baby dragons, looking up at her with wide eyes.

She petted his head, and he turned his attention to Luke, who was watching her and the baby dragon. Motu gave him a curious glance, and Luke smiled.

"Hello, angel," he said, voice smooth. Her stomach twisted at his sweet tone, and she watched as he crouched down to pet the baby dragon with his ringed fingers. She expected Motu to bite him—would welcome it, even—but instead, Motu made a purring sound, leaning into Luke's touch.

Luke smiled, pleased.

Emmeline glared at the little traitor.

"Motu," she hissed, and the baby dragon looked up at her with big purple eyes. Guilt pricked at her. She gathered Motu up into her arms and kissed his face.

Luke rose up, watching her with an amused expression.

"Motu?" he asked, arching a brow.

"It means little fatso," she told him.

"I know." His lips twitched. "A bit rude, don't you think?"

"Not at all," she replied. "We mean it affectionately. Motu knows that—don't you?" She smushed the baby dragon's face, and Motu swatted at her hand with his paw, not enjoying her playful aggression.

"Cute," Luke replied, but when she glanced up, she saw that he wasn't looking at the baby dragon—he was looking at her. There was fondness in his warm brown eyes that made her feel immediately flustered.

She swallowed, looking away. As she did, she spotted Anh.

"Anh!" Emmeline called, going over to meet the old lady, who was dressed in a classy matching tweed skirt and blazer. Anh was chatting with Minh but paused to greet her and Luke.

"Hello, dears. And who is this little darling?" Anh asked, petting Motu.

"My brother's baby," Emmeline replied. "On babysitting duties . . . Not to worry, though. He won't cause any trouble."

"A little trouble never killed anybody," Minh said from his reading chair, cracking open his book again.

Anh affectionately rolled her eyes at her little brother. "A little trouble most surely *has* killed somebody, but never mind you." She turned to Emmeline and Luke. "Right this way."

They followed her to the back of the bookshop, past a group of teenage girls squealing over a new romance, a couple exchanging book recommendations, and a bookseller pulling out a six-book fantasy series for a middle-aged man. Emmeline smiled to herself as she saw some familiar faces—friends of friends, or family members of clients, or old classmates.

Anh punched in the code, letting them into the office. Inside, there was a desk with a computer and printer, in front of which there were two seats. On the other wall, there was a labeled filing cabinet. Luke closed the door behind them, and she realized how small the office was compared to the lofty bookshop. Warmth spread through her, and she set Motu down to take off her coat.

Before she could, she felt gentle hands on her shoulders. "Allow me," he said, voice low by her ear. As he slipped her coat off, his hands brushed against her bare shoulders; she was wearing a lacy slip blouse on top of leather pants. Though his touch was fleeting, it sent a shiver down her spine, making her skin prickle with goosebumps.

Emmeline turned, watching as Luke hung up her coat, then took off his own. He wore black trousers and a black button-down shirt, the top buttons of which were undone to reveal three chain necklaces lying flat on the bare skin of his chest. She had the insane urge to reach out and touch them.

Shaking her head, Emmeline turned to Anh, who was watching them with an amused glance. Emmeline's cheeks flushed, and she straightened her back, focusing.

"The log-in information for the computer is written down here," Anh said, tapping a notepad. "All the reports and data for the business have been downloaded onto the computer, and they are all most likely also printed out and filed in the cabinet. Should you need anything else, feel free to ask Ola in the front. Minh most definitely will not know anything useful."

"Perfect, thank you so much," Emmeline said, giving Anh a bright smile.

Anh nodded, heading for the door, which Luke opened for her. She glanced back at both of them, eyes twinkling. "Have fun."

With that, the old lady left them alone in the office.

Emmeline released a breath and, sensing she was a bit more relaxed now, Motu strayed from his position by her feet, poking around the office.

"Motu, no," she warned, as he opened his mouth to chew on a wire. The baby dragon closed his mouth, and Emmeline headed for the filing cabinet, opening the first drawer, which was labeled with the current year. Luke stood across from her, looking through the drawer with her.

The office was quiet save for the shuffling of papers, until a voice broke the silence.

"So you're babysitting," Luke said.

"Why are you trying to talk to me?" she asked.

"Fine." His jaw clenched. "Forget it."

Guilt pricked her. Perhaps she shouldn't be *so* petty. "Yes," she replied. "I'm babysitting for my younger brother for the next six weeks."

Luke's eyes widened. "Six weeks?" He whistled. "That's a long time."

"Don't get your hopes up that I'll be distracted," she said, eyes narrowed. "I'm still going to beat you for Anh's investment."

Luke was unbothered by such a comment; instead, his expression was pensive. "Aren't you Drakkons not allowed to hatch your dragon eggs until you're old enough to look after the baby dragon yourself and take responsibility?" he asked.

She furrowed her brows, not following. "Yes."

"So why did your brother hatch his egg if he couldn't manage it?"

She blinked. "Well, he can," she replied, voice defensive. "He's just busy with school right now."

"And you're not busy with work?" he asked.

Her skin prickled. He was right, and he was the only person to have batted an eyelash at the fact. Samreen had simply replied that Haris was her brother—of course Emmeline had to help him. They all took it as a given.

"I can handle it," Emmeline replied, tone clipped.

"I'm sure you can," Luke replied. "But why burn yourself out? You need to set better boundaries."

Shock rippled through her. It didn't matter that what he was saying had some truth to it. Who the hell was he to speak to her in such a manner?

"Yeah, I do," she said, and he looked satisfied for a moment before registering that the anger on her face was directed at him. "So stop talking about things you know nothing about."

He blinked, taken aback. "I wasn't trying . . ." he started, but she turned her attention to the file in her hand, ignoring him. She needed to focus, anyway.

Walking over to one of the chairs, she sat down to look over the financial report in front of her. She'd need to see how much room there was in the budget for the coffee shop before beginning her plans.

They worked in silence while Motu occupied himself with a chew-toy. Emmeline could sense the baby dragon was slowly losing interest, and an hour later, Motu disregarded the toy entirely, climbing up onto the chair she was sitting on and jumping off. After he had done that about ten times, she felt her patience snap.

"Motu, behave," she said, on edge.

Motu looked up at her with an expression of utter betrayal,

and she sighed. This was what happened when one was not stern with a baby dragon; the animal grew spoiled. She would give her brother a lecture about this later—another thing added to her to-do list.

Rubbing her temples, she went back to the financial reports, highlighting key elements. Motu scratched at her legs with his paws, and she looked down to find him angrily pouting at her.

She put her index finger to her lips, hushing him, and his expression grew more upset. He let out a whimper, scratching his face with his paws. Luke glanced over.

"Acha, na," she said quietly, trying to coax him into relaxing, but it was too late. The baby dragon was upset, and he began growling.

Not only was it distracting, but embarrassment flushed through her. What would Luke think? That she couldn't even handle one baby dragon?

"Tch, Motu, bas," she scolded, and Motu hissed at her, jumping up onto the table. He kicked her stack of papers and they went fluttering in the air. Emmeline's jaw dropped open.

"Motu," she warned, but he was having a full-blown temper tantrum now. He leapt from the table, flying around the small office space, being deliberately destructive. He flew into the coat rack, knocking it over. Their coats toppled to the ground.

"Motu, stop!" Emmeline cried, appalled at the baby dragon's behavior. She reached for him, but he flew up, away from her. "Motu!"

"Here, let me help," Luke said, getting up and coming to her side.

She whirled on him. "I don't need your help!"

He made an irritated sound. "Just let me—"

Motu flew to the other side of the desk, and Luke followed with Emmeline right behind him. There weren't many places for Motu to go in the office, and he quickly turned, changing course. At the same time, they both reached for Motu from opposite ends.

The devilish baby dragon ducked, causing Emmeline and Luke to crash into one another.

"Woah!"

Luke fell back onto the desk chair and Emmeline fell with him, landing directly on his lap. Her hands fell to his shoulders, while his hands went to her hips, holding her steady.

For a moment, they both froze, staring at each other. Her blood rushed through her veins.

Then, his gaze dropped to her mouth. Desire pulsed through her, making her lips part.

She felt his grip on her tighten, fingers pressing in, and her breathing grew shallow. She was losing all sense, but she used the very last shred of her wits to push his chest.

"Let go of me," she said, though her voice didn't sound nearly as commanding as she wanted it to.

He immediately let her go, and she stood, skin burning.

Her knees felt weak, and she glanced over at Motu, who was now sitting calmly on the ground; she could have sworn he was smiling at her, happy to see her punished for having scolded him. She glared at the baby dragon, though he wasn't truly the cause of why she was feeling so flustered.

Emmeline glanced back at Luke, who was still seated languidly in the chair, knees spread apart. She felt dizzy.

"This isn't working," she blurted out.

His brows knit together. "What?"

Luke stood up then, until he was right in front of her, and she involuntarily took a step back.

"This," she said, gesturing to the both of them. "Us being here at the same time. It isn't productive."

As he cocked his head to the side, Emmeline rolled her shoulders. She tried to regain control of the situation and *not* think about how it felt to be in his lap, the solid feel of his chest, the way he had held her flush against him. It would have been so easy to—

She cut that thought off before it went further, blinking fast to stave off the faint feeling spreading through her. "We need to decide on a schedule of when each of us can be here and the other cannot."

He thought about it for a second. "That's petty," he said. "Not to mention immature."

She rolled her eyes. "Oh, bite me."

"Don't tempt me." His gaze scorched through her, and her skin warmed. Leveling her breathing, she reminded herself that he was purposefully lewd just to bother her. He was an incorrigible flirt. There was no need to think anything of his words.

Straightening her shoulders, she focused. "If we divide our hours at the shop, we don't need to spend time in each other's company. A prospect I'd gladly welcome."

As she spoke the words, she understood how petty and immature it sounded, but she didn't care. She couldn't think straight when she was around him! Being near him felt like being around a live wire, and any moment she'd be electrocuted. To death.

Luke's lips twitched as he regarded her, as if he could read her mind. "Okay, I'll humor you," he said. She swallowed. "Like anyone else with a job, I work about nine to five, Monday through Friday." He paused condescendingly. "I assume you do, as well?"

"Yes," she begrudgingly admitted.

"Hm." He pretended to think. "So we're free at the same time. If we divide that up, it limits our already limited time. Not to mention being needlessly tedious." He took a step toward her, leaning forward. "Feels like a lot of trouble."

Realizing he was right, Emmeline held back a groan. She clenched her jaw, trying to think and, as she did, he considered her closely, dark eyes unreadable.

"Now, I don't mind trouble," Luke said plainly, and then his tone shifted. "Though I don't understand what for." He cocked his head to the side. "What is it, Sterling? Can't handle being around me?"

Though his assumption was arrogant and ridiculous, Emmeline paused before responding, and he took the split-second hesitation to pounce.

Savage pleasure spread across his face, his dark eyes glinting like a blade catching sunlight.

"That's it, isn't it?" he said, satisfaction dripping from his words. "You can't handle me."

She scoffed. "I can see the years haven't done anything for your inflated ego," she gritted out. "I just thought it would be *easier* not to be in each other's way. I can handle being around you just fine. I am a professional, after all."

"Okay, sure." He shrugged easily, not believing her. She glared, and his voice turned to a dare: "Prove it, then. We don't need to work different times."

"We don't," she snapped, and he considered something.

"Actually, you know what? We should be here at the exact *same* time," he added. "I don't trust you not to hide files away or to try and sabotage me."

That was, unfortunately, also a good point. She narrowed her eyes at him. "I don't trust *you*, either," she replied.

"So we're in agreement, then," he said. "We'll come to the bookshop only when the other is here. Deal?"

He held out his hand for her. Her gaze dropped to his outstretched hand, and her pulse quickened.

Why did she have the sense that she had been tricked into something? It felt like she was treading dangerous territory, but there was no way she was backing down from the challenge in his gleaming eyes, the smirk tilting his lips as if he was waiting to call her bluff.

Emmeline lifted her chin. "Deal."

She took his hand in hers, shaking it. His large hand tightened around hers, and an electric jolt went through her at the contact. As if sensing it, he ran his thumb across her knuckles

Then, he gave her hand a slight but firm tug. She stumbled forward, and her breathing hitched. She inhaled the smell of his cologne: cypress and spruce. Why, oh why, did he have to smell so good?

Feeling disarmed by how close they were, she gazed up at

him with wide eyes. His gaze dropped to her mouth, and her lips parted involuntarily. Her stomach burned.

A slow smile spread across Luke's lips.

Emmeline had the distinct feeling she had no idea what she had just agreed to.

CHAPTER 10

The next day was Saturday, thank god; Emmeline needed a day off. In the morning, she took a long, hot bath, then headed straight for the Baby Dragon Cafe, taking Motu with her.

Luckily, the little menace helped distract her thoughts from constantly straying to Luke, though the sight of the baby dragon also reminded her of the situation in the office, how she had ended up in Luke's arms. The memory made heat flush through her, and she scowled—but how could she be angry with such an adorable creature? Especially when he gave such good cuddles.

With a sigh, Emmeline dismounted from Torch on Main Street. It had begun snowing, little flurries of snowflakes dancing in the air and sticking to her skin. Motu opened his mouth, trying to catch them, and she steered the baby dragon into the cafe, seeking shelter.

The place was packed. As she stood in line, her thoughts went to Luke again. She didn't know what was worse, his probing questions or the feel of his fingers pressing into her hips as she'd sat on his lap.

She did *not* need to think about that.

But she couldn't get his question about the baby dragon out of her head, either: "And you're not busy?"

Of course she was! Who was he to question such a thing?

Emmeline rubbed her temples. She needed caffeine. Luckily, it was almost her turn to order, and she looked around for Saphira, who she was supposed to be meeting along with Aiden, probably, since the man was never farther than a three-foot radius from his wife, if that.

Emmeline didn't spot her friend through the crowd. The establishment was busier than ever with the expansion and extended hours, which was good for business—both Saphira's and Emmeline's, as Emmeline sourced the cafe's coffee.

The expansion had been executed wonderfully by Theo, and there was lots more space, which was ideal for these winter months when the outside garden wasn't in use.

Motu hopped along as she went forward in line, until it was Emmeline's turn to order.

"One large karak chai," she said. "And a cake rusk please."

She pointed to the hard biscuit in the display case. It sat in a jar along with a sign that read 'The Baby Dragon Bakery by Theo Noon'. Beside that was the bakery's emblem: a cupcake with wings. She spotted other fusion desserts like gajar halwa cheesecake cups and chocolate milk barfi squares. There were also basic bakery items, such as croissants, donuts, mini cakes, and scones.

Motu pawed at her leg, and she glanced down at his

big purple eyes. "And some burned naan chips," Emmeline added to the order.

The barista handed those to her first, and she set the bowl down in front of Motu. The baby dragon munched happily as the barista gave her a piece of cake rusk on a plate. Emmeline stood to the side to wait for her chai as Motu happily ate his chips, bouncing in place, his hyper-levels slowly increasing.

"Behave," she said, careful not to be too stern or she'd elicit a tantrum. Luckily, Motu settled. Emmeline considered that the other baby dragons around him were probably having an effect.

In the early days of the cafe, all the baby dragons had been a bit chaotic, but now they knew how to behave, and the cafe ran harmoniously. Some baby dragons slept in little nooks, while others played together, mindful of the customers and definitely careful not to spit fire anywhere.

"Here you go," the barista said, handing her a large mug of chai.

"Mm, thank you." Emmeline stood by the wall, Motu at her feet as she took a sip and looked around. There were a few really young baby dragons; at under six months, they were delicate and vulnerable and as such were dressed in little knit sweaters. Some even had mittens on their tiny paws! She even spotted a baby dragon with a cable-knit trapper hat, complete with a puffy pom-pom on top.

Too cute!

Emmeline looked down at Motu, wanting to wrangle him into such an adorable outfit. He followed her gaze, and, understanding, took a pause from munching to hiss at her.

She rolled her eyes. "Alright," she conceded. "But you have to admit they're adorable."

Before she could attempt to convince Motu further, Saphira came floating down the stairs. Emmeline lifted a hand and Saphira came over, her braid swinging.

"You're early!" Saphira said.

"I needed this," Emmeline replied, holding up her mug.

"Hello, darling." Saphira petted Motu, and he leaned into her touch. "He's your brother's, isn't he?"

Emmeline nodded. "I'm stuck babysitting because Haris failed one of his classes."

"You and your baji duties never finish," Saphira said, letting out a breath. Emmeline took another sip of chai. "How's Millie? And the baby?"

Pulling out her phone, Emmeline showed Saphira pictures, telling her about the trip as Saphira listened intently with a fond smile. Emmeline took a bite of the cake rusk, pausing her storytelling to compliment the bakery item.

"Mm, this is good," Emmeline said. "Crispy but not too hard, and not too sweet, either."

"Oh, good!" Saphira said, relieved. "Theo's been playing with his recipe for that very reason!" She glanced over Emmeline's shoulder. "And speaking of—"

Emmeline turned to see the baker entering from the front door, his girlfriend tucked into his coat. Lavinia wore a huge scarf wrapped around her face with fluffy pink earmuffs and thick-soled boots, giving some height to her short frame, though her boyfriend still towered over her.

Saphira waved, and the couple came over.

"Ohmygoodness, who is this?" Lavinia asked, crouching

down to Motu. He looked curiously at her earmuffs, and Lavinia took them off, sticking them on Motu's head. The baby dragon was displeased, trying to get the earmuffs off.

"Babysitting for my brother," Emmeline explained, as Lavinia took her earmuffs back.

"Aw, fun!" Lavinia said, standing up. "I miss babysitting."

"I remember you watched your mom's friend's dragon for a bit!" Saphira said.

Lavinia nodded, tucking her straight hair behind her ear. "Biter. I miss that cutie-pie."

"We just saw her last week," Theo said, and Lavinia rolled her eyes.

Theo smiled, kissing Lavinia's temple, eliciting a smile from her as well. Though they had only been dating for a year, they had been best friends since childhood, and Emmeline loved how comfortable they were with one another, as if they were made from the same clay. Her heart ached.

"You're welcome to take this rascal off my hands," Emmeline joked. Motu looked up at her with betrayal in his purple eyes. "I'm kidding!" she told him, reaching down to smush his face in her free hand. "You're my little cutu."

"Motu was Torch's egg, wasn't he?" Saphira asked, and Emmeline nodded.

Lavinia gasped. "That means you're a grandma," Lavinia said. "Because Torch is your baby, and Motu is Torch's."

Emmeline gave Lavinia a threatening look. "I'm going to pretend like I didn't hear you just say that, Lavinia," she said.

"Oops!" Lavinia hid in Theo's side, and he wrapped his arms around her, hiding her in his coat. Saphira laughed, as another joined their group.

"Having fun without me?" Ginny asked, her baby dragon flying at her side.

"Hey!" Emmeline hugged her youngest cousin hello as Fang went down to knock heads with Motu.

"Motu, share with Fang," Emmeline said, but the baby dragon gathered his naan chips into his arms, hiding them behind his wings. Fang snarled. Motu jumped, alarmed, then spread his wings open, pushing the chips forward. Fang munched on one.

"Looks like Fang is a little bully just like his mama," Emmeline joked.

Ginny smiled, taking that as a compliment. "The whole gang is here?" she asked. "Here I was thinking I was special."

"We're just missing Aiden," Saphira replied. She bit back a giggle, and Emmeline raised a brow, suspicious. Saphira was particularly glowing today, lit from within with some sort of happiness that seemed extraordinary.

Saphira caught Emmeline's expression and, just as Emmeline opened her mouth to ask, Saphira blurted out the news.

"I'm pregnant!" As soon as the words were out, Saphira gasped, clapping a hand over her mouth. The rest of them were silent with shock.

Then Aiden came in from the back, snowflakes in his dark hair and on his coat. Saphira's eyes were wide. Aiden took one look at his wife and started laughing, shaking his head. "She told you, didn't she?" he asked, brushing the snow off his coat before wrapping an arm around her.

"Oops." Saphira canoodled into his side, sheepish, but Aiden only grinned. The rest of them erupted in congratulations, giving hugs and kisses. Fang and Motu were unsure what was happening, but they watched with pleased expressions.

"I had a whole set-up outside in the garden," Aiden said, when the first round of congratulations was over.

"I know, I'm sorry!" Saphira said. "I couldn't hold it in any longer."

Aiden snorted, looking over at the group. "Mind you, we found out three days ago," he told them.

"Three days is a long time to keep a secret!" Saphira argued.

"It's very early, so we've only told my parents and now you guys," Aiden said. "If you can be discreet. Particularly at family dinner later this week—don't need the entire extended family to know just yet."

"You only told Ginny now?" Emmeline asked, offended on her behalf, and Ginny smiled.

"No, they told me at the same time they told my parents. I just wanted to be here for the fun," she said, scooping Fang up into her arms and giving him a happy kiss.

"Speaking of fun—tell me if there's anything specific you guys want to eat and drink, otherwise I have little treats prepared for us," Saphira said.

"And we can go sit outside," Aiden added.

"Whatever you have prepared is good for us!" Lavinia said.

With a nod, Saphira went to the kitchen to let them know, while Aiden led the rest of them out to the garden, which was closed for the winter months. It was snowing lightly, the world white and bright, and Aiden had set up a big table with chairs and garlands of flowers, variations of white and pink along with greenery.

Aiden and Saphira's dragon, Sparky, was beside the table, catching snowflakes on his tongue. He was full-sized now, too big to come inside, and he took up most of the space in the garden. When Fang and Motu spotted him, they flew over, and Sparky played with them.

"Oi, Sparky," Aiden said. "A little help?" He gestured to the bonfire, and Sparky trotted over, easily lighting it. "Good boy," Aiden said, petting him. Sparky licked Aiden's hand.

Emmeline was always glad to see Aiden with Sparky. There was a time where the two didn't get along at all, but now their bond was unbreakable.

Saphira came, and they all took a seat, gathering around the fire as snow fell softly. Shortly thereafter, one of the cafe workers came out with a spread of snacks: hot chocolate, s'mores dip, caramel popcorn, along with chicken patties and little fried potato samosas.

They sat and munched on snacks and chatted. It was a much-needed break from the chaotic week she had had. While her to-do list was constantly running at the back of her mind, when she was here with such delightful company, it was easier to just relax.

"Ginny, did you see the text I sent you last week about the Baby Dragon Book Club?" Emmeline asked. Ginny hadn't responded.

"I did," she replied now, not seeming interested at all.

"A book club for baby dragons? Ohmygod, stop, that sounds adorable!" Saphira said, holding a hand to her heart.

"If I had known about it, I would have joined Sparky, but he's not a baby anymore."

"It could be good for Fang!" Emmeline told Ginny. "It's supposed to help baby dragons socialize and make friends, as well as behave better." While Fang was very well-behaved, she had noticed at Ginny's birthday party that he only wanted to spend time with his rider.

Ginny groaned. "That sounds awful."

"Come on, it'll be fun! I'll join with Motu!" He certainly could stand to be better behaved.

"Okay, fine," Ginny acquiesced. "Fang could possibly do with more socializing. The other day . . ."

Emmeline went to pour herself more hot chocolate from the thermos just as the baby dragons were playing nearby. Motu knocked into her, and she jolted, hot chocolate spilling onto her hand.

"Ow!" she hissed, scalding the side of her hand.

Motu's eyes widened.

"Oh no! Are you okay?" Saphira asked, alarmed.

"It's fine," Emmeline said, grabbing a napkin. She dabbed at her hand as Motu came to her side, licking where the skin was red. That helped to soothe the pain. Motu looked up at her with apologetic eyes, pouting, and she gave him a smile.

"It's okay," she said gently, touching his face.

"Does it hurt?" Aiden asked.

"I'm fine." Emmeline forced a smile, not wanting anyone to worry even as her skin pulsed. "Ginny, what were you saying about Fang?"

As Ginny continued her story, Emmeline felt unsteady,

though it wasn't from the burn, but a memory, long buried and resurfacing now.

That night at the bookshop, the night she and Luke met. They had been there for hours, drinking the terrible tea as they talked about so many different things. A baby dragon had knocked into someone; their cup of tea had upended, heading straight for Emmeline's hand.

Except the hot beverage had never landed. Luke had blocked the tea, catching it all in his own hands.

Emmeline had known she was just there as part of an elaborate plan to get revenge, but when he had done that, she had felt unmoored. As if he was somebody she could truly like. She had felt pity that they hadn't met under different circumstances.

She had convinced herself it was just his way of tricking girls into thinking he genuinely cared—but even she could recognize the fallacy in that. Why let himself get burnt for her? His skin had turned red. She remembered that.

The memory hurt.

Even after she left her friends and the cafe an hour later, she couldn't shake the feeling. Yearning beat through her, though she didn't know for what. Emmeline pressed a hand against her chest, trying to push the feeling away, but it felt bone deep, embedded in a place she couldn't extract it from.

Had it been there all along?

Concern spread through her at the prospect of working so closely with Luke at the bookshop. Even being around him this past week had felt like too much. Would she survive five more weeks in close proximity?

Lost in thought, Emmeline went down Main Street, turning onto Elderberry. Motu flew beside her as she took in a deep breath of winter air. She would call Torch to her side soon; she just needed to collect herself for a moment first. Her dragon would immediately sense Emmeline was troubled; she didn't want to worry Torch.

A cold wind pushed against her, and she squeezed her eyes shut against it. It had stopped snowing, but everything was covered in a layer of ice, and even the wind felt like it carried tiny shards.

Keeping her eyes closed for a moment longer, she continued walking.

Until she felt someone grab her from behind, jerking her back. Her eyes flew open just in time to see a car skidding on the road, narrowly missing her as the driver regained control of his car.

With the breath knocked out of her lungs, Emmeline reeled, turning to see who had saved her.

It was Luke, his face livid. "Are you trying to get yourself killed?" he cried. Emmeline blinked, heart pounding. Motu had fallen back, but he flew to her side now, holding onto her leg.

Her hands shook. What if something had happened to Motu?

"I . . ." Emmeline opened her mouth to respond, but no words came out.

"Answer me, damn it," he said, shaking her shoulders. The movement jolted her awake, and hot emotion spread through her.

"What do you care?" she asked, anger seeping into both

her tone and her expression. He scowled at her, countenance livid.

"Of course I care!" he snapped.

Her pulse quickened, and the question was out before she could stop herself: "Why? Why would you care?"

She glared up at him, and his jaw clenched. Time seemed to slow and stop as they looked into each other's eyes. There was so much hidden in the dark depths that she couldn't understand, even though a part of her nagged that it should have been obvious.

Luke released his grip on her then, taking a step back. He gave her a dirty look. "You're smart enough, Emmeline," he said. The sound of her name made her shudder. "Figure it out."

Before she could respond, he stalked away.

CHAPTER 11

Luke had been on Elderberry Lane by chance that Saturday, and he'd spotted Emmeline instantly. Anytime he was in the Hills, a part of him always hoped to run into her, but that afternoon, she looked troubled, closing her eyes against the wind, and the scene had played out like one from a horror film: her feet carrying her onto the street, just as a car skidded on the ice.

He'd lunged to reach her, pulling her back.

When Emmeline's eyes flew open, her gaze immediately went to Motu, worrying over him, and for some reason, the gesture had sent him over the edge. She took care of everyone else, but who took care of her?

Her negligence regarding herself had made him angry, and then she had had the audacity to ask him why he would care whether she got hurt or not.

A week later, as they worked together quietly in the Tales & Tails Bookshop office, the stupid question still pissed him off.

Of course he cared. He couldn't bear the idea of her getting hurt—how could she not know that? It was why, despite what she did, he had never retaliated. It would have been so easy to hold a grudge, but he didn't want to hold a grudge—he just wanted to hold her.

A fact he desperately tried to ignore. He was supposed to be focusing on this proposal, after all. He was still facing a range of problems at Tempest, and this was his last chance at saving the business.

He was already behind on this month's rent, a fact he'd been reminded of. For the last nine months it had felt like there were always too many bills to pay, both from the business side of things and for his mother's medical care.

Luke focused his attention on his laptop. He was sitting in the bookshop's office. Even from behind the closed door, he could hear the busy bookshop outside as customers asked booksellers for recommendations or directions.

He had decided the first floor would be best for the coffee shop, and was now doing research into menus. Since the Baby Dragon Cafe was a roaring success and only a block away, he knew the bookshop's coffee shop would need a different focus.

So far, he was considering a focus on different coffee-brewing methods. He was an aficionado himself, but most cafes only had basic options like espresso-based drinks (such as lattes or cappuccinos) or regularly brewed black coffee. The Baby Dragon was the same, but they had a wide drinks menu with a variety of drinks from chai to matcha to tea to refreshers. So a coffee focus in the bookshop would not infringe on the cafe's business.

He stole a glance toward Emmeline, who had been

working in diligent silence. Her hair was twisted and held in place with a massive clip, her bangs falling in front of her face. She had been quiet all week, and it was not at all what he had expected when he'd proposed they should only come to the bookshop at the same time.

He had thought being together would create more opportunities, like the situation last week, when she'd ended up in his lap. Was he to blame? The memory was one that had tortured him, but he couldn't stop revisiting it, just like all his other memories of her. He was becoming a real masochist.

But she kept to herself, and he found he didn't mind that too much, either. He liked being in her presence, watching her.

There were so many new details to catalogue: her hair had always been long, but it was longer now, cut in a way that somehow always gave a sense of movement; where she used to keep her nails painted the same blood-red as her lipstick, now they were bare; she always had at least two drinks nearby; and a hundred other tiny details.

"What?" Emmeline asked, voice sharp as a razor as she glanced over at him. They were both sharing the desk, sitting on the opposite end from the computer in chairs.

He blinked. "What?"

"Don't act dumb," she said, sitting back in her chair. "You keep looking over at me. I've been noticing all week."

"And you think *I* have an inflated ego?" he snorted, trying to act cool even though she was absolutely right; he had been watching her all week.

She released a short breath from her nostrils. "I can't

believe you're here at all," she muttered, returning her attention to her laptop.

"What's that supposed to mean?" he asked, intrigued.

"Your business." The words were clipped. "I can't believe you copied my idea."

Shock poured through him, and he froze. Did she really not remember?

"You're kidding," he said, dumbfounded.

"No, I'm not," she replied. "You should have come up with your own idea instead of taking mine."

His disbelief was promptly replaced with anger. It wasn't the accusation that upset him, but the fact that she genuinely didn't remember how they had come up with the animal-roasted coffee idea at the same time.

It was the morning after they'd slept together.

She never thought about that time together, did she? Clearly not. She didn't remember it at all, when he had memorized every moment, replayed it again and again like a broken record.

That night, the way it had felt to be around her all evening was unlike anything he'd experienced in his life. Kissing her for the first time had been like unlocking a new language that had always existed deep inside of him but he'd never understood before.

They continued to get up to no good until the bookshop slowly emptied out and Minh told them it was time for closing. Luke had been disappointed at the thought of the night being over. As they headed out into the cold, he had planned to ask her out for dinner the next day, when she'd surprised him by asking if he wanted to come back to her place, her family home, though no one was in.

Of course he'd said yes. They went back to hers, and he had been jittery like he was a teenager on a first date. She was acting so confident, but he could tell she was nervous, too. He caught the way her hands slightly trembled, just the slightest chink in her armor, and he'd held her hand.

The night they slept together was probably the best night of his life.

The next morning, he'd roused early to find the sun slanting into her room through the blinds, which hadn't been fully closed. He glanced over at Emmeline and saw that her brows were scrunched. Sunlight was shining across her eyes.

Luke lifted a hand, shielding her face from the light, and her expression relaxed. After a few minutes, his arm got sore, but she was sleeping so peacefully, he couldn't bear to let his hand drop. He finally shifted until he was on his side, his shoulders blocking the sun, and he'd watched her until he'd fallen asleep again.

In the morning, he woke up to her alarm going off. She released a growl, slapping the alarm off aggressively.

He looked over as she groaned, clearly unhappy to be risen. Her expression was like that of an angry kitten. She rubbed her eyes, smudging her makeup further.

Then, she seemed to remember he was there, and she turned her face to his. Her dark eyes widened.

She looked like she wanted to say something but was nervous. Before she could, he asked, "Coffee?"

Surprise lit her face, and she said, "Yes."

Luke sat up, then realized he didn't know where the kitchen was. She'd smiled, gaze dropping to his bare chest.

"Let's get dressed," she said, her lips pink with a faded

lipstick stain. There was kajal smudged around her eyes, and her hair was messy.

Slipping on a silk robe, she showed him to the guest bathroom, where he showered and got dressed. By the time he was out, she was perfectly done up again, all signs of last night gone as they went to the kitchen.

There, he sat at the counter while they discussed the merits of various coffee-brewing techniques, pour-over versus drip versus cold brew. He didn't know she was as enthusiastic about coffee as he was.

"You're as bad as me," he said, and she smiled from across the counter.

"I like all types of coffee, but I feel like pour-over gives the best flavor profile," she said, pulling out a bag of coffee from the cabinet to put in the grinder. "I just wish the roast was darker."

"I get this brand, too," he said, recognizing the label. "That is, unfortunately, the darkest profile there is."

As the coffee beans ground, someone entered the kitchen with a baby dragon in her arms; it must have been her family's dragon caretaker. Emmeline left the coffee grinder to scoop the black-scaled baby dragon into her arms.

"Are you up from your nap?" Emmeline asked her baby dragon, carrying her over. She set the dragon down on the counter. "This is Torch," Emmeline told Luke.

"Hello, angel," Luke said, holding a hand out to Torch. She looked at Luke hesitantly, purple eyes assessing, but then slowly stepped closer. Luke touched his hand to Torch's cheek, and the baby dragon hissed at the contact. Her scales were hot, and Luke withdrew his hand.

"My hands are cold," Luke said.

"She hates that," Emmeline affirmed. Torch opened her mouth wide, then sparked out a little flame in the direction of Luke's hand. The heat immediately warmed his fingers, but he fanned the flame away before it caught on his shirt-sleeve.

Emmeline chided, "Torch, we don't shoot fire at people. I've told you this already!"

"Hey—" Luke started, standing, just as Emmeline's gaze fell to the flames on the half-empty bag of coffee. Grabbing a towel, Emmeline swatted at the bag until the flames subsided.

An idea flickered in Luke's mind. At the same time, Emmeline turned to him with wide eyes.

"What if—" They both said at the same time.

Luke laughed. "You go."

"Dragon fire is intense," Emmeline said. "What if I roasted coffee with a dragon's flame?"

They were so similar; pleasure bloomed in his chest. "I was just thinking that," Luke said, "though more so in terms of a chimera. I've got a baby chimera at home—Sharptooth."

"Dragon-roasted coffee," Emmeline said. He could see the gears in her head turning.

"And chimera-roasted coffee," he added. "That would make a good business. Maybe we can be business partners."

Emmeline brewed the coffee, and they hung out for it, enjoying one another's company—until she showed her true face and broke his heart.

"It wasn't *your* idea," Luke said, snapping back to the present, to him and Emmeline in the bookshop. "It was ours."

She furrowed her brows, though recognition flickered in

her dark eyes. Coals of anger burned to life within him. He couldn't believe it. She really didn't remember.

"You may have gotten Inferno up and running two years before Tempest," he said hotly, "but that's only because I actually had to spend time finding investors. Daddy didn't just hand me the money."

Her lips parted. "You don't know what you're talking about."

"Don't I?" he pressed. "What twenty-two-year-old gets together enough capital to start her own business?"

"I worked hard, just like anyone else," she replied, but her voice had lost some of its edge.

"Poor little rich girl," he sneered.

Her face twisted. "So what if my father helped me out?"

"So nothing. Just don't accuse me of copying your idea when it was *ours*."

They were both breathing heavily, on the edge of their seats as they faced each other.

"Fine!" she snapped. "You didn't copy my idea. Happy?"

But he wasn't, not at all. She *had* to think about that time; it couldn't just be him.

"Stop trying to distract me," she said, blowing a stray tendril of hair out of her eyes. It bounced up, then back in place, landing by her lips. His gaze dropped.

"I . . ." he started, but she was already looking away. He clenched his jaw.

He hadn't been trying to distract her, but he *was* being distracted himself when he really shouldn't have been. He needed to focus.

Two weeks of six were already done, and while he'd made

progress on his proposal for the coffee shop, there was still a long way to go. Muttering an oath under his breath, he returned to his laptop.

Trying to regain his bearings, he looked at his notes, checking over the projected financials for his plans for the coffee shop addition. It took him about ten minutes to stop his thoughts from racing, but the calculations were a good way of getting his emotions under wraps.

After some time, he stood to search for the contractor on file for the bookshop. Now that he had an idea for what the project would cost, he needed to reach out to the contractor to get a quote, which he would most certainly try to negotiate.

When Luke went to the filing cabinet to search for the contractor's file with the business's history, he found something else. It was a profit report from the last three years that had evidently been misfiled; both he and Emmeline had been looking for this. The store manager Ola had said she would find it for them, but now he wouldn't have to wait for that.

An idea sparked in his mind.

"I found the profit report," Luke said, holding the file up.

Emmeline glanced up from her laptop, standing up from the chair she was sitting in. She came over to the filing cabinet to see, and after she'd had a glance to corroborate his claim, he quickly closed the file while she was still looking.

"Finders keepers," he said smugly, and her mouth jutted open.

"Not fair! Let me see it." She reached for it, and he shook his head.

"Nah."

Narrowing her eyes, she made an irritated sound. "You're being petty."

"Don't care," he replied with an easy shrug. He truly didn't. She had been quiet all week, and then she didn't even remember the idea of animal-roasted coffee was theirs. Now, he wanted nothing more than to piss her off.

"Don't be a child." She folded her arms across her chest.

He gave her a pleased smile. "I think I'm going to keep this."

Her eye twitched. "Fine," she snapped, going back to her chair. "See if I care."

Following behind her, he sat down in his seat. As Emmeline went back to typing on her laptop, he opened up the file.

Emmeline's fingers slowed on her keyboard as she looked over, and he bit back a smile.

"Hmm," he loudly mused, jotting something down in his notebook.

He pretended to be absorbed by the file, making exaggerated sounds of interest, as if he was discovering groundbreaking information. He could feel Emmeline's intrigue, her darting glances increasing in frequency.

Thoroughly entertained, he made more notes, smiling to himself as he sensed Emmeline losing her patience.

Until finally she snapped.

"Give it to me!" she said, holding out her hand.

Luke stood, stepping away from her with the file. "Why should I do that?" he asked.

"You've had it for long enough." Emmeline stood as well, glaring as she reached for the file.

He held it up, out of her grasp. She may have been tall, but he was still taller. She made an appalled sound, coming closer to reach for it again. He craned his arm back, and she reached over him, her chest brushing against his.

Amused, he wrapped his free arm around her waist, holding her in place against him.

Hissing, she stomped on his foot, and he grimaced, though he still held onto her, keeping the file out of reach.

"I was thinking of giving it to you," he said as his foot throbbed. "But that wasn't very nice."

"I'm not a nice girl," she told him, flashing her teeth. "Now give it to me before I do something worse."

For some reason, her threatening him made his pulse race. This is what he had been expecting when he got her to agree to coming to the bookshop at the same time as him. It was the most excitement he'd had all week, and the hurt he'd felt earlier faded away, replaced with adrenaline.

Luke cocked his head to the side, considering her. His arm was still locked around her waist, her body pressed against his as she reached in vain. Heat spread through him.

"Alright," he conceded. "I'll give it to you—on one condition."

She made an impatient sound. "What?"

He paused, thinking. "Forget it," he said, pretending to change his mind. "You won't accept it anyway."

"What. Is it." She gritted the words out. Her cheeks were pink. He shouldn't have enjoyed bothering her so much, but he did. "You don't know the lengths I'm willing to go."

Her voice was a dare, and so, he dared her back.

"A kiss," he said.

Her lips parted, eyes widening. She stopped moving. His hold on her waist loosened. She could have stepped away then if she wanted, but she was standing entirely still.

"Come on," he said, voice lowering. "It's not anything we haven't done before."

He wanted to remind her of their past, to torture her with it the way he was tortured. She may have pretended she didn't think of that time, but her sharp intake of breath at his words made him think that maybe she did.

It couldn't have meant so little to her—not when it meant so much to him. Perhaps she truly did need a reminder.

He knew she would never agree, but he could tease her. His gaze dropped to her lips, and her cheeks flushed. She bit her lower lip, flustered.

She *did* think about it.

It was enough for him to know that it wasn't all in his head. The past and the present. She felt it, too, she was just better at hiding it, at resisting. It was probably the clever thing to do, truly, but when could he ever be trusted to be clever around beautiful women?

Especially not Emmeline Sterling.

It was why he was about to hand over the file without his condition being met when she surprised him by meeting his gaze dead-on, a determined glint in her eyes.

"Alright," she said.

He froze, blood roaring through his ears.

"What?" he asked stupidly. Luke hadn't considered that she'd actually agree. His pulse quickened just at the thought, and then she inched closer.

"What?" she repeated, voice sultry. "Nervous?" She

batted her lashes, and any feeling of superiority he felt vanished.

He was no longer in control of the situation, not at all.

Trying to stay cool, Luke swallowed the lump in his throat, but it was hard to deny the effect she was having on his body.

"Like you said," she continued, putting a hand on his chest. "It isn't anything we haven't done before." His heart pounded as she drew nearer. She leaned forward, voice dropping to a whisper. "Do you remember?"

He started short-circuiting, the situation entirely out of hand as her fingers played with his necklaces, long nails scratching the skin of his chest. The sweet scent of jasmine invaded his senses, making him dizzy.

Emmeline looked up at him, and he wanted to drown in her kajal-lined eyes. Her gaze dropped to his mouth, her lips parting. He still couldn't believe this was happening, but who was he to complain? Anticipation fizzled through him. He drew closer to her.

Just as her lips skimmed his, he felt cold air across him.

Confused, Luke blinked and realized two things at once: Emmeline was smiling triumphantly a foot away from him, and the file was gone from his hands. Instead, it was in her grasp.

She had distracted him to get it.

"You didn't actually think I'd give you the satisfaction, did you?" she asked, gloating. He wanted to steal a kiss—surely that would put an end to her gloating—but he couldn't take such a liberty without knowing she wanted that, too.

She had played him, but he wasn't angry. His heart was still beating much too fast, and he knew she was affected, too. He could see a blush high on her cheeks, noticed the way her hands were slightly trembling despite her confident tone.

They were micro-changes, but with her, he was always paying attention.

Luke walked past her, stopping just behind her. Emmeline paused, turning her cheek toward him. He brushed aside her hair, baring her ear.

"Trust me," he said, voice low. "The satisfaction is all mine."

She touched a hand to her cheek, all her gloating gone.

CHAPTER 12

Working with Luke was insufferable, but Emmeline had no other option.

Most of the week had passed without any hitches, but she was still thinking of his little stunt with the file the next day: the way he'd locked an arm around her waist, pulling her close to him. He'd had the audacity to ask for a kiss—the memory made her blood hot. With anger, of course, and with something more.

Something that was getting more and more difficult to deny.

At least her plans for the coffee shop were coming along, though she wasn't being nearly as efficient as she should have been. She didn't know what was wrong with her, but she suspected Luke's presence wasn't helping, and nor was the mischievous baby dragon she had to take care of. Motu was a handful; in the evenings, she could sometimes leave him with Torch for a few hours and it was fine, but then when she got home, he wanted all of her attention.

He was in Torch's paw now as they flew down to see Millie and the baby. Emmeline wished she had more time to visit or even to stay over for a few days, but she already felt like she was being pulled in a hundred directions. She had just dropped off a care package for Saphira with some mommy-to-be self-care items. She had been meaning to do that all week, ever since Saphira told them the news, but she just hadn't had the time.

Now, as she flew down south to her sister's, she had two hours in the sky, and the wind rushing against her face was a welcome feeling to quiet all else. Though she couldn't quiet Luke's words from the night before.

He was right in that she was very privileged. She'd never shied away from that; she didn't know why she got so defensive when he said it in the bookshop's office.

He was *also* right in that he didn't copy her idea. She remembered now; they had both had the idea at the same time.

Emmeline had only made such a misstep because she had tried so hard to block out that time they had spent together, but she couldn't block it out any longer.

That evening at Tales & Tails, spending hours together before sharing their first kiss squeezed between the stacks. He had been so hungry for her, hands pulling her closer, and she'd surprised herself with how hungry she had been in return.

After Minh had basically kicked them out, she had invited him over to her place, where they slept together. It was a necessary part of the plan, though she couldn't pretend she didn't enjoy it. A part of her had even wished it was real, that come morning she wouldn't have to do what she had planned to.

It was why when he'd offered to make coffee, she had said yes without realizing. She just wanted it to last a little longer. Then, after they had spent the morning together, it was all getting too real, and she needed to make him leave right then or she was afraid she never would.

So she broke his heart and blocked out the memories—until now. He had been hurt that she didn't remember; it had been evident on his face. Guilt knifed through her at the memory, but she shook her head.

"There's no need to feel bad," she muttered to herself. "Not after his little stunt with the file."

When he'd asked for a kiss, a part of her had been thrilled at the thought of giving in—but she knew she'd be able to distract him and get the file. Her triumph had been short-lived. He had hardly looked bothered—he'd *smirked* at her.

At least she'd got the file, but she soon found it wasn't even that useful. He had been putting on a show to make her want it, to purposefully vex her, and it had worked. He was driving her insane. She didn't understand his games, his emotions, or what he was playing at.

Emmeline let out a groan, and Torch turned her head back, slowing her flight speed.

"It's fine, girl," Emmeline said, stroking her scales. Torch faced forward again, but Emmeline continued to stew.

Luke was making her lose focus. The realization made her pause. What if that was what he wanted? To get in her head so she would lose Anh's investment?

Irritation flashed through her. That wasn't going to

happen. Emmeline clutched the handlebars tighter. She would beat him. And then she'd never have to see him again. She could go back to pretending he didn't exist.

Though she had a sinking feeling that it would be easier said than done after these six weeks in each other's company . . .

Thankfully, Emmeline shortly arrived at Millie's, and she didn't have to think about Luke or the bookshop or work or anything.

"I'm here!" Emmeline called, entering through the front door. Noah and Ira ran to attack her with cuddles, and she hugged them tight.

"Motu!" Noah cried with glee. Emmeline was promptly forgotten in favor of the baby dragon. Motu's eyes widened as the four- and two-year-olds reached for him. With a hiss, he flapped up, latching onto Emmeline's shoulders.

"Tch, Motu, don't be a baby," she said, plucking him out of the air and setting him down on the floor. "These are your friends!" She turned to her nephew and niece, then. "Be nice, okay."

Closing the door, Emmeline went in, first going into the kitchen, where Samreen was washing the dishes.

"Hi, Ammi," Emmeline said, giving her mother a kiss on the cheek. Her mother was neatly dressed in trousers and a gray sweater, her dark hair in a fuss-free twist.

"Hello," Samreen replied. "How was the flight?"

"Not bad," Emmeline replied, walking past her to head into the living room, where Millie was sitting on the couch next to her husband. Millie's dark hair was pulled up in a high knot, and she was wearing one of her husband's

T-shirts. They were both watching baby Eve, who was asleep in a bundle of blankets in Millie's arms.

"Hey," Emmeline said, leaning forward to kiss her sister's cheek, then bop Eve's nose. At the contact, Eve twitched a little, and Millie hushed her.

"Hey," Millie said, giving Emmeline a tired smile.

"How are you guys holding up?" Emmeline asked. Millie opened her mouth to reply, but before she could, Motu flew into the room, chased by Noah and Ira, who were laughing with glee.

"Guys, shhh," Liam said gently. "Eve's asleep."

Noah made a face. "She's always asleep. She's so *boring*."

Emmeline snorted, turning to her nephew, who was pouting. "When you were a teeny tiny baby, all you used to do was sleep, too, you know," Emmeline said.

"No way." Noah shook his head.

"Yes, way," she replied.

"Noah, catch him!" Ira ordered, jumping up to reach for Motu.

The baby dragon looked thoroughly harassed by the two toddlers. He landed on top of the couch, then hid behind his wings.

Ira tried climbing over her father to reach him, and Millie quickly pulled Eve out of the way before the baby got kicked in the head.

"Millie, are you still holding that baby?" Samreen asked from the kitchen. "I told you not to spoil her with too much lap-time."

Millie turned to Emmeline and made a face of distress. "Save me," she mouthed.

Emmeline stood. "Hey, Millie, can you show me that thing in your room?"

Millie stood as well. "Ohmygosh, yes, thanks for reminding me," she said.

"What thing?" Samreen asked from the kitchen.

"Oh, just something!" Emmeline replied breezily, as Millie deposited Eve into Liam's arms. "We'll be back in a second!"

"Liam, hold the fort," Millie whispered, voice an order. Liam's eyes widened, but he nodded.

"You got it, babe," he whispered back, shielding the baby as the toddlers and Motu wreaked havoc. Taking the opportunity, Emmeline and Millie ran upstairs, making a beeline for her bedroom.

Two seconds later, they heard Ira ask, "Hey, where's Mama?"

Millie gasped.

"The closet!" Emmeline said. Without turning on the lights, they rushed into Millie's walk-in closet, shutting the door. They sat down against the door, barring it from opening if the kids did follow.

Emmeline turned on her phone's flashlight, setting it on the floor, while Millie crawled forward and fished out a bag from one of the drawers.

"Contraband," Millie said, showing her the bag of chocolate-covered espresso beans.

Emmeline laughed. "Ohmygod, yes." The chocolate made the espresso bearable for Millie, and they used to eat these all the time in university while studying.

Millie sat back down beside Emmeline, and they both popped the beans into their mouths, relishing the sweet chocolate and bitter espresso. "You know I actually never get these," Emmeline said. "It feels like such a uni thing."

"I keep this bag for special occasions," Millie said, taking out another. "Uni feels like forever ago."

Emmeline blew out her cheeks. "When life's biggest challenge was a discussion post."

"Things get so complicated the older you get," Millie agreed, offering Emmeline another bean. Their shoulders were pressed together, and just the contact made Emmeline reset. Seeing her sister always grounded her, and all the tension from the week slipped away in the quiet of the dark closet.

"Those were such golden days, and we didn't even realize it," Emmeline said. She was reminiscing on the time her and her sister lived together, went to school together, did everything together.

Millie turned to Emmeline. "I love Ammi, but I'm struggling a little with how intense she can be," she said. "I mean, I appreciate all the help because managing the kids and a newborn would be too much, but like . . ." She widened her eyes.

Emmeline snorted. "Don't worry, she's driving me up the wall, too," she told her sister. "She calls me every other day to ask after Motu and the boys and Dad."

"Good lord," Millie said, shaking her head. "She asks too much of you."

Emmeline knew it was true, and she was tired of it. *Why must I take care of everything, and everyone? You do in fact have other children!* They were words she imagined saying to her mother often, but they never came out.

"It's okay," Emmeline said, instead. "How's Eve been?"

At that, Millie smiled. "Adorable, though Noah's kind of right: all she does is sleep, so she *is* kind of boring."

Both sisters laughed.

"You're just used to toddler chaos," Emmeline said. "And anyway, be grateful she's not up half the night crying like Ira used to be."

"God, you're right." Millie shuddered at the memories. "Now tell me how things are going with the bookshop. Have you run into Luke again?"

"*Have* I?" Emmeline started, blood quickening in her veins at the mention of Luke.

Emmeline told Millie all the infuriating details of the past ten days, expecting her sister to be angry on her behalf but surprised to find Millie squealing and then, worse, *giggling*.

"Stop giggling!" Emmeline ordered.

Millie only cackled. "Why? This is perfect. He's your *match*."

Emmeline pouted. "I hate him," she said.

Millie frowned. "Why?"

Emmeline gave her a look, but still her sister didn't understand. "He broke your heart," Emmeline finally said. "You cried for a week!"

Millie's jaw dropped open. "Are you okay?" she asked, slapping Emmeline's arm.

"Ow!"

"You hate him because of me?" Millie confirmed. "I'm literally married! We are hiding from my three children as we speak! I don't even remember what happened between us."

Emmeline scoffed. "Well, *I* remember," she said, crossing her arms.

"Don't," Millie replied. "You've got enough going on without holding onto a grudge for something I literally couldn't care less about. Let it go."

Millie was always too forgiving, but Emmeline was her older sister. It was her job to be protective, though deep down, a part of her knew that it wasn't only that.

That perhaps the real reason she kept Luke an arm's distance away was because she was afraid of what she might feel if she let him get close to her.

And that thought unsettled her.

CHAPTER 13

On Sunday morning, Emmeline rubbed her temples as she rushed to the bookshop.

She had informed Luke she would be coming in today, though it was the weekend. Sunday was the bookshop's busiest day, and she wanted to study the bookshop at its peak to deduce how many workers the coffee shop would need over the weekend versus throughout the week. While she hadn't told Luke as much, he had confirmed that he would be there as well, bright and early.

Unfortunately, she hadn't slept well the night before, so she was already in a crabby mood. They had come back from Millie's later than planned because Ira had wanted Emmeline to do bedtime with her. Millie had said Emmeline should just stay over, but Emmeline already had plans to go to the bookshop today, so she had soldiered through and flew back at night, something Motu was decidedly not happy about.

Of course, once it was time to go home, the baby dragon had suddenly realized that Noah and Ira were his long-lost best friends whom he could not bear to be parted from. Emmeline was now his number one enemy, for she had ripped him away from those he loved most.

He had been fussy when they'd returned to her place, bothering her for an hour before finally falling asleep. As such, Emmeline hardly got any sleep herself, which had led her to oversleep this morning. She had rushed to get ready and drop Motu off at her dad's, where the caretakers could watch the baby dragon while she rushed to town.

She had planned to pick up breakfast from the cafe, but she didn't get a chance. Now, as she entered the bookshop, she heard her phone ringing, and pulled it out to see it was her mother.

"Hi, Ammi," Emmeline said. She smiled and waved at Minh and Ola with her free hand, then spotted Luke heading for the office. She followed to set down her things.

"Hi," Samreen replied. "Did you drop Motu off at home?"

Emmeline entered the office, where Luke was hanging up his coat, his back to her.

"Yes, he's with the caretakers," Emmeline replied as Luke pulled out his notebook, paging through. "I have to get some work done today."

Samreen sighed a very motherly sigh, and Emmeline's eye twitched. "It's Sunday," Samreen said. "You should have spent the day with your father and brothers."

Emmeline closed her eyes, guilt needling through her. Her mother was always making her feel guilty. No matter what Emmeline did, it wasn't enough.

"I know," Emmeline replied, opening her eyes. "I'm going to swing by later."

Even so, she felt bad. Maybe she shouldn't have scheduled any work today, but she had been at Millie's all day yesterday, and she was running woefully behind on her proposal.

This was a busy time, and during a busy time, one had to work extra hours.

Samreen hummed. "Okay," she said. "They've been ordering in, so try and cook something when you go. If you can."

"Yes, Ammi," she replied, pinching the bridge of her nose, thumb brushing against her nose-ring. She noticed Luke watching her then, and she bristled. She had forgotten he was there. "I'll talk to you later, okay?"

Emmeline hung up, throwing her phone into her purse. When she glanced up, Luke was still watching her.

"Hasn't anyone told you it's rude to eavesdrop?" she snapped.

"Excuse me," Luke replied, dark eyes glinting. "Hasn't anyone told you it's rude to take a call in an office where others are trying to work?"

He was right, which only worsened her already vile mood. She glowered at Luke, hoping it would keep him away, but he only raised his brows, as if vaguely amused.

"You're perky this morning," he said, seemingly unbothered. She hissed.

"Here," he said, handing her a thermos. "I brought you chai."

Emmeline stilled. He had brought her chai? Precisely what she was missing and sorely needed now?

For a moment, tears pricked her eyes, and the amusement

on his countenance shifted into concern. Embarrassment spread through her, and she quickly looked away.

"Why would you do that?" she asked, genuinely not understanding. Then, it was his turn to look away.

"Don't worry, it wasn't on purpose or anything," he said, voice cavalier. "I ended up making extra and thought it would be better to bring it along instead of throwing it out."

"Oh," she said, though she still hesitated about taking the thermos from him.

"Besides, you can be quite devilish before your morning caffeine, so I thought it would be good to have on hand in case you didn't get any this morning," he continued, and the fact that he knew such a thing made her feel a sharp emotion she couldn't quite pin down.

He said the words easily, as if they were excuses he had practiced. She didn't know if she should believe him or not, but the fact remained that she desperately needed caffeine.

Hesitantly, she took the thermos, taking off the lid. Steam rose from the top. "Thank you," she said, looking up at him.

He smiled. "'Course."

Just as she was about to take a sip, he said, "Oh, and I poisoned it." She paused, pulling the cup away from her mouth to glare at him. He gave her a boyish smile. "Just kidding."

"I am going to choke you," she threatened, then took a sip.

"Dirty talk, Sterling?" he said, checking his watch. "This early in the morning?"

She almost spat the chai out at that, and he snickered to himself. She clenched her jaw.

After setting down her things, she took off her jacket, revealing one of her favorite black dresses: a lacy number that fell to just below her knees. The bookshop was always warm, so she wasn't wearing any stockings today, just knee-high suede boots. After hanging up her jacket, she slung her purse back on her arm. Luke sat down in his usual seat, but turned when he saw she wasn't sitting down beside him.

Grabbing the thermos, she stalked outside. A moment later, he had followed her out.

"I see we're changing tactics," he said.

"*We* are not doing anything," she replied curtly, walking over to the side of the bookshop, stopping by a bookshelf. He followed.

"Any particular reason you wanted to come in on a Sunday?" he asked, watching as she pulled her notebook out of her purse. Taking a sip of chai, she narrowed her eyes at him.

"Wouldn't you like to know," she replied. He waited, curious. Maybe this was how she would get back at him for being so irritating, by not telling him.

Emmeline was in the center of the bookshop, with a clear view of the front door and the front desk. Sipping her chai (which was really quite good), she watched as customers entered through the front door, the first of the day. It was a couple with a blue-scaled azura baby dragon bouncing by their feet.

"Fine," Luke said. "Don't tell me." He leaned against the other side of the bookshelf. She was momentarily distracted by the long stretch of his torso, the muscles of his arms as he folded them across his chest.

Blinking, she shook her head. *Insufferable.*

Emmeline turned her attention to the bookshop. She could feel Luke watching her, but she refused to glance over at him. Instead, she made a note of when the couple had entered in her notebook. A few moments later, the front door dinged; an old man entered.

She continued watching, making notes whenever anybody entered. About fifteen minutes later, the couple with the azura baby dragon left without purchasing anything, and she wrote that down as well. Then, five minutes later, she saw the old man go to the front desk to pay for a book.

She wrote that down. Along with studying how busy the bookshop got, she was studying how long customers spent in the shop, since customers who stayed longer would be more inclined to purchase a coffee as they browsed as opposed to customers who were only popping in to quickly make a purchase.

"Ah, so that's what you're doing," Luke said, not even hiding the fact that he was reading her notes from over her shoulder. Closing her notebook with a snap, she threw it back into her purse. She turned her face to glare at him.

As she did, she startled; she hadn't realized he was standing so close.

Her pulse quickened as she stared into the depths of his dark eyes. There were fine lines around his eyes, a sign of age that hadn't been there when they were twenty-two. For some reason, she wanted to press her finger along the crease, to feel just how much he had changed.

Seven years was a long time. There was so much about him she didn't know—and suddenly, she realized she wanted to learn more about him.

"I don't know what you're talking about," Emmeline said, taking a step away from him.

"You're studying how long customers stay in the shop," he said. "I'll bet you're trying to work out what percentage will be likely to buy coffee as they browse."

"No," she replied, but he was clever, which was irritating. Unfortunately, his competence was also very attractive.

"Good idea." He flashed her a smile, then disappeared and reappeared thirty seconds later with his notebook and pen.

Emmeline scowled. The front door dinged with another customer, and she turned her attention there, trying *not* to focus on the irritating presence of Luke beside her.

He stayed with her throughout the day, watching and jotting down notes. She tried to find some way to get rid of him, but no matter how she moved around the store, they ended up back in each other's space.

Even so, her bad mood gave way. It was impossible to stay upset for long when you were surrounded by shelves and shelves of books, three entire stories full. Emmeline watched as some people quietly browsed while others showed book covers to their friends and partners.

A white-scaled baby dragon flapped through the air, landing on top of one of the bookshelves, wings spread as it looked down. Another baby dragon—a red-scaled garneta—held onto a stack of books while its rider browsed, patiently sitting at the end of the bookshelf while it waited. She watched as a basalta baby dragon bounced over to the fireplace, blowing a little flame of fire onto the wood, which crackled.

With a smile, she inhaled the scent of woodsmoke, which

mingled with the smell of ink and paper. She continued taking notes and tracking the customers, getting a good idea of the market.

A little while later, feeling warm, she gathered her hair and twisted it up. As she did, she realized Luke was watching her, his pen stopped mid-motion.

"What?" she snapped, securing her hair with a clip. He closed his notebook, coming over to her in a few long strides.

Her heartbeat quickened at how close he was, the intent expression on his face. She gave him an odd look, unsure what he was doing as he lifted a hand up. Before she could react, he reached up and undid the clip in her hair, letting her long tresses unfurl and fall down.

"I like your hair down," he said, voice earnest. Her cheeks felt warm. At the same time, indignation flashed through her.

Where did he get the audacity from to say such things to her?

"And I like your mouth shut," she replied. "But we can't all get what we want."

He cocked his head to the side, as if in thought. "I don't think that's true," he said, his gaze flicking down to her lips. "Not if I remember correctly."

Emmeline blinked, heat pouring through her. He smirked. What was wrong with him? He was utterly ridiculous and absurd.

"You *don't*," she snapped, snatching her clip from his hand. Turning on her heel, she stalked away. Unfortunately, she couldn't do anything about her racing pulse.

She had been minding her own business—why would he say such a thing? Releasing an irritated breath, she rubbed her temples. He was just trying to get under her skin, to distract her, she reminded herself. She wouldn't let him.

Instead, she re-focused on the customers in the store. She watched as an old man browsed the shelves, taking his time. He pulled out different books, reading the back copy, then opening the pages to the first chapter. After reading a page or two, he either set the book back on the shelf, or dropped it off at one of the tables. As he browsed, his baby dragon bounced by his feet, happily following along.

The blue-scaled dragon flew up to look over his rider's shoulder, and the old man lifted the book, showing the dragon, as if the baby could read. Emmeline smiled to herself. After about fifteen minutes of browsing, the old man paid for two books, and Emmeline jotted down notes from his visit.

Along with tracking trends, Emmeline tried to find some way to get back at Luke for his little stunt with the file last week, but she couldn't find any opportunity, which was annoying.

Until she spotted a mischievous baby dragon nibbling on the end of a book. Its owner noticed and released a long-suffering sigh.

"No," a woman scolded, pointing a finger. The red-scaled baby dragon begrudgingly dropped the book, leaving behind teeth marks; it was clearly hungry.

Just then, Luke went to get a cup of tea from the back. As he did, she saw him drop his notebook off on an empty display table, leaving his hands free.

Emmeline looked at the baby dragon, an idea flickering to life in her mind.

CHAPTER 14

Emmeline had a bag of fried bitter gourds in her purse. The snack was meant to appease Motu, but today, it would serve another purpose. She pulled a handful out, and the garneta baby dragon perked immediately, sniffing the air.

It turned its head, searching, then spotted Emmeline, who bit back a smile. The dragon's red eyes widened, and Emmeline casually walked across the bookshop. She heard the sound of the dragon's wings flapping behind her, and she went over to the empty display table where Luke's notebook was.

Just then, Luke turned around with his tea. Swaying her hips, she knocked her purse over, and it swiped across the table, pushing the notebook off.

"Oops," she mouthed, and he cocked his head at her. She bent over to pick up the notebook and, as she did, she slid a few fried gourds under the cover. Then, she set the notebook back on the table and continued walking forward, as if going for some tea herself.

Luke furrowed his brow at her—but then his gaze jumped behind her.

"Hey!" he cried, setting down his tea and rushing past her. Emmeline turned to see the baby dragon had latched onto his notebook with both paws and was chewing on it. "Give that back!"

Luke went to grab the notebook, and the baby dragon growled, biting down harder as Luke pulled. The baby dragon's wings flapped in the air as it tried to fly away, tugging Luke forward a step.

Laughter bubbled up in Emmeline's chest, and she covered her mouth with her hand, watching as Luke fought with an adorable and hungry baby dragon.

Eventually, the baby's rider caught wind, and she rushed over, scolding her pet.

"I'm so sorry!" she said to Luke, pulling the notebook from the baby dragon's mouth. The damage wasn't catastrophic, but one side was soggy with drool. Luke gave the woman a weak smile, and she grabbed her baby dragon, scolding it as she walked away.

Once she was gone, Luke made a face. Emmeline snickered.

"Eugh," he said, gingerly holding the other end of the notebook. He opened the flap, then paused. "What the hell is this?"

Her mirth quickly disappeared. Even from here, she could see an oil stain, left behind by the fried bitter gourds.

As if sensing Emmeline's meddling, Luke snapped his head around to look at her. She avoided his gaze, though not before she saw his eyes flash. Her heart rate spiked in response.

Turning on her heels with a little yelp, she walked in the opposite direction, but she hardly made it two feet before she felt his hand on her wrist.

With a firm tug, he had her spinning toward him, colliding into his chest before she knew what was happening. Eyes wide, she placed her hand against his chest for balance, inhaling the scent of cypress and spruce from his skin.

"What the f—" she began, then stopped as his gaze went to the side, to where he was holding up her other hand. The words died on her lips as the damning evidence was clear for both of them to see: her stained fingers.

Luke raised a brow. Emmeline was momentarily disarmed.

There was no point denying it now, but that wasn't the reason it felt like the ground was quivering beneath her feet. His thumb was pressed against her pulse, and she wondered if he could feel it quicken beneath his touch.

A thrill shot through her to have him so near.

"Seriously?" he asked, vexed, and she tried to recall what all of this had been for. She lifted her chin.

"That was for all that drama with the file," she said.

His eyes flashed, the irritation giving way to something else. His grip on her wrist loosened, but he didn't let go of her just yet, and she didn't pull away. He was assessing her carefully, and she swallowed the lump in her throat.

"Don't mess with me," she said, trying to sound threatening, but the words hardly came out as confidently as she wanted them to.

He continued looking at her. "Why is winning so important to you?" he finally asked.

Was he being genuine in his curiosity?

"Why does it matter?" she replied, hesitating.

As if sensing her thoughts, he dropped her hand, shrugging. "You're a determined person. I just want to know what drives you."

She wasn't sure what compelled her to respond; she could have easily walked away. Maybe it was the tenderness in his brown eyes, or maybe she was too tired to resist today.

Her gaze jumped away from him. "I don't lose," she said. "I make sure of it."

Though her stomach was in knots, she forced herself to look at him. "I'm the oldest," she explained. "Then it's my sister, then my two brothers, who are six and seven years younger. I've always been the one who looked out for everyone else. And to do that, I have to be on top of things, to make sure everything goes according to plan."

Luke made a pensive sound, listening. It was a little strange to talk like this; she was so used to being the one who listened. With her family, she was the one in the background, but with him, she felt as if she had been brought into focus.

It would have been easy to end the conversation there, but there was a feeling of something loosening in her chest. His gaze on her was intense, and she continued, the words spilling out.

"Things are a bit complicated with my mom," she said, swallowing. "We get along, and I love her, but she can put a lot of pressure on me, which then makes me put a lot of pressure on myself—" Luke's brows furrowed, and she quickly corrected. "But it's not a bad thing! It's what pushes me to succeed."

"Success is good," Luke agreed, "but there's nothing wrong with failure."

She had an immediate reaction to that, her nose wrinkling with her elaborate nose-ring, and his lips twitched.

"You're disgusted by the very thought," he said. It was true; failure never felt like an option for her. "But even you must realize everyone has a limit." He looked around pointedly. "You didn't bring Motu today; you needed a break."

"A *break* is different," she said, then thought back to her conversation with her mother from this morning, about how she should have spent the day with her father and brothers. "And it's only for a little while. I'm going to get him back after I leave here."

He cocked his head to the side. "Aren't you tired?" he asked.

The kindness in his expression had her taken aback. Of course she was tired—a part of her was always tired—but she was so used to it now that she hardly ever registered the fact.

How had Luke of all people noticed?

Her silence was answer enough, and his lips turned down. "Why don't you just say no?" he asked, as if it was that simple. "I've never seen you have a problem telling me what you think."

"That's different," she replied. "You're you. My family is . . ." She let out a breath. "I can't say no to them, no matter how thinly stretched I am."

She hated that she sounded like she was complaining; she didn't mind, not really. She wanted to be there for her family; it was how she expressed her love for them.

"I like taking care of the people I love," she said.

His expression warmed. "That's admirable," he said. "And I think I understand a bit more about you, now. You said you don't lose, which means that you're calculated—you don't take bets that won't give you the outcome you want. You like being in control." He paused then, voice softening. "But not everything can be in your control, Emmeline."

The thought of that freaked her out—it was why being around him made her feel so unnerved, too, but she couldn't say that. What had Millie said? That Luke was her match. That frightened her, but it thrilled her, too. She couldn't deny there was a part of her that relished difficult situations for the satisfaction that came from overcoming them.

Instead, she asked, "What about you? What drives you?"

He looked surprised, as if he hadn't expected her to ask. But why wouldn't she have?

He let out a little laugh, shaking his head. "You won't believe me."

She wrinkled her brows. "Says who?"

Still, he hesitated, clearly not wanting to respond to her question. He glanced away, clenching his jaw.

Suddenly, hurt flashed through her. She had answered his questions; she had been vulnerable. Now, he wasn't affording her the same courtesy.

Why had he asked to begin with?

She had thought that perhaps they were connecting, that maybe it was time to let go of the tight grip the grudge from years ago had on her heart—the way Millie had suggested—but any softness she felt disappeared.

"Fine," she snapped. "Don't tell me."

His expression fell. "I'm not . . ." He broke off, clenching his jaw. "I know you," he said. "You'll think I'm making it up."

His words only increased her ire. "That's an unfair accusation to make."

"I don't think you want to talk about what's fair," he said, a warning in his tone.

A volatile feeling spread through her, and she looked around. They had been standing on the side of the bookshop, everything else fading away, but it all came back to her now, the buzz and noise of customers in a busy bookshop.

With a scoff, she stalked away from him. This had been a waste of time. Anger flashed through her. Talking to him had been a stupid idea.

She should have never told him anything, no matter how open his eyes were as he gazed at her. She had thought there was such a softness to the brown of his eyes, something warm and inviting, but it was only a trick of the light.

It was early evening, by then. The light from outside the windows was fading fast, and Emmeline checked her phone. She had a message from her father, asking when she would swing by, along with frantic messages from her brother asking her why Motu was in such a crabby mood.

She replied to both, then threw her phone in her purse before turning her attention back to her notes. She was here to *work*, she reminded herself—though that was evidently difficult to do with the way her mind was racing.

What did Luke mean by asking her all of those questions? What did he mean she wouldn't believe him?

Lost in thought, she didn't notice Luke until he was standing right in front of her. She glanced up. For a moment, she thought he would answer her question, and her pulse quickened.

But he only said, "I'm heading out."

Emmeline gave him a curt nod of her head, turning her attention back to her notes. In her peripheral vision, she saw him leave; the front door dinged after him. Her shoulders sagged, and she frowned.

Releasing a groan, she snapped her notebook shut. She might as well leave now, too. Throwing her notebook into her purse, she went to the office to grab her coat. Luke's words rang in her ear: *"I don't think you want to talk about what's fair."*

Emmeline's pulse quickened. He thought she hadn't been fair in her treatment of him all those years ago, but he had broken her little sister's heart, and so she had broken his. She had always stood by that decision, but now, a needle of guilt pricked her at the memory.

Releasing a long breath, she looked around the empty office. She spotted his thermos on one of the small tables. He must have forgotten it because it was the one she had drunk from.

With a frustrated groan, she thought of the chai he had brought her this morning, how she couldn't quite get a good read on him, or her own emotions. Frowning, she glared at the thermos.

As she walked past, she collided into the edge of the table, hitting her knee.

Before she could swear in pain, she watched as the thermos tipped and the last few sips of her now cold chai spilled over the front of her dress. Liquid seeped through the lacy fabric.

Along with irritation, shock went through her. She had been clumsier these past two weeks than she had been all year, and she knew it was because of Luke. He was getting under her skin.

Appalled, she dabbed at the front of her dress with a napkin. Luckily, she always had a spare riding outfit on Torch. Emmeline left the bookshop, calling down her dragon, who arrived a few moments later.

Grabbing her spare bag, she went back into the bookshop. She would quickly change before heading to her parents' place.

She headed for the bathroom, only to see there was a line. Glancing down at her stained dress, she frowned. She looked around, trying to think of another solution, when her gaze fell to the closed office door.

She could just change in there.

Turning on her heels, she went to the front desk. Minh wasn't in today, but Ola, the bookshop manager, was at her usual spot behind the desk.

"Ola," Emmeline said. "I managed to spill chai on myself, so I'm just going to change in the office quickly." She held up her bag while Ola gave her a sympathetic look.

"Oh dear—yes, do get changed," Ola said. "If I need anything, I'll knock."

Nodding, Emmeline headed for the office, shutting the door behind her. She released a long breath, looking down at the stain on her dress again. Glaring at it, she kicked off her long boots.

Standing barefoot on the rug, she quickly pulled up her dress, wanting to get out of it as soon as possible.

Unfortunately, it seemed her bad luck hadn't quite finished. As she tugged the dress, the lace fabric caught on her bra hooks. She yelped, tugging again, but the fabric was fully stuck, her arms entangled in the dress.

"Ugh!" She tried to pull the dress again, hoping the force would pull the fabric from the hooks, but the dress only snagged on her hair clip, tugging at her hair. Pain shot through her scalp.

"Ow!" She cried, swearing. "Fuck!" She tried pulling free again but lost her footing, stumbling sideways. Her knee knocked into the table, and she swore again, the words lost to the commotion of things falling to the floor with a crash. She released a groan of frustration.

This situation couldn't get worse, could it?

Then, she heard the door open. It must have been Ola, checking in.

"Thank goodness," Emmeline said, turning in the direction of the door. "Ola, you need to help me."

She heard the door shut, then the sound of a raspy response: "Um."

Emmeline's heart rate spiked. That deep voice was decidedly *not* Ola. Swearing to herself, she turned around—though that wasn't exactly protecting her modesty, either.

"What are you doing?" she seethed. "I thought you left!"

She desperately tried to pull the dress off, not caring if the fabric tore at this point, but she (unfortunately) only bought things of quality, so it would not rip that easily. Her arms were entangled in the fabric above her head, unable to reach down to free the dress.

"I came back to . . ." Luke paused. "I heard a commotion."

"So you just barge in here!"

"Who uses an office as a dressing room? I didn't know if you were okay or not!"

"*Now* you care!"

"I always care," he muttered defensively.

There was no time to unpack that, not when she was standing in nothing but her underwear. Mortification swept through her, making her skin heat.

Silence hung between them until Luke cleared his throat. "Are you . . . stuck?"

At the last word, she could hear the amusement in his voice. That was enough to make any embarrassment she felt immediately disappear. In its place, she only felt anger. She was still upset with him for refusing to answer her question.

"Shut up," she growled, but that only made him laugh, which grated on her nerves.

"You are, aren't you?"

Her vision turned red. "You'd better not be looking," she seethed.

"Oh, I am definitely looking," he replied simply, unapologetic.

"Stop!" she snapped, still facing the opposite direction, though that didn't shield him from a good view. *Ugh!*

"Relax," he said. "Nothing I haven't seen before."

He was the worst person in the world. She hated him.

"Shut up." At this point, she would just rip the dress off. It didn't matter that it was one of her favorites. She tugged the dress up, but the fabric stayed stuck in place, refusing to tear.

She groaned. "Are you just going to stand there or are you going to help?"

Now that Luke was here, he might as well be useful.

Besides, there was no need to be shy around him. She straightened her posture, refusing to feel unsettled because of him, no matter how loudly her blood roared in her veins.

Her question was met with silence, and Emmeline turned around. She could just about see him through the fabric bunched around her head. He was standing very still.

"Well?" she asked.

CHAPTER 15

Everything was going unexpectedly.

Luke had been irritated at first about Emmeline's little prank with his notebook, but it had faded quickly when he'd sensed an opportunity to talk to her. He hadn't expected her to fully respond with so much honesty, but she had.

Then, she had surprised him again by asking him the same question. Sudden fear had gone through him at the thought of being vulnerable.

The last time he had opened up to her, she had broken his heart, after all.

So after she stalked away, he finished up his work and left, but he hardly made it a few feet onto Elderberry Lane before he was overcome with a tightness in his chest, as if he'd left something vital behind. Her face had flashed in his mind; she had been hurt when he'd refused to answer her question.

Guilt had pricked at him, so he had turned back to the bookshop to answer her question, to tell her about his mom.

He was still afraid she might believe it was a ploy, like he was just pretending to be a good son, but he could deal with that if it happened.

But then he'd heard a crash and her muffled swear. He'd rushed into the office to make sure she was okay and saw her in her underwear.

All coherent thoughts had promptly rushed from his head.

"Well?" she snapped, bringing him back to the fact that she had asked him a question.

While her body language was confident, he saw the way her arms trembled. He remembered she was asking for help to untangle herself.

With some difficulty, Luke found his voice. "Alright," he agreed. Her dress was bunched over her head and arms.

"Don't look," she ordered, being bossy despite the fact that she very much needed his help. "I mean it."

"Fine, fine." Obeying, he closed his eyes and began walking forward, moving slowly.

"Where are you?" she asked impatiently, and her voice was very far to the left.

"How am I supposed to help if I can't look?" he snapped, frustrated in more ways than one.

She scoffed. "Don't tell me you haven't undressed a woman before."

"I assure you, I've undressed plenty," he replied hotly. Irritation ran through him; here she was insulting him while simultaneously asking him for help. Her bedside manner could surely use some work. He swiveled to the left, heading in the direction of her voice.

"Riiiight," Emmeline replied, drawing out the word. He

wished the dress would have covered her mouth entirely so she wouldn't be able to speak, either.

"The girls I undress are usually not entangled in their own clothes," he replied, and as he said the words, some of his frustration turned to amusement. His voice softened. "How did you even accomplish this?"

"I don't know," she whined, sounding much closer, as if she was right in front of him. "Now hurry up, my arms are getting tired."

He blindly reached for her, his knuckles brushing against her stomach, and she inhaled a sharp breath. "Ugh, fine, you can look, but don't ogle," she warned. "I'll be able to tell."

"Don't worry," he replied sharply. "I have no desire to."

His words were a flat-out lie because when he opened his eyes, that was all he wanted to do. Heat zipped down his spine with the intensity of a lightning bolt. He wanted to touch her, but he refrained, holding his hands into tight fists at his side as he took a step toward her.

Swallowing the lump in his throat, he glanced over her, looking for the source of all this trouble. The dress was caught from behind.

"Turn around," he said, voice rough. She did as she was told, and the view from behind was just as torturous as it was from in front. He forced his eyes up.

The lace was caught on the hooks of her bra; the easiest solution would be to undo the bra, but just the idea of that was enough to send his brain short-circuiting.

He looked up at the ceiling, taking a deep breath before laser-focusing on the tangled fabric and hooks. He brought a careful hand to the dress. Her skin prickled with goosebumps, but he felt hot all over.

"Why were you changing in here, anyway?" he asked, hoping conversation would break some of the tension beating through him, but when he spoke, he was appalled at how rough his voice sounded. He surreptitiously cleared his throat.

"The line for the bathroom was too long," Emmeline replied, voice quiet. "Why did you come back? For the thermos?"

He paused. A part of him was still smarting from her rejection all those years ago, and his guard had gone up at the thought of being vulnerable with her. It would have been easy to use the thermos as an excuse, but he didn't want to do that.

The ridiculousness of this situation made it feel less scary.

"No, not for the thermos," he said, his hands moving slowly on the fabric of her dress. He was careful not to touch the bare skin of her back as he gingerly pulled the fabric from her bra hooks. Just being this close to her made his entire body go haywire.

"Then why?" she asked. "You left."

His heart pounded. "I wanted to apologize," he said. "I should have answered your question."

She was quiet. "Oh," she eventually said.

"I thought you wouldn't believe me because you don't seem to hold a very high opinion of me," he explained. "But if you ask me again, then I promise I'll answer."

She didn't respond. He had untangled the fabric by then,

and he moved his hands to her ribs, slowly turning her around.

"You keep surprising me," she whispered, facing him now. Her words were filled with awe.

Gathering the fabric of the dress, he pulled it up over her head—until it snagged again.

"Ow!" she cried out. "My clip!"

He winced. "Sorry."

Gently, he slipped his hand under the dress, moving up until he felt where the clip had gotten tangled in the fabric. He held it in place as she stood still, then used his other hand to pull off her dress.

As he dropped the dress to the ground, she lowered her arms, releasing a breath.

Then, she looked up at him. His hand was still in her hair, but he couldn't bring himself to move. They were standing inches apart, and he could feel the warmth of her body. His stomach burned. Before he could stop himself, his gaze dropped to her mouth.

He couldn't remember what they had been talking about. Both of them were quiet, entranced. Until he took another step forward, their knees bumping into one another's. Her sharp intake of breath filled the hushed space between them. The blood quickened in his veins.

"Em," he whispered, voice soft as he lifted a hand to cup her face.

She leaned into his touch, brows furrowed. A troubled expression came over her face, as if she was warring with herself, but in the dark depths of her eyes, he saw an undeniable truth: she wanted this.

Perhaps just as badly as he did.

Desire beat through him as she lifted up onto her tiptoes, and he leaned in—

A knock sounded on the door, making them both freeze.

"Everything okay?" It was Ola. "I heard a commotion."

Reality came crashing down. Emmeline jumped back, and Luke turned around, his face hot. He felt weak in the knees, unsteady.

"I'm fine, thank you!" Emmeline called out as Luke clutched a hand over his chest, willing his heart rate to steady.

It was so easy to forget about everything else when he was around Emmeline.

He couldn't think straight.

CHAPTER 16

On Torch, Emmeline flew through the freezing evening air, trying to calm her blood and the desire beating through her.

They had been so close to kissing. It was so easy to lose herself around Luke, to forget about all of her carefully thought-out plans and ideas. It was perhaps the only time she felt so in the moment—entirely untethered from everything but him: the scent of his skin, the soft pad of his fingers cupping her face, the warmth of his body.

"Get a grip," Emmeline scolded herself. Torch turned her head, concerned, and Emmeline cleared her throat. "Nothing, girl." She patted Torch's scales, and her dragon faced forward again, soaring through the air to take her to her parents' place.

There, she wanted to collapse on the couch the moment she entered, but she knew that if she did, there would be nothing stopping her thoughts from focusing on Luke, and she could not handle that right now.

Instead, she strode with purpose to her father's office, where wood was burning in the hearth. Her father was sitting at his desk, reading a book, and the familiar sight helped ease some of the edge off her nerves.

"Hi, Dad," she said.

He looked up from over his glasses, his face lighting up. "Emmy!" Charles said, closing his book. "When did you get here?"

"Just now," she replied, going over to kiss her father's cheek. "How are you doing? Where are the boys? And Motu?"

"Oh, they've all gone out," Charles replied.

Emmeline's eye twitched. Why had her mother made her feel guilty for working on a Sunday when neither of her brothers were even home?

"Up for a game of chess?" Charles asked, setting his book to the side. She let out a long breath, giving her dad a smile.

"If you're prepared to lose," she replied. "Then, of course."

Charles laughed, pulling the chess set out from his desk drawer as Emmeline sat on the chair across from him. They started the game, which she had always been good at. Chess was all about planning ahead, mapping out how the game would go and adjusting accordingly.

Comfortable silence filled her father's office as they played, interrupted by the occasional sound of pieces moving across the board. She inhaled the sweet scent of woodsmoke, listening to the fire crackling in the background.

It was enough to distract her for a little bit, but as she waited for her next turn, her focus frayed.

She thought of the way Luke had whispered her name. He had never called her that before. It was always "Sterling" or occasionally "Emmeline," never "Em," as if he could barely speak.

The scrape of his voice played in her ears, over and over.

Charles picked off another knight from the board, then paused before making his next move. "Is everything alright?" he asked, looking at her carefully.

Emmeline jolted. "Of course," she replied automatically, forcing a smile.

Charles furrowed his brows. "Are you sure?" he asked. "Everything okay with work?"

Her father looked down at the chessboard as she blinked stupidly. When she followed his gaze, her mouth jutted open. They had hardly been playing for ten minutes and she had already lost half of her pieces.

Swallowing the lump in her throat, Emmeline gave her father a tight smile. "Just a bit tired, that's all," she replied.

"Why don't you go lie down for a bit?" Charles asked. With a nod, she stood, exiting her father's office. The house was quiet—much too quiet. Luke's voice filled her mind, the way he had apologized for not answering her question.

"If you ask me again, then I promise I'll answer."

She thought she had him all figured out, but he kept surprising her, and she wasn't sure if that was a good thing or a bad thing. Her pulse raced, making her feel unsteady.

Clenching her jaw, she went to the kitchen, hoping some water would help. As she went to the sink, she saw it was filled with dirty dishes. Emmeline frowned, then immediately rolled up her sleeves.

She pulled open the dishwasher, her frown deepening as she saw that it hadn't been unloaded. "These men cannot do anything, I swear," she muttered to herself, pulling out the rack.

Since it was Sunday, the cleaning lady hadn't come, and Emmeline set about unloading the dishwasher, then loading it, grateful for the distraction, even if it was irritating how useless the men of her family could be.

After the sink was emptied, she opened the fridge to find random containers of leftovers.

"Of course there's nothing proper to eat," she muttered, snapping the fridge door closed. She yanked the freezer open, pulling out meat to defrost.

As she waited for that, she wiped the counters, and then, when she was finished with that, she spotted crumbs all over the floor.

"Ugh!" Emmeline grabbed the vacuum, the hum of the machine filling her ears as she pushed it back and forth. Her arms were burning by the time she was finished, but once she was done vacuuming, she grabbed the mop.

Just as she got started on the tiles in the kitchen, she heard her brothers entering through the front door. Emmeline glanced up and saw Naveed entering the kitchen with a bag.

Once he saw her expression, her youngest brother froze.

"Uh, hey," he said, giving her his best boyish smile. Emmeline paused her mopping to cut her youngest brother a glare. Despite being twenty-three, he gulped, rightfully afraid.

"The cleaning lady was just here yesterday and this place is already such a mess," Emmeline scolded. "It really isn't difficult to put your plate and glass in the dishwasher after you've eaten. And if you drop crumbs on the floor, just pick them up!"

Her brother looked around, confused. "It's not such a mess," he said.

She huffed. "Because I already cleaned up!"

"You didn't have to," he said, going around her to set the bag he was carrying on the counter.

"Of course I did!" she groaned, continuing mopping. Naveed headed for the exit, then paused to look at her curiously. He pushed a hand through his long hair.

"Why are you . . .?" Naveed asked, trailing off.

"Why am I what?" Emmeline replied. "Mopping? Because the floor is dirty."

"No, you're . . ." He trailed off again, but this time gestured to her.

"What?" she asked, impatient.

"You're aggressively cleaning," he said.

She was going to throttle him. Her brother must have sensed the intent in her eyes because he shut his mouth and made a prompt exit.

She continued mopping, muttering under her breath as she went. When she finished, the floors were sparkling. Inhaling the clean scent, she went to put the mop away.

She returned to the kitchen just as Haris was quietly exiting with a glass of water, his socks leaving footprint marks on the still wet tiles.

"Hey!" she said. "I just mopped!"

Wincing, Haris turned to her. "Sorry." His voice lowered as he muttered something to himself, and she narrowed her eyes at him, hand going to her hip.

"Excuse me?"

"Naveed told me you were crashing out," Haris said.

Her jaw dropped. "I am *not* crashing out!"

Haris arched a brow, unconvinced. Her chest tightened.

"Anyway," Haris continued. "Are you staying for dinner? Or did you just come here to take your frustration out on our kitchen?"

She glared at her brother. "Don't be smart with me," she said. "And, yes, obviously I'm staying, since you people don't know how to fend for yourselves. I was about to cook."

He gave her a confused look. "But we already brought dinner." He pointed to the bag Naveed had left on the counter.

"Oh." She frowned. "I took meat out to defrost."

"Just put it back," Haris said with an easy shrug. "And relax."

"I am relaxed! I've never been more relaxed!"

"You're acting like Ammi."

Oh god. She was becoming her mother. That was enough to get Emmeline to pause. She released a long breath, and Haris nodded. "I'll call the others—I'm starving."

Emmeline pulled out the plates to set the table and, shortly thereafter, Naveed came into the kitchen to reheat the tray of food they'd brought home. Once the oven dinged, he brought the tray to the table, removing the foil to reveal roasted chicken atop a bed of buttery rice. It smelled divine.

They all dug in, chatting about different things: Naveed's finance job, Haris's medical school classes, random members of their extended family.

As Emmeline ate and talked with her family members, she found herself relaxing, talking and laughing along with them. She showed them pictures of Eve from her visit to Millie's yesterday, telling them all the funny things Noah and Ira had said, her heart warming as she thought of her adorable nephew and nieces.

"She's all calmed down now," Haris said to Naveed, voice a fake-whisper. "No need to be afraid anymore."

"Damn," Naveed replied in an equally terrible whisper. "I was hoping she'd clean my room."

Emmeline rolled her eyes. "You guys are so funny. Truly."

They continued eating, and she felt much better once there was a hearty meal in her stomach. Just as she was finishing, Naveed stood, picking up his plate. As she scooped the last bite of rice onto her spoon, he grabbed her plate from underneath her, too.

"It really isn't difficult to put your plate in the dishwasher after you've eaten, you know," Naveed told her. She raised a brow.

"Hey, don't be smart with her," Haris said, pointing a finger. They were both mimicking her, clearly enjoying themselves.

"Hilarious. A real comedy act," Emmeline said drily, pushing her chair back. The boys laughed, and her lips twitched.

Together, they picked up the rest of the dishes, and Charles stuck them in the dishwasher. Then, they went to the couches in the living room to hang out, and a little while later, one of the caretakers brought Motu in.

The baby dragon lit up when he saw Emmeline, flying straight to her. She hardly had a chance to bring her arms up to catch him as he all but tackled her, almost sending her flying back.

The weight of him against her chest was soothing. Tears pricked her eyes as Motu nuzzled his head against hers, and she held him closer.

"No longer your enemy, huh?" she asked. Motu had seemingly decided to forgive her for tearing him away from Millie's kids and bringing him home last night.

Motu was getting a bit too big for such cuddles, so Emmeline sat on the couch, and he nestled over her lap, cuddling against her stomach. She petted his scales and he purred happily.

"That little heathen is so much better behaved than he was," Charles said, smiling at Emmeline before fixing Haris with a stern glance. Not that Haris was even slightly chagrined—he only looked pleased with himself.

"See?" he said, folding his hands behind his head. "I told you it was a good idea for you to watch him."

Emmeline shook her head at Haris; he was such an annoyance. But he was her younger brother, so even though he irritated her, she was still fond of him.

"There's nothing Emmeline can't handle," Charles said.

She had always thought so, but the more time she spent with Luke, the less confident she was. She pushed the thought from her mind, focusing on Motu, who looked sleepy now.

"I should head home," she said, standing with the baby dragon.

They all had work in the morning. After saying goodbye, Emmeline headed home, hoping that she would be so tired once she arrived that she could focus on unwinding, then simply fall asleep.

Unfortunately, not even her favorite silk pajamas, a fastidious skincare routine, a hot oil head massage, and a steaming cup of mint tea could calm her thoughts. After

Motu was sound asleep, she was alone in her quiet home, and she couldn't stop herself from thinking of Luke.

"What is wrong with you?" she muttered to herself, picking up the cup of tea from the vanity table in her bedroom. She took a sip, hoping the mint and honey would relax her nerves.

Her thoughts returned to what Luke had said, how she didn't hold a high opinion of him. She wasn't sure if that was true or not. If she was being honest, she was not exactly proud of how she had behaved all those years ago.

He had hurt Millie, yes, but she had hurt him, too, so wouldn't that make it even?

She glanced at her reflection in the vanity's mirror. Her dark hair was oiled and pulled back in a braid, her face bare of makeup. The only embellishment was her nose-ring, but even with that, she looked young. Her dark eyes were wide and lost.

"Why do you insist on hating him if the record is clear?" she asked herself. It was unreasonable, and she hated being unreasonable.

Deep down, she already knew the answer to her question. If she didn't hate him, then . . .

She trailed off. Shaking her head, she reached for her phone.

Luke had said that if she asked him a question again, he would answer.

CHAPTER 17

Emmeline was to meet Luke in Bayview after work finished at Inferno.

She could have met him at the bookshop, where they would both be headed afterwards, anyway, but she didn't know how the conversation would go. If it went well, she could get work done at the bookshop after, but if it went poorly, she would want some space away from him for a little while before getting back to work.

He had apologized, which she appreciated, but that didn't mean all of her guards were down. In truth, she was scared. She was barely holding herself together, and she was afraid of what she might feel for him if she let herself—but she wouldn't let herself feel anything unless she knew he was genuine.

There was the possibility that he was only acting this way to distract her. He was her rival, after all. She knew winning Anh's investment was just as important for him as it was for her. It had been three weeks, bringing them halfway to their deadline, and she needed to focus—something that seemed impossible to do if things continued the way they were with Luke.

There was no denying that he had gotten under her skin—but his hand had been so gentle in her hair. He'd apologized. He'd brought her chai.

She didn't know what his plan was: hence, this test. "What drives you?"

That was her question, and he'd refused to answer. If he answered her now, then he was genuine. If he didn't, then he was just playing with her.

Meeting in Bayview was the best course of action because it gave her an excuse to visit. She had hardly been to that part of Starshine Valley, and she wanted to see the lake. Arriving early, Emmeline took in the sights. As throughout the rest of the valley, a blanket of snow covered every tree, bush, and patch of grass, along with the lake itself, though parts were cleared out for ice-skating on the frozen waters.

The area was cute, fitted with a walkway that wound along the lake. There were benches for people to rest, along with small shops: a cafe, a bakery, a bookshop. As Emmeline walked down the path, she spotted a few people jogging in athletic clothes, then saw some old couples walking together. There were mothers pushing strollers and fathers with toddlers; teenage girls giggling over coffee cups; and solitary young men reading on benches.

Some were accompanied with chimeras of various ages, and Emmeline smiled as she walked past a baby chimera holding onto a twenty-year-old guy's beanie, its snake tail curled across the guy's shoulders. She hadn't seen a baby chimera before; it was adorable with its little goat face and stubby horns.

Emmeline continued walking, until she spotted a small truck selling hot chocolate. The sweet scent of the drink wafted toward her. She walked up and scanned the menu, which had about twenty different options. Eventually, she settled on a classic blend.

With her drink, she walked over to a bench, sitting to stare out at the silver lake. Some teenagers played ice hockey in one section, while others skated in another. The sky darkened, the sun about to set.

Emmeline checked her phone; Luke was late. She nibbled on her lower lip, trying not to think the worst: that this was what he wanted, for her to wait for him only for him to stand her up.

"Mommy, look!" a little girl said, pointing. Glancing up, Emmeline spotted Torch, who was flying above with Motu in her paw. The little girl wasn't the only one staring in awe.

Emmeline smiled to herself. Since this was the chimera area of town, her dragon would be a novelty. While she hadn't been to Bayview much, it was nice. Unlike the Hills, but lovely all the same.

The hot chocolate was sweet and warm, and she took another sip, gaze straying to where there was a toboggan slide set up. It looked to only be open on the weekends, but there were some people pulling up their own toboggans and even a few chimeras flying the toboggans on to the top. Passengers shot down the steep slide, both children and adults shouting in glee. It looked fun—probably as thrilling as a dragon diving down in the sky.

Emmeline checked her phone again, then frowned. Luke was ten minutes late now, with no message. Standing, she walked back and forth, sipping her hot chocolate until she reached the end. She went to toss it, just as a man a few years older than her tossed a crumpled piece of paper into the trashcan at the same time.

Her gaze met his, and she paused. He was very good-looking, with wavy black hair and stubble across his cheeks and jaw. There was a nasty scar slashed across his throat, the skin white and raised. There was another scar over his brow and in indent in one ear.

"What did you get?" he asked, giving her an easy smile.

"The hot chocolate?" she asked. He nodded. "A classic."

He didn't hesitate: "How about I get you another?"

"Oh." She hadn't been expecting that, but she wasn't entirely averse to the idea, either. She was used to men offering her such things.

"I'm Flint," he said. His voice was deep and raspy. "Give me a sec."

Before she could respond, he headed for the hot chocolate truck. Emmeline checked her phone, wondering where Luke was. Then, Flint was back. She put her phone away as he offered her a fresh hot chocolate, steam rising from the top. The sweet scent filled her lungs. With a shrug, she took the cup.

She was standing here waiting anyway, and one little hot chocolate was no harm; she was hardly going home with him. Besides, Flint was handsome. She always enjoyed handsome men. Though his beauty had a dangerous quality to it, the way the flash of lightning did, with the promise to scathe.

He was the type of man she would have—years ago—

cautioned Millie (with her terrible taste) away from, but Emmeline had handled plenty of men like him before. She wasn't worried.

"You're not from around here," Flint said, tilting his head as he assessed her.

"Oh?" she asked. "Then where am I from?"

He took the chance to check her out, his gaze slowly going down, which amused her. She was used to men who were forward. They knew what they wanted and weren't afraid to show it, which made them the most uncomplicated.

After everything being so complicated with Luke, this was a welcome distraction. She liked when guys fitted into neat boxes; it made it easy for her to manage.

"Let me guess," he said, looking her over. "Dragon rider?"

Surprise lit through her, but she didn't show it, not wanting him to think she was impressed. "Beginner's luck," she said casually. "There's only three other animals to choose from, anyway."

He shrugged easily, then pointed a finger up. "The dragon circling above kind of gave it away," he said. She looked and, sure enough, Torch was flying overhead.

Emmeline's lips twitched. "Someone's sharp."

"I get the feeling you like sharp," he replied smoothly, earning a laugh out of her. She was about to respond when Flint's gaze shifted to something over her shoulder. His expression soured.

Emmeline glanced back—Luke was there, looking royally pissed off. Anxiety spiked through her at his expression.

He stalked up to her and Flint, practically radiating tension as he came to stand by Emmeline's side. She could immediately sense he was angry, though really *she* should have been upset since he was the one who was late!

"Luke," Flint said curtly, nodding. So they knew each other.

Luke didn't respond. Instead, he turned to Emmeline, dark eyes stormy. "Go," he said, voice hard. Her brows crinkled. He'd never spoken to her like that, his voice a command. She opened her mouth to argue, but he ground his teeth together. "*Now.*"

Her blood beat hotly in her veins. First, he was late, and now he was ordering her around like a toxic jealous boyfriend. How dare he tell her what to do!

As she geared up to fire back a response, she saw the tight expression on his face. He was at the very edge of bursting, glaring at Flint, who didn't seem too pleased to see Luke, either, though *he* wasn't acting like a barbarian about it.

Something told her not to argue with Luke right then. Suppressing her anger, she turned to Flint.

"Thanks for this," she said, raising the hot chocolate in a "cheers" motion. Before she could bring her hand back down, Luke snatched the to-go cup from her. He took a stride away from her and tossed the cup into the garbage.

Her mouth dropped open.

She was about to quarrel with him, but Luke wasn't even looking her way. He was staring Flint down with his arms crossed.

Fuming, Emmeline stalked away. She walked along the pathway, stopping in front of one of the empty benches. She sat down, then stood again, too worked up to stay seated.

Releasing a frustrated sound, she began pacing back and forth. The sun had set by then, the sky a deep shade of navy blue. It was too early to see the stars.

Emmeline glanced over, where Luke was exchanging heated words with Flint, who looked peeved. Obviously they didn't like each other, but she didn't care. That still didn't give Luke the right to behave in such an uncivilized manner with her.

She continued to watch as eventually Flint left. Luke released a long breath, as if trying to steady himself. He was practically twitching, and though she was angry with him, seeing him so distressed made her unsettled.

It was the first time she had ever seen Luke so upset. Not even when she had broken his heart all those years ago had he been this agitated, like a kettle shrieking. She could have sworn steam was coming out of his ears, and for a moment, she felt a little guilty, as if it was her fault, somehow.

Then, Luke turned in her direction. He stalked over, his anger directed at her, and any remorse she felt quickly went away. She was the one who should have been angry he was late, after all. And yet, his eyes were blazing, his hands in tight fists at his sides.

Turning her cheek, she crossed her arms over her chest as he came to a stop beside her.

"Do you have any idea who that is?" Luke asked. She ignored him, and he grabbed her elbow, pulling her to face him. "Do you?"

She turned, narrowing her eyes at him. "Oh, now you're speaking to me in more than one-word orders?" she asked, voice dripping with venom. Luke made an irritated sound, looking away for a moment before snapping his gaze back to hers.

"Don't piss me off, Emmeline," he said. She threw his hand off her arm.

"What is wrong with you?" Anger burned through her. "How dare you order me around like that? Who the hell are you?"

He scoffed. "When you've taken complete leave of your senses, that's what you get," he replied. "Are you insane? You just take any drink from any stranger you met five seconds ago just because he's hot?"

Emmeline paused. Luke kind of had a point, but she was not going to admit that. Besides, she could handle herself, and even if she couldn't, Flint was correct in noting that Torch had been circling above. Her dragon wouldn't have let anything happen to her.

She didn't explain any of that.

"It was just a hot chocolate!" she cried, genuinely baffled by his reaction. "It's five p.m. on a Monday evening! And we're down by the lake, not in some club!"

Luke ground his teeth together. "Stay away from Flint."

She couldn't believe this. "You don't get to tell me who to stay away from!"

"I do when you have exceptionally bad taste in men!"

"No wonder I went after you!" The words were out before she could think better of them.

Emmeline froze.

Luke's face twitched, confusion breaking through the rage. "But that was just to get back at me," he said. Her heart pounded. "You weren't actually interested in me."

She paused, unsure how to respond, and the moment was enough for his anger to come back in full force as he seemed to replay her words.

"And don't compare me to fucking Flint!" he snapped.

His expression was furious, as if she had offended him deeply. She had no idea why he was so upset, but he was behaving entirely out of character. He wasn't explaining anything; he was just ordering her about.

"You're right—he's much nicer than you!" she snapped back.

Luke's face flashed with hurt. Before she knew what was happening, he bridged the space between them, seizing her shoulders. "You don't know anything," he said, shaking her.

"If you're not going to tell me, then obviously I don't know!"

He clenched his jaw, looking away from her. With a frustrated huff, he released her, turning. He pulled out a whistle and blew; shortly thereafter, Sharptooth arrived, swooping down behind him. Adrenaline beat through her as she watched him head toward his chimera.

"You're leaving?" she cried, appalled. "I thought we were going to talk!"

"I can't talk to you right now," he replied.

Pain slashed through her. "But you said if I asked again you would answer," she said, hating the way her voice wobbled. She sounded like a child, and she hated that, too.

He turned back to face her, expression turbulent. "Please don't ask me anything right now," he said, jaw clenched over the words.

"But you said—"

"I changed my mind!" he cried.

She flinched. *How could he do this?* He said . . .

He really was just playing with her.

The realization shouldn't have surprised her so much, and yet. She shook her head.

"You were right," she said, voice empty. "I don't have a good opinion of you. I was hoping to change that—but it seems there's no need."

He looked gutted by that, and she was glad.

"Torch!" she called.

Luke's dark eyes filled with regret as Torch swooped down, landing behind Emmeline. Motu was in her paw, and the baby flew to Emmeline's side, holding onto her leg.

Both the baby dragon and Torch could immediately sense that Emmeline was upset. Torch growled at Luke, eyes slitted into a glare.

In response, Sharptooth inched closer to Luke, growling just as deeply. The animals stared each other down as Emmeline went to mount.

"Torch, come on," she said. Luke took a step toward her.

"Emmeline, wait—" he started, but it was too late.

She was gone.

CHAPTER 18

Luke flew home, his mind spinning. The last two hours had turned his brain to mush, and he was still reeling from all that had happened.

He had been pleased when Emmeline had messaged him to meet after work. She had wanted to meet him in Bayview, which had only pleased him further. He had thought he could show her all of his favorite spots: the hot chocolate truck, the kids playing ice hockey, the toboggan slide.

Unfortunately, he'd arrived late. He'd taken his mother, Rhea, to a doctor's appointment, from where his brother, Farhan, was supposed to pick her up, but Farhan had gotten busy with an after-school meeting with one of his middle school students. He would have texted Emmeline to explain all of this but, in perfect luck, his phone had died.

He had planned to explain in person, but when he rushed down to the lake, he saw Emmeline laughing with Flint of all people, which made him lose his mind. Flint was certified terrible news; he was involved in the gang that ran the illegal dragon races. Not only that, but a few years back, he had drugged the youngest of the Din girls at a party.

Though Luke didn't have any sisters of his own, the Din girls were as close as he got, and the youngest, Lilliana, had hardly been eighteen at the time.

Luke didn't care if Emmeline could take care of herself; seeing her around Flint had sent him into a panic.

Then she had the audacity to be angry with *him*. For someone so clever, she really could be so dense. Couldn't she tell he was only looking after her? Trying to protect her? And why would he do that—because he cared about her, damnit. But it was like she refused to see that.

How couldn't she understand? It should have been obvious.

Maybe he hadn't handled the situation well, but he couldn't think straight. Dark possibilities ran through his mind, driving him over the edge as he thought of Emmeline in danger . . . Emmeline taken advantage of . . . Emmeline hurt.

It had been impossible to keep a lid on his temper, to be around anyone for a moment longer, which was why he'd called Sharptooth.

He couldn't speak to her—he could hardly speak now, even as he made it home. Anger beat through him and, after dismounting from Sharptooth, he stood out in the cold, catching his breath. His chimera nudged her head against Luke's side.

"It's alright," he gritted out, petting Sharptooth's head. "It's fine."

But it wasn't fine. He wanted to hit something. Instead, he

dug his hands into the snow. The cold helped a bit, and when his fingers became numb, he headed inside.

He had thought he would spend time with Emmeline, that things would go well, and then maybe he'd get some work done at the bookshop, but now, he didn't have the energy for anything.

He thought of Emmeline laughing with Flint again, and he slammed the door shut with such force that it rattled on its hinges. He kicked off his shoes and threw off his coat, then stalked into the living room and collapsed onto the couch.

Closing his eyes, he pressed his temples. He had a headache, now, too. Fantastic.

"Back already?" a voice asked.

Luke opened his eyes to find his younger brother Farhan sitting on the lounge chair across from him, a mug of chai in his hand. At twenty-eight, Farhan was two years younger than Luke. The brothers looked alike, but Farhan's black hair was slightly shorter than Luke's, and while Luke stayed clean-shaven, Farhan sported a neatly trimmed beard.

Their mother was sitting on the other chair with a shawl across her shoulders. There was an additional blanket on her lap, atop which sat her knitting. She still hadn't finished the sweaters she was making for the baby chimeras, Butternut and Squash, both of whom were sitting happily by Rhea's feet, munching on biscuits.

"Yeah," Luke replied.

"I thought you had a date or something?" Farhan continued, snagging a biscuit from the plate sitting on the table between him and Rhea. "Though I'm not really sure who has a date on a Monday evening—"

"Shut up," Luke replied, rubbing a hand over his face. He was still feeling foul.

"Someone's in a great mood," Farhan said cheerily. "What, did she stand you up or something?"

"Tch, Farru, stop bothering him," Rhea said, setting down her knitting to take a sip of chai. "Being stood up is sure to put one in a bad mood."

Was that a hint of amusement in his mother's voice? His family sure was great at rubbing salt in a wound.

"I don't wanna talk about it," he said, brooding.

Rhea and Farhan exchanged a glance. "Was it Emmeline you were meeting?" Rhea asked. "I can't imagine anyone else you would be upset over."

"Emmeline?" Farhan repeated, shocked. "Emmeline Sterling? Dude, no wonder you're upset she stood you up."

Luke sighed. "You guys are seriously the worst," he said, sitting up. He didn't want to talk about it, but they obviously weren't going to stop bothering him, so he might as well tell them the details they were clearly keen for. "Yes, I was supposed to meet Emmeline."

Farhan whistled. "Good for you."

"What's that supposed to mean?" Luke asked. Farhan arched a brow, looking at Luke as if he was being obtuse.

"You've been committed to being obsessed with her for, like, seven years," Farhan said with a snort.

"Even Ayman and the girls know about Emmeline," Rhea added, referencing her best friend and her three daughters. The Din girls were just as nosy and desperate for gossip as any younger sisters.

"Great." Luke rubbed a hand over his face. "Just further the humiliation."

"Oh, jaan, I'm sure she had a good reason not to come," Rhea said, voice pitying.

"Yeah, quit being such a baby," Farhan added, taking a sip of his chai. "Have a biscuit."

"She didn't stand me up!" Luke cried. "I saw her down by the lake. With Flint." Even saying Flint's name made Luke's temper flare up again, and he scowled.

"Fucking Flint?" Farhan said, immediately upset. "No wonder you're pissed off." A dark expression crossed his face, both brothers matched in their dislike of him.

Even Rhea was upset by the mention of Flint. Of course, she knew what had happened all those years ago between him and Lillie.

"Yeah," Luke huffed, stewing.

Butternut and Squash sensed Luke and Farhan's vile moods, and the baby chimeras each bounced over to one of the brothers. Butternut fluttered his little wings until he landed in Luke's lap, rubbing his face against Luke's arm. Squash did the same with Farhan.

Luke released a long breath, petting the baby's furry face. Butternut licked Luke's hand with his little tongue, and Luke smiled. The sound of Rhea's knitting needles filled the quiet space, until she set the needles down.

"I know," she said. "Let's play a round of ludo. That'll fix your evening right up."

Luke snorted. Despite how old they had gotten, they would always be little kids to their mom.

"Mama, come on," Farhan said, cracking a smile. "Losing will hardly make Luke feel any better."

"Losing?" Luke arched a brow. "If I recall properly, you're the one who always loses."

Farhan snorted. "Yeah, right."

They set up the board game on a table in front of their mother, both boys sitting on the floor on either side of her as they played. It was hard to say who was trying to cheat the most, but that was half the fun.

In the end, both brothers lost, and Rhea won, but he didn't care. His mother was right; the game did fix his evening, though that was more from the company of his family than from the game itself. His mother looked brighter than he'd seen her in days, her eyes wide open instead of drooping closed from fatigue. She laughed easily, beaming at her sons.

Afterwards, he and Farhan tag-teamed dinner—creamy chicken handi with naan—and they all ate together. By then, Rhea was tired, since it was getting late. Farhan helped her up to her room.

"Don't forget your mail, jaan," Rhea reminded Luke from the stairs, and he grabbed the stack from the front table.

He shuffled through as he made it to his room on the ground floor. Because he still lived at home, they had sectioned this part of the house off into a kind of studio apartment with a separate outside entrance so he could still have privacy and, once he closed the door, he let out a long sigh.

Closing the door behind him with his foot, he continued rifling through the mail. There were a few junk envelopes, but then he spotted some that he knew were bills for Tempest.

They were marked with a bright red OVERDUE stamp across the front, and he winced.

He swore under his breath, shuffling past them only to find more bills, these ones from the hospital for his mother.

"Today is truly the worst," he muttered to himself. He dropped the stack of mail onto his dresser, running both hands through his hair.

Sitting down on the edge of his bed, he buried his face in his hands, closing his eyes. He focused on the rhythm of his heart, beating steadily but slowly increasing as tension seeped through him.

He had wanted to talk to Emmeline, to see if they could move forward together, but he realized now what a terrible idea that was. His entire evening had been derailed because of how she made him feel, and he didn't need that, not right now.

He should have been focusing on his business, on pulling it out from the dire straits it was in. He *needed* to win that investment. He needed to take care of his mother, the way he always did.

Emmeline was his rival. He couldn't risk forgetting that fact.

CHAPTER 19

After Luke had flown away, Emmeline had been too wired up to go to the bookshop to work on her proposal, so instead, she had gone home, where she had cooked way too much food. She ended up packaging up most of the food for Saphira, dropping it off at their cottage with a note that said, *For you and the baby* ♡.

That had helped a little.

The next day, as Emmeline headed to Tales & Tails, she wondered how Luke would be. She was sure he would apologize, and she was intent on making him grovel for a while before forgiving him. She knew he'd have some sort of explanation, but she wouldn't accept it, not right away at least.

"Hi, Ola," Emmeline said, passing by the manager at the front table. "Minh." They both waved, Ola from where she was bagging a book, and Minh from his reading chair, though he didn't glance up from his book while he did.

With Motu flying beside her, Emmeline headed for

the office, weaving between customers. She smiled at the booksellers, watching as one of them tried to rescue a distressed baby dragon that had managed to get stuck in the window display. Recognizing the garneta breed from the Baby Dragon Book Club, she went over to say hello to Vaneeza Kiani, who was trying to coax her baby dragon out with burnt naan chips.

"Hey, need any help?" Emmeline asked. "I have fried bitter gourds." At that, Motu perked up; he really was such a little fatso. Shaking her head, she pulled the bag out of her purse and gave him a few, which he happily gobbled up.

"Honestly, yes," Vaneeza replied with a little laugh.

Emmeline pulled out the snack, and Ember perked up from the smell. The bookseller moved the rest of the books out of the way, clearing the path for Ember to come out from where he was stuck in the corner of the window.

"Ember," Emmeline cooed, shaking the bag. The baby dragon perked up.

"Come on, angel," Vaneeza said, holding her hands out. "Come on."

Ember wiggled out of the corner, squeezing out.

"Good girl!" Vaneeza said. "Come on."

The baby dragon jumped up onto the table, then leapt into flight, flying into Vaneeza's outstretched arms.

"Good girl," Emmeline said, feeding her some of the fried bitter gourds. By Emmeline's feet, Motu flapped his wing, smacking her leg. She glared down at him, while he opened his mouth wide.

"Here," she said, giving him some of the snack, as well. She met Vaneeza's gaze, and they shook their heads, laughing.

"Thanks for the help," Vaneeza said. Emmeline waved her free hand. "We missed you last night."

Too upset from her encounter with Luke, Emmeline hadn't gone to the book club meeting last night. She let out a short breath. "I'm sorry to have missed it, too," she said, wincing.

Ginny had sent her an annoyed text for not being there, as well, and Emmeline had already promised to make it up to her. The first meeting they had gone to was fun; there were about ten people there, different ages with different breeds of baby dragons. The bookseller leading the club had been a sweet, middle-aged man, explaining how he didn't have a dragon of his own but he loved to see the baby dragons of the community.

"Hopefully we'll see you next week?" Vaneeza asked, and Emmeline smiled.

"Definitely!" she replied. "I just got caught up with something this week."

Remembering exactly *what* she had gotten caught up with last night made her heartbeat quicken as she said goodbye to Vaneeza and headed for the office. When she reached the closed doorknob, she paused. *Was Luke already here?* She hesitated for a moment, and Motu flew into her shoulder.

She gave the baby dragon a look, and he returned the gesture, as if asking her, *What are you waiting for?*

Taking a deep breath, Emmeline opened the office door, entering. Her pulse spiked when she spotted Luke sitting in his usual seat, his back to her. She expected him to turn and say hello, but the only hint that he'd noticed her arrival was a slight stiffening of his shoulders.

Emmeline's brows furrowed. She closed the office door

behind her, then set down her bag and coat. Still, Luke didn't turn, the quiet office filled only with the sound of keys clicking as he typed on his laptop.

So you're not going to say anything? she wanted to bite out, but why should she speak first? He was the one who needed to apologize. Emmeline clenched her jaw, pushing the words back.

Lifting her chin, she sat down and got to work, though her mind was hardly functioning. She glanced over at Luke's rigid posture.

He was supposed to be groveling, and here he was being cold. Her temper flared. Suddenly, she couldn't bear to be in the same room as him. Closing her laptop with a snap, she grabbed her things. Motu flew up beside her as she threw open the office door, heading out to work on the main floor. She didn't care that the door slammed on her way out.

As she sat down on one of the reading chairs, Motu settled by her feet, his body warm against her leg. Releasing a short breath, she pulled open her laptop. A moment later, she felt Motu rub his face against her knee. Glancing down, she saw the baby dragon looking up at her, big purple eyes concerned.

With a sigh, she reached down to pet him, and he nuzzled against her hand. Her heartbeat slowed, steadying, and she got back to work.

As she focused, he eventually got up from her feet, going to roam around. One of the booksellers was restocking the shelves, and Motu flew over, helping him. She watched fondly as Motu put a book in his mouth, flying up to the top shelf to hand it to the bookseller on the ladder.

"Thanks," the bookseller said, petting Motu's head, and Motu flapped his wings happily, clearly pleased with himself.

Emmeline let him play around, keeping an eye on him from above her laptop to ensure he wasn't causing trouble, but he seemed to know not to go out of her sight or to wreak any havoc, thankfully.

As her baby dragon played, she worked on the coffee shop proposal. She had already worked out the menu—with a focus on different coffee brews made with coffee sourced from Inferno, of course—and was looking over the quote the contractor had given her for the renovation. It seemed reasonable and, since the bookshop had worked with the contractor before, she figured it would be the best rate, but she had reached out to two other contractors as well, just to compare.

Now, she was working out decor details—she wanted the vibe to be different from any other cafe in this area, particularly the Baby Dragon Cafe, since that was just a street away. Her plan was to lean into the bookish side of things—maybe even have themed drinks based on characters from famous novels.

She also wanted the to-go cups to be covered with book quotes. Plus, she wanted the furniture in the seating area to be fuss-free and minimalist in design rather than spacious and comfy; that way, customers would feel more inclined to browse the books as they drank their coffees, rather than sit down.

Working on the proposal was enough to distract her, but then, about an hour later, she saw the office door open from across the bookshop. She watched as Luke exited with his things, closing the door behind him.

Despite herself, she held her breath, waiting to see if Luke would come over to her.

But he didn't. Instead, he slipped on his coat and headed for the door. As he did, he glanced her way, just as she looked up. Their eyes locked across the bookshop, and a crease appeared between his brows. His brown eyes were so sad.

For a moment, she thought he would change course, come to her, but he didn't. She must have been imagining the expression on his face because he didn't say a word. He just left.

He left, again.

It shouldn't have hurt, but it did. Terribly, tears welled in her eyes, and she hastily blinked them away.

"Don't be ridiculous," she scolded herself. "Fuck's sake."

She squeezed her eyes shut, but as she did, his face flashed in her mind. She didn't understand why he looked so anguished when he looked at her. *She* was the injured party, here. Wasn't she?

It was all too complicated—all too much.

And she needed to *focus*. It was week four of six, and while she'd made good progress with her proposal, there was still a long way to go to make her presentation perfect.

She straightened her back, turning her attention to her work.

Three evenings later, Emmeline and Luke still hadn't exchanged a single word since their disagreement.

He hadn't tried to explain why he had reacted the way he

had. It was stupid of her, but she wanted to know what had made him to behave in such a manner. The curiosity was eating at her. A silly part of her believed that maybe he had good cause—but then why wouldn't he tell her if so?

He seemed adamant on avoiding her entirely, completely freezing her out. In the almost four weeks they'd been working together, she'd never seen him so focused, and often, he only stayed at the bookshop for an hour before heading out, rather than staying for the entire evening the way he used to.

She was still angry with him, but such behavior made her feel . . . abandoned, which was ridiculous, she knew. They weren't friends. They most certainly weren't anything *more*. Him avoiding her shouldn't have bothered her.

But it did. And that only made her feel worse.

She wanted to understand.

Which was why, after another silent evening, Emmeline mounted Torch and headed for Bayview. Maybe she could find Flint and ask him. It would obviously be only one side of the story, but it would give her a better idea of why Luke was behaving the way he was with her.

The weather was bitingly cold tonight, frigid and unrelenting. She buried her nose in her neck scarf, trying to look through the icy wind at the lake to search for Flint.

Torch landed by the hot chocolate stand, and Emmeline dismounted. Motu flew out of Torch's paw to join her, staying by her side as she looked around. The baby dragon struggled to fly in the wind, and even Emmeline braced against the cold. She stopped walking, looking around, and Motu settled by her feet, his scaled body warming her leg.

Searching, Emmeline spotted a low glow of fire far away

on the lake. It looked to be a bonfire, a group of adults surrounding it. Maybe she could ask somebody there if they knew where she could find Flint.

Emmeline started in that direction, walking along the frozen lake. The wind was worse on the open lake, tiny shards of ice cutting against her eyes. She made it about halfway when she heard someone coming after her.

"Emmeline!" Luke called over the wind. Her heartbeat quickened, and she slowed, but didn't turn.

"What!" she cried back. Where had he even come from? Irritation flashed through her, though a part of her crackled with anticipation as she heard him jogging to catch up with her.

"Where are you going?" he asked, jogging to cut in front of her path. She was forced to stop, and she crossed her arms over her chest. Motu looked between both of them, his little face worried.

"What does it matter?" she asked.

Luke clenched his jaw. "You're impossible," he groaned. Despite her coat, a chill ran down her spine.

"Then why don't you go back to ignoring me!" She had to shout over the wind, which seemed to be intensifying now that she had stopped walking. It pushed against her, propelling her in Luke's direction, but she dug her feet in.

"Come on," he said, reaching for her arm.

"No," she said, throwing him away from her. "I'm going to find your *friend*."

His face blazed, and for a moment, she almost shrunk back, his expression was so fierce. But she didn't. Instead, she lifted her chin and met his burning eyes with her own. He muttered a curse under his breath.

"I told you to stay away from him," he told her.

She wanted to throttle him. "Since when do you get to order me around?" she replied, livid. "I'll do whatever I want."

His hands clenched into fists at his sides. They were both breathing hard, dark eyes clashing. It was the most words they'd spoken to one another in days, but it wasn't nearly enough. She wanted to yell at him, for him to yell at her, for them both to *talk*. The silence had been eating at her.

Motu whined, unhappy, and a moment later, Torch swooped over to join them. The dragon landed with a thud at Emmeline's side, snarling at Luke. When Torch did so, Emmeline heard the flapping of wings, and soon thereafter Sharptooth was there, landing on Luke's side, across from Torch.

Both animals were agitated, taking protective stances. The icy wind howled, and Luke reached for Emmeline again.

She swatted his hand away. "Don't touch me," she said. Luke held his hands up, but Sharptooth turned in Emmeline's direction. She roared at her.

More surprised than afraid, Emmeline faltered back.

"Sharptooth, back off!" Luke cried.

Emmeline lost her footing, and her feet slipped on the ice. Before she realized what was happening, the sky tilted and she fell back hard, hitting her head against the frozen lake. Pain shot through her.

"Em!" Luke cried, reaching for her. Her head was spinning, but she heard Torch growl at him, and an alarm beat through her.

Torch was not happy, and an unhappy dragon was not a good thing.

As she tried to sit up, she saw her dragon step toward Luke.

"Hey, it's okay," he said, voice gentle and coaxing. "Torch, it's me."

But Torch only released another unforgiving growl.

"Torch, it's okay," Emmeline said, but her voice was weak, lost beneath the howling wind.

She tried to rise to her feet, and Luke took a step toward her to help. Torch bit at the air in front of him, the sound of her teeth snapping together a clear warning.

Then, everything happened so quickly.

In response to Torch, Sharptooth fired.

"Sharptooth, no!" Luke cried as Emmeline rose to her feet. Torch's wings came in front of her as a shield, though Emmeline still felt the heat cut through the freezing night.

The moment the flames subsided, Torch's wings fell and she jumped forward to retaliate. Sharptooth was waiting, and the sky lit with flames as both animals attacked.

Emmeline's heart lurched. In a fight between a dragon and a chimera, a dragon would always win, and hers was a basalta breed, one of the biggest and strongest. One of the best.

"Torch, stop!" she called.

But it was too late. Torch roared and the flames overcame Sharptooth's. The chimera was pushed back, bringing Luke into the crossfire.

"No!" she cried, her heart rising into her throat. She reached for Luke, but it was futile; she was too far away.

Sharptooth opened her wings to protect herself and Luke, but Torch's fire was strong. The blast was enough to burn the chimera's wings. Sharptooth cried out in pain, falling over with a thud onto the snow, which sizzled beneath his burned wings.

"Sharptooth!" Luke cried, crawling to the chimera's side.

Tears blurred Emmeline's eyes, and she ran over to the chimera and Luke.

"Luke," Emmeline started, but he held his arm up.

"Stay back!" he cried, not looking at her. Guilt knifed through her, and she brought a hand over her mouth, horrified with what had transpired.

"Luke, I'm so sorry," she said, voice broken. Torch seemed to have sensed her mistake then, sitting back with her head lowered. Luke shoveled snow onto Sharptooth's wings with his hands, trying to ease the burn, but the snow immediately hissed and melted, not providing much reprieve.

Luke made a helpless sound, panicking.

Emmeline's mind raced. She pulled out her phone, dialing Lavinia.

"Emmy—" Lavinia started.

"Lavinia, I need your help," Emmeline said, hyperventilating. "Please. Torch fired at a chimera and he's hurt. Can you come?"

"Hey, take a deep breath," Lavinia said. "I don't normally do this, but where are you? I'll grab some supplies and meet you."

CHAPTER 20

It had all happened so fast. Things had escalated before Luke could stop them.

They were arguing, both of them angry, and then Emmeline had slipped, falling, and nothing else mattered except for the way his entire heart had seized, as if somebody had plunged a hand into his chest and squeezed. He had understood then that whatever they were fighting about was stupid, that it wasn't worth it. All he wanted was to make sure she was okay.

He hadn't realized how agitated Torch and Sharptooth were getting, both protective and fierce. Not until it had been too late.

This should have never happened.

Luckily, the burns weren't too bad, and Emmeline's veterinary friend had set Sharptooth right. He had met Lavinia before when he'd taken the baby chimeras to the Animal Hospital; she was competent. He'd trusted she would do a good job, and she had.

All of that nasty business was over now, leaving him in the

aftermath. He was in the barn, watching Sharptooth sleeping. She would heal in a few days, Lavinia had said.

Even after Lavinia had left, Emmeline had stayed. She was still here, now, having sent Torch and Motu away. He had texted Farhan to come over and keep Rhea and the baby chimeras busy and not to ask anything.

I'll explain later, he'd written.

Fine, but you owe me, big time, Farhan had texted back.

Now, all that was left was quiet. He and Emmeline hadn't spoken to one another. He didn't know what to say. It felt as if this could have all been avoided, like it was all his fault, and he was ashamed. The barn was filled with soft golden light from one of the lamps, and they both stood by it, watching Sharptooth sleeping.

Emmeline fussed with her fingers. He saw her chin was trembling.

"I'm sorry," she said, her voice a whisper. He looked over at her, and she brought her eyes up to his. They shone with unshed tears. "Luke, I'm so sorry. This is all my fault."

His chest tightened with pain. "Hey, it's not," he said, going to her side. She squeezed her fingers tight, her knuckles going white. Her shoulders shook from the force of it, and he reached for her hands, pulling them apart.

"It was an accident," he said, not letting go of her hand. "I know that Torch was only looking out for you."

"I should have . . ." She broke off, shaking her head. "I should have . . ." she muttered to herself, and he could see the way that statement was unfolding in a dozen ways in her head, all the things she could have done better, all the ways she felt she should have taken control of the situation.

"Hey," he said, voice gentle. "It's okay. Things happen."

"It's not okay."

"It is," he said.

She quickly blinked away her tears. He had never seen her cry, but he'd seen her close a few times now, and each time was like a punch in the gut. Whenever he saw her eyes well with tears, he wanted to do anything and everything in the world to make them go away.

He wondered if she ever cried in front of anyone, if she ever let herself be anything but strong. But he could see she was breaking now, and so was he.

"How's the head?" he asked, touching his other hand to the back of her head. He was glad her hair had been down; if she was wearing one of those massive clips of hers, it would have hurt much worse.

She winced a little. "Okay," she replied easily, automatically. "A little headache never killed anyone."

He frowned. He had noticed she always did this—acted fine even if she wasn't. And she clearly wasn't. She was like a lightbulb on the verge of fading, dim and flickering.

Luke let go of her hand and went to where there was a basket atop one of the piles of hay. He rummaged around until he found a painkiller and a small bottle of water, bringing both over to her.

Emmeline raised a brow. "You're giving me chimera medicine?" she asked.

His lips twitched. "No, I keep these here for me when the babies get too hyper and give me a headache."

"Oh." Her lips tilted, and she took the medicine. He felt marginally better. "Thank you," she told him. "And I'm sorry. Again."

He furrowed his brows. "I'm sorry, too. For . . ." He trailed off, blowing out his cheeks. "For everything. For how I've been behaving all week. I've been terrible."

She looked down at her hands. "You have been," she said. "But I'm sorry, too. I could tell you were upset but I kept provoking you."

He shook his head. "Stop apologizing. Please." He brought his hand to her chin, tilting her to face him. "I shouldn't have been so easily provoked."

"I only came out to Bayview today to ask Flint what had happened between you two," she said, voice quiet. The mention of Flint made Luke's temper spike, but he swallowed his anger.

"You could have asked me," he said. Her dark eyes held complaint in them, and he winced.

"I couldn't," she said. "You were angry all week, and even before that, you stormed off and didn't answer my question." She looked away, and her next words were hardly a whisper. "Even though you said you would."

She was right. Guilt needled through him. "I'm sorry," he said. "Again. For everything. Flint is just—the worst. He's part of the gang that runs the dragon races."

While it was the dragons that raced, it was the chimera owners who arranged the races and flew spectators up, at least the ones who didn't have dragons of their own. No other animals participated in the races; griffins could just barely fly high up to the mountains where the races took place, and while chimeras could, they didn't have the speed or aggression to race.

Her eyes widened. "Oh, I didn't know. But you're right. Anyone involved in running the racing is someone to stay away from. Theirs is a whole different world. I remember my cousin Danny telling me as much when he used to race."

"Flint is especially bad, so I react poorly whenever he's concerned," he said. "That's not an excuse, it's just . . ." He released a long sigh, then reached for her hand. "Em, I don't want to fight anymore."

It was true. He was either fighting her or himself, and he was tired of both. He was so tired.

"I don't want to fight anymore, either," she replied, squeezing his hand. Releasing a breath, she sat down, leaning against a stack of hay, and he sat down beside her, their shoulders pressed together.

She didn't move away, and he relished the solid feel of her. He wanted to be her anchor, to be the thing she held onto when she was falling apart.

The hay was soft beneath them, comfortable even, and for the first time in a long time, he finally relaxed.

"Why *are* we fighting?" he asked. "I can't remember anymore."

She nibbled on her lower lip, and he watched her throat move as she swallowed. "Well, it all started when you broke Millie's heart," she said. The words were practiced, as if she reminded herself of them often, but her voice held no conviction.

"If it means anything, I never meant to," he said. "I thought she was great, but once I realized I wasn't interested, I wanted to be clear so there was no misunderstanding."

She played with the ends of her long hair. "I know, I'm sorry," she said. "You never did it with any ill intent—not like I did. Everything I did, I did to hurt you."

"You were just trying to take care of your little sister," he said. "Anyone can see how much you're willing to do for the ones you love."

She turned to look at him. "It was still wrong." Releasing her hair, she took a deep breath, then said, "Clean slate?"

He nodded. "Clean slate."

Her eyes softened, as if she was finally relaxing, now, too. Their gazes were locked, and it felt like the beginning of a book he knew would become his favorite story.

He was seeing a new side of her now, true vulnerability, and he could see she was frightened by it, but she didn't look away. She stared into his eyes just as intently, and he thought he could drown in the dark depths of her eyes. They were such a dark shade of black it was hard to tell where her pupils began and ended, and he inched closer, staring, losing all sense of time and place. Her eyes widened ever so slightly, and his heartbeat quickened.

Carefully, he lifted his hand, bringing it up to brush a lock of hair behind her ear. His fingers lingered in her hair, his thumb grazing against her cheekbone. His chest ached.

She leaned into his touch, turning her cheek into his palm. Heat spread through him. Her lips brushed against his skin, sending sparks skittering through him.

Her gaze flicked to his mouth, and her lidded eyes made his stomach twist with desire.

She pulled back, then settled against his side, leaning her head on his shoulder. He lowered a little so she could be more comfortable, resting his head against hers.

He remembered what she had said once, about how she couldn't lose. It was why she was so cautious.

He finally understood a bit more of why she was resisting their connection, despite how obvious it felt between them. And it was okay; he didn't want to push her. He just wanted her to know that if she bet on him, she wouldn't lose.

They stayed like that for some time—until there was knocking on the barn door. Before Luke could respond, the door opened and Farhan entered.

"Mama said to call you in for dinner," Farhan said. "And Emmeline, too."

Embarrassment burned Luke's ears.

"Hi," Emmeline said, sounding amused. "Do I know you?"

Luke tried to give his brother a silent warning, and a mischievous glint entered Farhan's eyes.

"I'd tell you if I didn't care for my life," Farhan told Emmeline, giving her a boyish smile.

"Oh?"

Farhan strode over, offering Emmeline his hand. "I'm Farhan," he said, helping Emmeline stand. "Luke's brother. I'm sure he's told you nothing about me, since in comparison he seems pretty dull. I am the better Hayward man, after all. Ask anyone."

Emmeline finally smiled, and Luke cut his brother a look. "Quit being so charming," he said. He was the one who was supposed to be making Emmeline smile.

Farhan only rolled his eyes. "Ignore him, he's always like this," he stage-whispered to Emmeline. Then, he grinned. "Now, come on, I'm starving!"

CHAPTER 21

Things felt good between Emmeline and Luke now. There would be no more fighting.

It had already been too much, things going too far, and it was all so stupid. Luke hadn't been hurt—thank God—but he could have been, and just the thought made her stomach clench. She hated how she'd been behaving; how erratic everything had felt, how out of control.

A clean slate would put an end to all that.

While she still wasn't quite certain of exactly what her feelings were, she knew that she wanted to stop hiding from them. She wanted to feel—even if it made her feel like she was on the edge of a cliff, about to fall.

She followed Farhan out of the barn and into the cold. He was explaining how he was a middle school teacher, telling her about some of his students as they headed into the house. Inside, the home was warmly lit by the golden glow of lamps.

It was a small place, a little messy, but cozy. There was a woman asleep on the couch, knitting on her lap.

"Our mother, Rhea," Farhan said, voice quiet. Luke followed in after them, closing the backdoor. He took Emmeline's coat, going to hang it, and Emmeline's eyes dropped to the baby chimeras snuggled on Rhea's feet.

"And this is Butternut and Squash," Farhan said with a smile, scooping the baby chimeras into his arms. He brought them over to Emmeline, and she smushed their furry goat faces.

"How cute," she said, petting them as they cooed. "I love the names."

"I came up with them," Luke interjected, coming back to stand between her and Farhan. Emmeline bit back a smile. She could sense Luke wasn't enjoying the attention Farhan was getting from her.

"That's really cute," she said, smiling at Luke, and his face lit up. Her heart warmed. She hadn't known a few simple words from her could make him so happy, and suddenly, she felt a little shy.

She turned back to the baby chimeras, who were obviously identical twins. She searched for something to tell them apart but failed.

"How do you know who's who?" she asked, petting one of them.

"Honestly, I can't," Farhan said. "It's a guess every time."

Luke shook his head. "I'd expect better from a teacher," he said. Then, he lifted the right wing of one of the babies and the left wing of the other. They had matching birthmarks on opposite wings.

"Butternut's the one with the mark on her right," Luke said. "Squash is the other."

Squash wiggled in Farhan's arms, trying to jump free, and Farhan let him. The baby chimera leaped onto Luke, where Luke caught him with one ringed hand, holding him steady against his chest. The chimera's snake tail curled around Luke's forearm, and her heart squeezed.

"Oh, hello," a soft voice said, and they turned to see Rhea rouse from her sleep. She blinked slowly. "Why didn't you wake me?"

"You've had a long day," Luke said, going to her side. Rhea looked a little frail. She might have been sick because of the cold weather, Emmeline thought.

"Hi," Emmeline said, going over to her. "I'm Emmeline."

Rhea's face lit up. "Emmeline!" She opened her arms, and Emmeline leaned forward to give Rhea a hug. She really was frail. While Luke and Farhan were both tall, their mother was petite, though the boys clearly looked like her with their deep brown skin and dark hair.

"I'm so glad to finally meet you!" Rhea said, and Emmeline's brows twitched. She glanced over at Luke, who looked embarrassed.

"Emmeline," Farhan said, grinning at his mother.

"Ignore them," Luke implored her. "Please."

She didn't say anything, but that didn't stop her from recalling how Farhan had also acted like he knew who she was. A sneaking suspicion rose within her: Had Luke spoken about her to his family members?

And if he had, what had he said? She was afraid he'd left a bad impression, for surely she had been a thorn in Luke's side, but Farhan and Rhea were both perfectly kind with her. They were practically . . . giggling.

"You are staying for dinner, aren't you?" Rhea asked.

"I don't want to impose," Emmeline replied. "I should get going."

Luke gave her a funny look. "Don't be ridiculous," he said, voice non-negotiable.

"Yeah, don't be ridiculous," Farhan said, mimicking his brother.

Were all younger siblings certified menaces? Before she could try and protest, Farhan ushered her to the dining table, while Luke helped Rhea up.

"You sit here," Farhan said, depositing her in front of a chair.

"Well, let me help, at least," Emmeline said, not sitting yet. "What can I do? Should I set the table? Cut a salad?" She was about to head in the direction of the kitchen when Luke shook his head at her.

"No," Luke said, bringing Rhea to the table. "The only thing you can do is sit down."

Emmeline opened her mouth to argue, and he slightly shook his head at her. "Sh. Sit."

She had never realized just how bossy Luke was, but she found she didn't hate it. Obeying, she sat down as Luke helped his mother into the seat across from her. Then, he set the table while Farhan brought over a bowl of raita, a spiced yogurt dish with sliced cucumbers, tomatoes, onions, and cilantro.

Emmeline could guess what they would be eating, as the cold salad was usually an accompaniment for only a few things. Her stomach rumbled, and she was glad she was staying for dinner, after all. It had been a long day.

"Is Baba coming?" Farhan asked, going back to the kitchen to grab the pot from the stove. He brought it over as Luke finished setting the table, setting down a trivet for the pot to sit on.

"No, he won't be in until ten," Luke said. To Emmeline, he explained, "Our dad works late." Luke sat down in the seat next to her as Farhan put the pot down.

"Here we are," Farhan said, lifting off the lid. Steam rose from atop the brothy rice dish, filling the air with the comforting aroma of browned onions and cumin.

"Did you make it?" Emmeline asked Farhan as he sat down across from Luke. He nodded.

"Apologies in advance," Luke interjected, and Farhan rolled his eyes good-naturedly at his brother.

"No, it looks great," Emmeline said, thoroughly impressed. "You could teach my brothers a thing or two. The best they can do is instant noodles, and even that smells radioactive. I have to air out the entire house whenever they've cooked—the word *cooked* being used quite loosely here."

Rhea laughed. "These two had an instant noodle phase, too, and you're right, the smell is *horrible*. I banned it for precisely that reason." Rhea reached for the spoon, offering it to Emmeline. "Please, take first."

Emmeline wanted to protest, but she had a feeling none of the Hayward family members would allow that, so she acquiesced, putting a serving of the chicken pilau onto her plate. She offered the spoon back to Rhea, and Farhan took it, plating a serving for his mother before making his own plate.

Taking a bite, Emmeline sighed. It was delicious, warming

her to her core. Pilau was a perfect comfort meal, especially in winter, the rice soft and soupy with the spiced broth.

"Good, right?" Farhan said, gloating. Luke rolled his eyes as he piled food onto his plate.

"Don't be too impressed," Luke told her. "It's pretty much the only thing he knows how to make."

"Not true and you know it," Farhan said cheerily, unperturbed by his older brother's commentary.

"Did you learn from your mom?" Emmeline asked, as Luke poured water into her glass.

"No, no," Rhea replied with a fond smile. "He learned from my best friend, Ayman."

"She makes it all the time," Luke said.

"It's Jiya's favorite," Farhan said.

"The Din family lives two houses down, and we all grew up together," Luke told Emmeline. "The eldest, Basim, is Farhan's best friend, and he has three younger sisters, who are pretty much like our sisters, too."

"Not all of them," Farhan muttered under his breath. Luke gave him a funny look, and Farhan cleared his throat. "Emmeline, do you like pilau?"

"Yes, but I usually make it with mutton instead of chicken," she said.

"Don't say that too loud," Farhan said in a mock-whisper.

"We don't eat too much mutton in this house," Luke explained, glancing over at the baby chimeras.

"Oh. Right." Emmeline bit back a laugh. "That makes sense."

They continued eating, chatting about different things. Rhea asked Emmeline how her work was going, and

Emmeline was a little hesitant at first, because she was Luke's rival and all, but he didn't seem worried, so she relaxed as well. They were turning a new leaf, moving forward.

It was a wonderful evening and, after eating, the boys cleaned up while Emmeline kept Rhea and the baby chimeras company in the living room. Then, it was time to go. It was getting late and they all had work the next day.

"Thank you for such a lovely dinner," Emmeline said, kissing Rhea goodbye.

"Thank you for spending the time with us," Rhea said. She looked very tired by then, and Farhan came to her side.

"Why don't we get you to bed?" he said, and she nodded slowly. He gave Emmeline a smile, then the two of them were off. Luke returned with her coat, and she slid it on.

"Can I check in on Sharptooth before going?" she asked.

"'Course," he replied. They went out back to the barn. It had begun snowing a little bit, snowflakes making a slow and steady descent. In the barn, Sharptooth was still fast asleep.

"She'll be okay," Luke said.

"I'm glad."

They left, and Emmeline waited a moment before calling Torch. She knew her dragon wouldn't be far away, and a part of her didn't want to go just yet. She lingered, and Luke was in no rush to head inside.

The air shimmered with snowflakes, a few sticking to his dark hair, which was a bit messy now, but she liked it. She was so used to seeing him perfectly done-up. It felt intimate to see him like this, like he was only hers to see.

It reminded her of that night all those years ago. Her cheeks grew hot at the memories.

"Thank you for letting me have dinner with your family," she said. "Your mother and brother are really sweet."

A fond expression came over Luke's face. "They're pretty great," he replied, voice soft.

"I hope your mom feels better," she said. "Does she have the flu or something? She looked a bit under the weather."

Luke blinked, surprised. "You don't know . . ." He trailed off as if realizing something. "I never told you . . ." He paused, swallowing. "She's sick. She has been for a while, since I was in university."

Emmeline's mouth jutted open, shock pouring through her. She hadn't known. It was such a big thing, and she hadn't known.

"Is she undergoing treatment or . . .?" she asked.

He ran a hand through his hair. "There's not much they can do," he said, "but she takes medication and has some treatments to help manage the pain." He looked down at the floor, and her heart ached.

"I'm sorry," she said. Before she could think better of it, she bridged the space between them and brought a hand to his cheek, lifting his face to meet her eyes. "Luke, I'm sorry."

He leaned into her touch, comforted, and satisfaction spread through her.

"It's okay, I don't really talk about it," he said quietly. She pulled her hand away as he seemed to find his words. "It's . . ." he trailed off, taking a deep breath. "When you asked me what motivates me—it's her. It's why I still live at home. Farhan has his own place, but I stayed so I could look after her and help with medical bills. It's why my dad works late; we tag-team so she's not alone for too long."

She was even more shocked. She'd had no idea.

He had been right before; perhaps she wouldn't have believed him if he had told her the first time she had asked. She might have thought he was trying to make himself appear as better than he was, to trick her into thinking he was a good son and a good man.

But now she had seen him, she had met his mother, and she knew he was a good son.

A good man.

"Thank you for telling me," she said. "And if there's ever anything I can do, let me know. Please."

That earned her a small smile. "You don't have to take care of everyone, Emmeline," he said. For some reason, him saying her name sent a shiver down her spine.

"I know," she said. "But I like caring for people who are important, and she's your mom."

The words were out before she could stop them, and he paused. Admitting that his mother was important was a roundabout way of admitting that *he* was important to her, as well.

Which was scary. She bit her lower lip, thinking he might take the opportunity to tease her, but he didn't. Instead, he only looked touched, as if her words meant more than she could ever imagine.

"Thank you," he said, voice soft. "I appreciate that."

He leaned forward, and her breath caught in her throat. She held herself still, waiting to see what he would do. His gaze flicked down to her mouth, but at the last second, he turned, kissing her cheek.

It was the gentlest brush of his lips against her skin, hardly anything intense, especially considering that they had slept together the first night they met, but there was something so tender about the gesture.

Even the briefest touch was enough to set her skin aflame and her heart pounding. His lips lingered, and they stayed anchored in that moment, snow falling softly around them as if they were two figures frozen together in a snow globe.

When he pulled back, she missed him immediately. His throat moved as he swallowed. She could tell he wanted to kiss her, and she wanted that, too, but she was being careful.

Clearing her throat, she called Torch. Sure enough, her dragon appeared almost immediately, swooping down with Motu in her paw. The baby immediately flew toward her, and she hugged Motu.

Torch had been unhappy to leave Emmeline at Luke's, and some of that concern was still etched onto her scaly face—until she saw how comfortable Emmeline was now. The tension eased from Torch's stance, curiosity entering her purple eyes.

Emmeline looked at Torch, then at Luke, and Torch understood. The dragon sat, then lowered her head in front of him.

"She's sorry," Emmeline explained.

"It's okay," Luke said, walking toward her. He lifted his hand and petted her head. When he did, Torch twitched, irritated. "My hands are cold," he said, pulling away.

Torch's eyes widened with recognition, and she bounced, excited. She bumped her head against Luke's chest. He almost went flying, but he steadied himself, laughing.

Emmeline smiled fondly. "I think she remembers you, now," she said. His face brightened.

"I remember you, too," he said, petting Torch happily.

"Don't worry," she told him. "She finally learned not to warm people's hands with fire."

CHAPTER 22

Week four of six came to an end, bringing them to the new year.

New Year's was always bittersweet for Emmeline. She looked back and thought of all the things she had wanted to happen but hadn't come true; all the things she had hoped to achieve but hadn't accomplished; the way time continued to move but she didn't.

Because her birthday was right after New Year's, they always cut a cake for her at the New Year's Eve party, and that always made her feel both happy and like she was having an existential crisis.

She was turning thirty, now, and she had imagined something far different for herself: a partner, a family of her own, the way Millie and Aiden and most of her other cousins had. If she had to spend one more New Year's Eve single, she was well and truly going to lose her mind. Then again, she had said the same thing *last* New Year's Eve . . .

At the same time, she knew there was a great deal to be thankful for, that she *had* also accomplished so much that she could be proud of. The New Year was also a fresh start, the entire year spread ahead of her like a blank canvas. There were endless possibilities and so much to be hopeful for.

She tried to focus on the positive as she went through her yearly rituals. There was the New Year's Eve party for the entire Sterling clan at her uncle Edmund's. Saphira was glowing, and Aiden was stuffing her with food every chance he got, not at all being discreet about the whole pregnancy thing. She was sure their aunts had figured it out.

It was all lovely. She missed Millie and the kids and Samreen but, the next day, on New Year's Day, they flew down to see them all, which was fun and gave her time to debrief her sister, who literally made popcorn as Emmeline explained everything that had happened with Luke.

After spending the day, she had flown back at night, and now, on the second of January, it was back to work, which she found she was excited for. She was excited to see Luke again. She had gotten used to seeing him every day for the last four weeks, and now two days apart and she had . . . missed him?

Was that what this feeling was?

The thought made her antsy, but she tried not to think about it for too long. Instead, after having breakfast, she ran errands then went directly to Tales & Tails. The bookshop was still closed for an extra day for the holiday, even though it was Saturday, but Minh had said she and Luke could pop in if they wanted to.

The bookshop was quiet and hushed when Emmeline entered. It was strange to see the shop so empty, though Motu evidently enjoyed the fact. Now, it was just Emmeline.

Once they entered the empty shop, he flew through the air, taking the opportunity to jump from atop one bookshelf to another.

"Motu," Emmeline warned. "No masti, okay? Behave."

He gave her an innocent look, then jumped again. Emmeline blew her bangs out of her face. As long as he didn't knock a bookshelf over, it was fine.

Closing the door behind her, Emmeline went to the tables, setting down the bags she had brought in. Since the shop was closed, she could take up as much space as she wanted.

Most of her proposal for the coffee shop was done, she just needed to finalize some details, then dress up the presentation. Today, her goal was to make a final decision regarding the coffee shop's color scheme. She had already worked out the general vibe, which would be bookish and black-and-white, but she wanted to add a splash of color, as well.

The bookshop did such a wonderful job of feeling bright and vivid with all the different sections—the pink and yellow romances, the blue and green fantasies, the vibrant children's section, the leatherbound classics. She didn't want the coffee shop section to feel dull or boring.

She had managed to narrow down the accent color to four options, and today, she wanted to see how the color would look in the bookshop itself. She had gotten approval from Minh to paint swatches on the wall; he'd had Ola move one of the bookshelves to the side to clear a portion of the wall that they could cover back up with the bookshelf again after.

As Motu continued jumping from bookshelf to bookshelf, enjoying the empty shop, Emmeline pulled an empty display table to the section of the wall she would be doing the samples on. It was central, across from the stairs, and she wanted the coffee shop to go there.

After placing newspapers along the floor and table, she put her supplies on top: paint tins, along with small trays and paint rollers. There were four different colors she wanted to check: a sage green, a custard yellow, a periwinkle blue, and a blushing pink.

She began with the sage green, painting a foot long patch over the white. While that dried, she painted a similar column beside it in the custard yellow.

As she worked, she saw Motu out of the corner of her eye, who was now sliding down the stair railing backwards. His wings were poised to go into flight as he shot off the end, but since he was backwards, the momentum was too much, and he ended up flying into a display table.

"Motu," she warned, as books fell to the floor. One opened over his head like a hat, and she set down her paint roller to pick up the fallen books. The baby dragon gave her an adorable smile as she put the books back in place.

"Be good," she said, this time stern. She gave him a sharp glance, and he sat calmly on the floor. She released a breath. "Good boy."

Setting down her paint roller, she went to her purse and grabbed a package of naan chips. Sniffing the air, Motu perked immediately. As she emptied the snack onto her hand, Motu made a pleased sound, bouncing over to eat them from her palm until they finished. She scratched his chin, and he happily flapped his wings.

She went back to the table with her paints. Just then,

the front door dinged, bringing in a current of cold air. Emmeline's stomach flipped as she glanced over to find Luke entering.

Shutting the door behind him, he cleaned his shoes on the front mat before looking up at her. A smile lit his face, and she felt her pulse quicken.

"Hi," he said, taking off his coat and walking over to her. He unwound a scarf from his neck, revealing the long line of his throat. His usual necklaces hung on his chest where his black shirt was unbuttoned.

The shop was warm, but it felt hotter now. He looked particularly handsome today, his dark hair falling in perfect swoops that made her want to sink her fingers in.

He arched a brow, and she realized she was staring.

"Hi," she replied, voice a squeak. *Oh god.* Why was she acting weird? Like a girl with a crush? Ridiculous.

His lips twitched, and he leaned down to pet Motu, who licked Luke's hand. As he went to set his things down in the office, Emmeline caught her breath. She turned back to the wall, cheeks warm as she dipped the roller into the blue paint.

"What are you doing?" he asked, coming to stand behind her a few moments later. His proximity sent sparks shooting down her spine. She could feel the heat of his chest, just inches behind her shoulder. If she leaned back . . .

"Checking paint samples," she replied, not turning around. This was not the moment to let intrusive thoughts win.

"Mmm," he hummed, and she could almost feel his chest vibrating behind her. She bit her lower lip. Then, she felt Luke's hand on her elbow, steadying her arm.

She turned with wide eyes and met his amused gaze.

"Careful," he said, nodding at her hand. She had loosened her grip on the paint roller, and the blue paint had gone into the green.

"Thanks," she replied.

"Course." He gave her an easy smile, then let go of her elbow. He stepped to her side, leaning against a bookshelf. "So how was your New Year's?"

"It was good!" she replied. "I was at Millie's. Her kids and Motu were bouncing off the walls, but that's nothing new. How was yours?"

"Also good," he said. "We just hung out at home. My dad had it off, so the four of us were together for the first time for a while, which was nice."

"Aw," she said, setting her paint roller down into the tray. "How's Sharptooth doing? Better?"

He nodded. "All healed," he said. "That friend of yours knows what she's doing."

She smiled. "I'll be sure to let her know you said that."

She felt more normal now, though he was still so handsome that a part of her chest felt like it would ache permanently.

Had he always been this handsome? How hadn't she noticed before?

Surely she'd known he was good-looking in an objective way, the way models were beautiful, but today, there seemed to be an extra quality to him, as if he was the only star in the night sky. She couldn't look away. She didn't want to.

She watched him go as he walked around with his notebook, as if confirming things he had written down.

He tapped his lips with the end of his pen, and she tried desperately not to stare at his mouth.

They fell into a comfortable silence and, as she finished off the last paint sample, she found herself glancing over at him. She liked the focused expression on his face.

A tendril of hair fell in front of his brow, and he pushed it back, but when she glanced back a few moments later, there it was again. She felt suddenly fond of that tendril, for some reason. Probably because she was losing her mind.

But it seemed she wasn't the only one. She could feel him glancing over at her when she wasn't looking, and every few moments, they locked gazes across the room. Each time they did, a thrill shot through her like a bolt of electricity, energy fizzing through her.

Motu continued playing, and when Emmeline glanced over next, she saw the baby dragon was bothering Luke, who was absent-mindedly petting him with his free hand. Her heart warmed.

Turning back to the paint swatches, she took pictures of each on her phone. Done with that, she closed the paint tins, but left out the trays so they could dry.

Then, she went to the bookshelves, unable to resist browsing in the shop empty of other patrons. She ambled through the rows of shelves, losing herself to the quiet of the books. It had been a long time since she had gone through the bookshop simply for the sake of enjoyment, reading through titles, searching for a new read.

She spotted a familiar title on the top shelf, and reached up onto her tiptoes to pull it out. She could just barely reach it, but there was no stool nearby, so she stretched, finally grabbing the edge. It slid out, landing in her hands, and she smiled.

Letters to Milena by Franz Kafka, the cover read, and she touched a hand over the words. Of course, she had read it dozens of times; each time she found herself connecting to a new passage.

Now, she flipped it open to a random part, paging through until she reached a passage she knew well. It was where Kafka wrote about how he wished the world was ending tomorrow. Then, he could take the next train, arrive at Milena's doorstep in Vienna and tell her to come with him; that they would love each other without scruples or fear or restraint. All because the world was ending.

It always made her heart squeeze, and for some reason, tears filled her eyes. She read the passage again, and in doing so, she didn't hear Luke come up toward her. It was only when she closed the book that she saw him leaning against the end of the shelf, watching her.

Hastily blinking, she pushed away her tears, giving him a shy smile.

"It's too easy to get distracted when surrounded by so many books," she said. He gave her a soft smile, walking over.

The space between the two shelves felt small then, as if they were in a private alcove. Her gaze went to his mouth. The first time they kissed was like this, in the narrow lane of bookshelves, surrounded by the scent of ink and paper.

Her heartbeat quickened, and she turned away from him, facing the shelf. Rising on her tiptoes, she lifted her arm to put the book back.

The top shelf was still too high, and before she could reach, she felt Luke come up behind her. His hand covered hers on the spine. Taking the book from her grasp, he slid it into place on the shelf.

He held his hand over hers, holding it against the bookshelf above her head and, slowly, she turned. Backed up against the shelf, she faced him. Desire beat through her as he leaned in, and she inhaled the scent of cypress and spruce, so deliciously wintry that she wanted to take a bite out of him.

Her heart hammered against her chest, wild and frantic as she looked up at him. His lids lowered as his gaze dropped to her mouth. Her breathing grew shallow.

Their bodies were so close she could feel the heat emanating from his skin. Anticipation pulsed through her, making her feel weak in the knees. Then, slowly, he lowered both of their hands, not letting go of her fingers as he brought her hand to his mouth.

He dipped his head, pressing a kiss to her wrist. A gasp rose in her throat, and she bit her bottom lip, feeling dizzy. He lifted his dark eyes to hers, watching her reaction. Neither of them said a word, but she was sure desperation was written on her face.

She clutched the edge of the bookshelf with her free hand, trying to hold herself steady. He moved his mouth lower, biting the edge of her sweater sleeve and dragging it down to reveal the skin of her forearm.

He pressed another kiss to the sensitive skin below her wrist. Sparks skittered down her spine. She released a shuddering breath, her entire body aching.

"Luke," she whispered, and he propped her hand onto his

shoulder. She clutched the fabric of his sweater as he stepped closer, the space between them disappearing entirely.

"Em," he whispered back, voice rough.

Ever so gently, he kissed her cheek, and she squeezed her eyes shut. She felt his thumb brush against her cheekbone, and she opened her eyes again to see his finger was wet. He had wiped away a tear. She hadn't even noticed when it had slipped out.

Their gazes locked.

"Aren't our eyes made to be torn out, and our hearts the same?" he asked, voice rough.

Her heart lurched. She knew where the rest of the passage went, it was one of her favorite parts: *You are the knife I turn inside myself; that is love*.

There was a confession on his face, and she was afraid, but still, she leaned in. *Finally*, her body sighed, just as his lips brushed against hers—

And they heard a crash.

CHAPTER 23

At the same time, Emmeline and Luke looked to where the noise had come from. Panic rose in her throat and she rushed out, Luke a step behind her, only to find Motu covered in paint.

He had jumped from paint tray to paint tray, knocking the last one over. Luckily, she had covered the table and floor with newspapers, but Motu was now multicolored, his black scales dotted with blue, pink, green, and yellow.

Her heart was still racing from the brush of Luke's lips against hers, but she now had to deal with this disaster of a baby dragon. He truly had terrible timing.

"Motu, no!" Emmeline cried as he jumped up, his wings flapping. Paint splattered in the air; she rushed forward, trying to stop the paint from hitting the shelves. Rogue flicks of paint landed on her, and she scowled.

"Stop!" she scolded. Motu froze. "Sit," she demanded, and he sat down in the tray of pink paint.

"Seriously, Motu?" Luke muttered, shaking his head at the baby dragon. Covered in pink paint, Motu looked up at both of them innocently, as if he hadn't just ruined the moment between her and Luke.

Her lips tingling at the memory, she went over and picked Motu up in her arms, not trusting him to sit still.

"I'll get paper towels," Luke said, disappearing. Paint quickly covered her hands and arms, dripping down onto her clothing as she stood on top of the newspapers.

"There goes this outfit," she muttered unhappily. Motu tried to give her an adorable expression, as if he had had great fun, and she narrowed her eyes at him. "Don't act cute with me."

By then, Luke had returned with paper towels, and she tried shifting Motu to one arm, but, god, he really was fat. She could hardly hold him. Luke bit back a smile.

"Why don't you set him down?" he said. "I think he knows not to jump, now." She nodded, and Luke moved the paint trays off the table, making space.

Emmeline looked at the baby dragon, eyes warning. "Don't move," she ordered, carefully putting him back down atop the newspapers covering the table.

Motu calmly sat down, and she sighed. Her hair fell forward, and she tried tossing it back, but anytime she moved, her bangs and the shorter layers came bouncing forward again. Her hands were covered in paint, so she couldn't move her hair back properly.

"Let me," Luke said, noticing her struggle. "Do you have a clip somewhere?"

"My purse," she replied, feeling surprised. She could have washed her hands, then gotten the clip herself.

She was so used to doing things herself, but he had

noticed and didn't hesitate to help. It was such a little thing, but it made her heart soften toward him.

Luke returned with her clip, then went behind her. She tilted her head back, and his fingers brushed against the back of her neck as he gathered her hair together. He twisted, and the slight tug sent her pulse racing. It reminded her of his hand in her hair when she was tangled in her dress, the warmth of his body seeping deep into her bare skin. She felt weak at the knees.

He secured her hair in place—albeit sloppily—but it was good enough.

"Thanks," she said.

"'Course." He touched her shoulder, and a shiver ran down her spine.

She wiped her hands on the paper towels as best she could, then set about getting Motu as cleaned as possible, though the dried paint wouldn't come off either of them without soap and water. As she did that, Luke started to clean up the paint trays.

"I can do it," she said.

"I know, but so can I," he replied. "Let me."

Had he always been this caring? This kind? How had she never noticed before? There was a tenderness to him that made her want to do all sorts of foolish things.

She wasn't very often at a loss for words, but she felt like a ship adrift today. As she continued to wipe Motu's paws, Luke put away the paint tins and supplies into the bag she had brought them in.

He gathered the dirty newspapers and tossed them as she cleaned up Motu's wings. The baby dragon was still covered with dry paint splatters, but she would give him a deep bath when they went home.

As Luke finished up, she went to the bathroom to wash her hands. In the mirror, she saw there were rogue splatters of paint across her cheek and neck; after her hands were clean, she wiped at the other spots. Evidently, she and Motu *both* needed a bath.

Once she'd done all she could, she went back out, where the mess was cleaned up. Motu sat calmly on the table. She continued wiping at a stubborn spot of paint on the back of her hand with a wet paper towel until it came out.

"This is the most color I've seen you wear," Luke said, and she glanced up to his lips twitching. She looked at the multicolored splatters all over her black outfit; she looked like a rebellious teenager intent on designing her own clothes.

"Hilarious," she said drily, but her lips twitched as well, as she walked over to him and Motu. It was ridiculous, and while he looked amused, she saw something else in his expression, a tenderness on his face as he looked at her. He must have sensed the question in her eyes.

"I like you in pink," he said, voice soft.

Her cheeks flushed, and she was sure they were the same shade of pink as the paint. She was hardly one to blush, but suddenly, she couldn't help it. She didn't know why.

She had never felt so shy around a man before. It was a new feeling, not entirely unwelcome. He kept surprising her and, in turn, her reaction to him kept surprising herself.

"You missed a spot," he said, pointing to her jaw. She raised the wet paper towel to wipe at it, but before she could, he took a step toward her, easily taking it out of her hand.

A jolt shot down her spine as he brought his other hand up, holding her chin. She was entirely immobile, letting him turn her face to the side. Her heart pounded against her chest. Then, he wiped along her throat.

Her breathing stopped altogether then at the contact, his touch searing through her. She swallowed, her throat moving against his hand. Her gaze dropped to his mouth, hoping they could pick up where they had left off. As if thinking the same thing, his eyes darkened.

But then they heard a knock on the front door.

She furrowed her brows. That was weird. "The shop's closed," she said.

"I'll go see," Luke said. He stepped away from her, and once he was gone, she released a shaky breath. Her body was overcome with sensations.

She glanced over at Motu, who needed to get cleaned up. Gathering her things, she gave her baby dragon a disappointed look. He was unperturbed, and she shook her head. After she collected all her things, she headed for the door, where she heard voices.

She looked and saw Luke was talking to a group of people, all crowded in front of the door. He seemed to be barring them from entering any further, trying to usher them out as he spoke in a low tone. It was three girls and two boys—she spotted one familiar face: Farhan.

Before she could say hi, one of the girls spotted Emmeline. Her face lit up, and she pinched one of the other girls.

"Emmy, hey!" Farhan said, waving a hand above the other heads.

"Hey, Farhan," she replied, going over.

Rubbing a hand over his face, Luke released a long-suffering sigh. Farhan pushed past his brother, entering the bookshop to give Emmeline a quick side-hug. "Love the look," he said, glancing down at the paint splatters. "Very teenager chic."

"Occupational hazard when it comes to baby dragons," she replied with a smile.

"We were just in the area so we wanted to pop in and say hi," Farhan said cheerily, and Luke muttered an oath under his breath. "This is my best friend, Basim." Farhan set about introducing the group, and she realized it was the Din siblings, the ones Luke had mentioned before. "That's Liliana, Jiya, and Hira."

He pointed to the girls, seemingly going in age order, with Liliana being the youngest. She was probably a year or two older than Ginny, with Jiya a year older than her, and Hira looked around Saphira's age.

"Oh, hi! It's nice to meet you all," she said. Basim nodded; he looked a bit stern and serious, very much the eldest child, while the girls looked excited.

"They were just leaving," Luke said, trying to shove them all out the door. Basim seemed ready to go, but the girls and Farhan all held their ground. Liliana, especially, was looking at Emmeline with wide eyes, like she was meeting a celebrity. Emmeline bit back a smile.

"You should join us!" Liliana said. "We were going to get hot chocolate. We were trying to convince Luke to come along, and I'm sure he'll join us if you are." She batted her lashes sweetly in a manner that told Emmeline she was used to getting what she wanted.

Before Emmeline could reply, Luke cut in. "No, I don't think she wants to," he said. Emmeline gave him a funny look as Liliana and Jiya exchanged a glance. Hira shook her head at Luke.

"Thanks for the offer," Emmeline said, "but I should get home and get cleaned up. Have fun!"

"You heard her," Luke said, pulling open the front door. "See you later!"

As they exited, Emmeline caught Farhan's gaze lingering on Jiya, and she recalled how Farhan had said chicken pilau was Jiya's favorite. *Hmm.*

"Bye!"

"It was nice meeting you!"

"Hope to see you again!"

The girls' voices tangled together as they all said bye, and Luke all but shoved them out. Once they were gone, he closed the door, leaning against it and releasing a sigh.

"Don't mind them," he said. "They're basically my annoying little sisters."

Emmeline smiled. They had reminded her of how she and Ginny loved bothering Aiden. "They seem sweet," she said.

That got a smile out of him. "Yeah, they're the best." He paused, thinking of something. "You know how I freaked out about Flint?"

"Yeah," she replied, confused as to why he was bringing all that awfulness up. He tensed, and she was afraid they would argue again.

"It wasn't just because he's part of the gang that runs the races," he said. "You met Liliana—well, she's always been reckless, and when she was hardly eighteen, she went to a party and attracted Flint's attention. He spiked her drink."

"Oh my god," she replied, horrified. Luke clenched his jaw, visibly agonized by the memory.

"She managed to call Farhan to say she wasn't feeling well, and we got to her in time, but . . ." He trailed off, shaking.

"That's horrible," she said. She understood now why he had reacted the way he had, especially when he saw Flint had given her a drink.

"Yeah." He ran a hand through his hair, releasing a long breath. "I got into a nasty fight with him and made him swear to stay away from anyone I cared about. It's what I held him to that day by the lake to get him to stay away from you."

Her blood roared in her ears, and shame burned through her. She had been so angry with him that day, and he'd only been protecting her.

"I'm someone you care about?" she asked, voice quiet.

He looked at her as if she was silly, a small smile playing on his lips. "Obviously."

"Oh." Her cheeks felt warm, and his eyes sparked with amusement. He looked as if he was enjoying this.

She cleared her throat, changing the subject. "The girls seemed nice," she said. "It would have been fun to hang out."

"Mm, it could have been," he said, stepping toward her. "But the thing is, I don't want to share."

She blinked. She had always known he was charming and flirty, but it had never had such an effect on her. Before, it had all felt shallow, like a trick, but now, it felt like he meant every word, and that only made her heartbeat quicken.

She'd been given plenty of compliments by men before

but, for some reason, it felt like it was worth more coming from him. It felt more genuine. She had been awful to him, and yet he was still kind to her, flirting with her, looking at her as if he wanted to devour her.

"Oh," she replied stupidly.

"Yeah." He grinned, his gaze scorching through her. A tendril of hair had come loose from her clip, and he tucked it behind her ear. His eyes were so brown, the color so specific she felt she had never seen it before anywhere else, as if the shade had been created solely for him and him alone.

Her cheeks felt like they were burning, and his eyes lowered, as if he could tell. His lips twitched. Gently, he brushed the top of her cheek with his thumb.

"So how about you get cleaned up and then *we* go out for hot chocolate," he said.

She blinked, taken aback. "Like . . . a date?" As soon as the words were out, she cringed.

Why was this all so embarrassing?

He grinned. "Exactly."

CHAPTER 24

Luke hadn't been surprised when he'd gone to the bookshop's door to find his annoying brother and the entire Din clan, but it had certainly made him feel more stressed.

Farhan must have told them Luke was at the bookshop with Emmeline and, where one Din sister went, the other two usually followed. Them being "in town" was no coincidence. He could sniff out a Din sister plot from a mile away; they had come to spy on him and Emmeline.

"I can't believe it's finally happening!" Liliana, the youngest sister, squealed.

"Only took *forever*," Jiya, the middle sister, added.

"I'm so happy for you, Luke," Hira, the eldest sister, said with a fond smile.

"Finally," Basim agreed, and Farhan grinned.

It was the stuff of nightmares. They were all acting as if he'd proposed to Emmeline and she'd said yes, not that they had simply agreed to stop fighting. The girls had wanted to come in and chat with Emmeline, and he'd had to physically bar them from entering.

"Will you guys shut up?" he hissed, hoping Emmeline couldn't hear.

"You're being no fun," Lilliana pouted. "You finally get a girl, and now you won't even let us interrogate her? You guys harass every guy I've ever been interested in!"

"Every guy you're into deserved to be harassed," Basim said with a scowl. Lillie matched his scowl with one of her own.

"You guys never let me live anything down," she snapped.

"Yeah, and do you ever learn?" Jiya asked with a snort. Lillie geared up to respond when Hira held up her hands.

"Bas, bas, we cannot get into this right now," Hira said, ever the peacemaker. "You guys are derailing the focus, which is Luke and—"

Emmeline had chosen that moment to enter, and he had gone into full panic mode. Any second now, one of them would say something stupid and embarrass him. Then, Lillie invited Emmeline out with them all, and he had to intervene before the situation got out of hand.

All's well that ended well—he had finally gathered the courage to ask her out himself, and she'd said yes. He had meant what he'd said: he didn't want to share. Not before he'd even had enough of her to himself. Even the barest brush of her lips against his had felt as magical as somehow traversing realms to enter the world of his favorite book, and he was keen to pick up where they had left off.

After packing up at the bookshop, they both went home and agreed to meet up again in the evening.

Today, he wouldn't be late. Which was why he was already down by the lake.

Sharptooth had dropped him off, and he was waiting for her ten minutes before she was meant to come. The sun had set about an hour ago, and the sky was a deep shade of navy blue, studded with stars that sparkled bright.

There was a layer of snow over his surroundings, and every storefront was covered with string lights and wreaths and ornaments. The entire town looked like it belonged on a postcard. It was the perfect romantic background to their first date, and he was keen to spend the evening with Emmeline.

Nerves skittered through him as he waited. He'd planned out a route that would hit all the best spots; now, he just hoped she would like it all. His hand tightened around the bouquet of roses he was holding. They were red, and even though he felt she would like them, he worried if they were the right choice.

Then, he heard the flapping of wings, and moments later, Torch landed behind him. His heartbeat quickened. He turned as Emmeline dismounted, and he was struck again by how beautiful she was.

She had always been stunning, but she seemed even more so now, as if only he could see the full breadth of her beauty. There was a new quality to her, some light that was coming from within as she walked towards him. Her face shone like the full moon.

"Hi," he said, smiling.

She smiled back. "Hi."

She was wearing her fur coat and matching hat, her dark hair loose and bouncy beneath. He was obsessed with her hair. She was wearing knee-high heeled boots and stockings.

There must have been a dress under the coat, but he couldn't see it; the coat was done up to her chin.

She had redone her makeup, with the usual smoked-out kajal around her dark eyes. Beneath her elaborate nose-ring, instead of a bold lip color like red or maroon, her lips were a light shade of pink. It made her look different. Softer.

"These are for you." He offered her the bouquet, and she took them, smiling.

"I love red roses," she said, looking surprised. Relief poured through him. "You're taking this date thing seriously."

"Of course," he replied, confused. "I take everything that has to do with you seriously."

Her cheeks flushed, and he'd meant it when he'd said he liked her in pink. It was even better when he was the cause. He wondered just how pink he could make her cheeks, and his mind immediately took a salacious turn as he imagined all the ways in which her face would flush with pleasure.

Heat zipped down his spine, and he ached to pull her into his arms, to kiss her right then. But he had waited this long—he could wait a little longer. At least until the end of their date. He knew once he kissed her, it would be the end of anything else, and he wanted to have a good date with her, a proper one.

It was the first time he'd ever felt such a way, this wish to be cautious despite how deeply he desired her.

Emmeline pressed her nose to the flowers, then put them on her saddle on Torch so she wouldn't have to carry them around. After a last pat goodbye, Torch took off, leaving the two of them.

"Did Motu get cleaned up okay?" Luke asked, as they started down the walkway.

"Yes," she replied. "He's a little devil, I swear."

"He seems better behaved than he was a few weeks ago," he replied, and she arched an eyebrow. He laughed. "I mean it. He listens to you, and I can tell he's really attached."

She smiled fondly at that. "It's been fun having him around, despite the chaos," she said. "Though it can be tiring—I dropped him off with my family for the evening so they can deal with him."

"Good," he replied. "I get you all to myself." She beamed. "I want to show you all my favorite spots."

"I'd love that," she replied, and they kept walking down the path.

"Of course, most people think Bayview is best in the summer," he explained, "and it is really beautiful then, too, but there's a special quality in the winter. It feels smaller, somehow, more enclosed and cozy. All the snow and lights and festive decor—and my favorite hot chocolate."

They had made it to the hot chocolate truck. Going to the front, Luke told her about the different flavors, explaining the different types of chocolates that were used, along with the flavors in different blends.

"There's twenty options, but you can make your own, as well," he told her.

"Have you tried all of them?" she asked. He nodded proudly.

"My mom is obsessed," he told her. "We used to come really often when we were kids."

She smiled. "Hm, well what would you recommend? They all look so good!"

"The milk chocolate with hints of molasses, pecan, and coffee," he said. "It's amazing."

She nodded, and he ordered for both of them, paying. They stood by the side, waiting, and when their orders were ready, he handed her a to-go cup, watching as she took a sip. Her eyes lit up, and she smiled.

"Mm, that's delicious," she said. "I can taste everything you said, and it all goes so well together!"

He was glad she liked it. He took a sip of his order, savoring the decadent flavor.

"What did you get?" she asked.

"A dark chocolate blend," he said. "It's rich and a bit bitter."

"Ooh, let me taste."

They switched cups, and she took a sip. "Mm, that's good, too! It's so different. I can't tell which one I like better."

He smiled. "I got it in case you wanted something different than yours," he said. "I know that one is pretty sweet. And this way you get to try two of my favorites."

"That's so nice," she said in a whisper. She looked so touched.

He had noticed that she was always surprised when he did nice things for her, as if she wasn't expecting it. But why wouldn't he? He saw how much she did for others; it was only fair that someone tried to care for her the same way she cared for others, and he wanted to be that someone.

They went and sat on one of the benches, switching their hot chocolates back and forth until the flavors mingled and mixed to become something better, bitter and strong and sweet.

"On to the next stop," he said, standing. They tossed their

cups, and he led her down the pathway beneath a canopy of fairy lights towards a little shop. The scent of cinnamon, ginger, and allspice wafted toward them.

"Ooh, what's this?" she asked.

"Gingerbread cookies," he explained. "In the summer, the shop sells ice-cream, and in the fall, it's apple cider donuts, but all winter they have gingerbread cookies."

"What about the spring?"

"Berry crumble."

"I love that."

They walked up, and he ordered them a cookie each. The old woman managing the store gave Luke a fond smile, handing him the cookies in parchment bags. They were still hot, and he brought them over to Emmeline, handing one to her.

"It's a winter staple," he said. "I've also been coming here forever."

Emmeline brought the cookie up to her nose, inhaling the smell of the freshly baked gingerbread. She hummed to herself, and he smiled. He would always do that, too.

"Go on, taste it," he said, waiting. She pulled the cookie out of the parchment, then went straight for the jugular, devouring the head in one bite. He laughed.

"I should have expected such savagery," he said, shaking his head.

"The head is the best part!"

"Poor gingerbread man," he replied, "but now he knows how I feel. You're always biting my head off."

"Rightfully so." She snorted. "You are always frustrating me."

"And what exactly is it that you think you do to me?"

She narrowed her eyes at him. "I thought you weren't going to fight with me anymore."

"Was that the agreement? I thought we weren't going to fight with each other."

She pretended to think about it, tapping her chin with her index finger. "No, I think you weren't going to fight with *me*. I never fight anyway." She shrugged, and he laughed, holding his hands up in defeat. She smiled to herself, pleased.

They walked around, finishing off the cookies. Clouds gathered out of nowhere, covering the stars, but it didn't matter because soon, snow began falling, a soft flurry of sparkling flakes glittering in the sky.

Emmeline looked up, her eyes wide with delight. He watched as a snowflake landed on her bottom lip, melting upon contact. His body ached.

A smile spread across her face, one of pure wonder and joy. He'd never seen her look like such a kid, and his heart went soft. It had snowed almost every day this winter, and yet, she was as awed as if it was her first time seeing snowfall.

"Winter's my favorite season," she said, turning to look at him. "I never get tired of it. Look!" Palms outstretched, she held her hands up to catch snowflakes. He smiled, not tearing his gaze away from her.

"Pretty," he said, but he didn't mean the snow. A flush crept up her cheeks again.

She had been acting shy in moments throughout the day, even a little nervous, and he hadn't expected such behavior from the usually bold and confident Emmeline Sterling—

but he found that he liked it. He wanted to know every version of her, every possibility and iteration.

Then, he noticed that she was catching the snowflakes with her bare hands. "You didn't bring any gloves?" he asked, brows furrowed.

She shook her head. "I forgot."

Secretly, he was glad, for it gave him an excuse. He reached for her hands, holding them between both of his. Her fingers were freezing, and he rubbed them between his palms, trying to warm them up.

She watched him, a fond expression on her face. "Thank you," she said, voice soft. He wasn't sure how to convey to her that anything he did was the very least she deserved, that he would do so much more.

He let go of her hands, reaching into his pocket. "Put this on," he said, giving her his left glove. She wrinkled her brows.

"Okay," she said, putting it on as he put the right glove on. She gave him a funny look, until he reached for her right hand with his left, tugging her closer as he stuck both their bare hands into his pocket.

"To keep you warm," he said.

Her eyes sparkled brighter than the stars.

They kept walking down by the lake, headed towards a line. They joined, and she craned her neck, trying to see what it was for.

"It's chimera sledding," he said. "We used to do it as kids." He wanted to show her all the little things he loved about Bayview.

Her face lit up. "Fun!"

As they waited in line, they talked, people watched, and

discussed random things. Emmeline pointed out nearly every baby that passed, smiling and waving to every single one. She had a very particular expression when she spotted a baby or child, and he could just imagine how fond her nieces and nephew would be of her. He didn't need to see her with them to know she was an incredible aunt.

Though the line was long, the time passed quickly, and soon, it was their turn. They sat down on the sled, which was a large red structure with cushioned seating. There was a thick wool blanket set to the side; after they took their seats, he spread the blanket over their laps.

She leaned closer, their shoulders pressed together, and he reached for her hand under the blanket, keeping her warm.

"You're a dragon rider, so I'm sure this won't be very exciting," he said, a little sheepish.

"No, it'll be fun," she replied. "It's like a scene out of a storybook for children; it makes you believe in magic."

He smiled to himself. She was magic herself, and she didn't even know it.

The sled rider introduced himself and the chimeras and, once they were settled, he whipped his reins, spurring the animals forward. The chimeras began walking, then increased their pace into a run. She squeezed Luke's hand, and then, the chimeras flapped their wings, taking off. It was a bit of a bumpy start, but soon, they were up in the air, sailing smoothly.

It was a slow flight, not very high up, but enjoyable all the same as they took a leisurely flight over the lake. Snow flurried in the air above them, and Emmeline's eyes widened with awe.

"What were the chimera's names?" she asked. "I didn't hear."

"Barney," he replied, and she furrowed her brows.

"Barney?" she repeated.

"No." He shook his head. "Baaaarney," he said, bleating, and she laughed out loud.

"And the other? Don't tell me it's modeled after the same lame joke."

Luke grinned. "Lambchop."

"Come on, that's just mean!" But she was laughing. He squeezed her hand, and she leaned against his shoulder, the two of them fused.

After the chimera ride, he was going to take her to a local spot for dinner. But before he could tell her, her phone rang.

"Just a second," she said, picking up. She stepped to the side, and he waited, watching as she smiled.

"Hey Saphira . . . No, I don't have any plans for tomorrow," she was saying. There was a pause as the other person replied, and Emmeline laughed. "We already celebrated my birthday with everyone on New Year's Eve! We don't have to do anything tomorrow."

Luke stilled. Wait a moment.

It was her birthday tomorrow?

CHAPTER 25

Luke waited as Emmeline continued to chat with Saphira, who seemed to be trying to make plans with her for her birthday.

"Okay, I have to go now, but I'll see you tomorrow, then, okay?" she said. "Love you, bye."

She walked back over to Luke, but it was only a few steps. "Sorry about that," she said.

"No worries," he replied. "It's your birthday tomorrow? Sorry to eavesdrop."

She got a little shy, then. "Yes, it is," she replied.

"You should have said! It's a big one." Her thirtieth!

She waved a hand, and he narrowed his eyes. He could see that she went out of the way for others, but when it came to herself, she seemed to do the opposite. It was so weird.

He had already wanted their date to be great, but now he was even more determined for it to be wonderful. He would stay with her until midnight, so he could be the first one to wish her happy birthday.

She covered her face with her hands. "The older you get,

the faster time moves," she said. "When you're ten years old, a year is ten percent of your life, but when you're thirty, it's only three percent. That's scary, isn't it?"

"It's not scary, it's exciting," he said, and he led her down the path around the lake. "Besides, you have so much to be proud of. And growing older is such a privilege." He thought about his mother. He didn't know how many years she had left, but he was thankful for the time he had had with her.

Emmeline considered that. "I've never thought about it that way," she said. "My cousin Danny and I were the same age; every year I get older, he doesn't. He'll always stay twenty-five. It's . . ." She trailed off, struggling to find a word, but there was no word for it.

"Were you two really close?" he asked. She nodded.

"My other cousins are much older, and in our age group, Aiden was really quiet and withdrawn," she said. "Danny was always so hyper and fun. He, Millie, and I were a trio at family dinner."

"Where's Millie now?" he asked. He had been cautious about asking too much about her before, in case it made Emmeline upset, but she seemed to have moved on from all of that.

"She got married right after college and moved down south," she explained. "Her husband, Liam, is actually the farmer who provides the coffee beans for Inferno."

"Oh, wow," he replied. "That's great."

"Mhm." Her eyes looked a little sad, and he understood.

"You must miss her."

She nibbled on her lower lip. "I get to see her, but it never feels enough," she said. "Not the way it used to be." There was yearning on her face, as if she ached for a bygone era, but then her expression warmed as she remembered something. "Let me show you my nieces and nephew."

She took out her phone, pulling up pictures of some of the cutest kids he had ever seen. They were clearly *her* nieces and nephew.

"They look just like you," he said, and it was definitely the best compliment he could have given because she smiled widely.

"I am obsessed with them," she said, scrolling through what must have been at least a hundred photos, and they all looked to be from this month. The children were certainly very cute, and they were obviously obsessed with her.

"I'm sure you're a great khala," he said. She beamed. "And I'm sure you're going to be an even better mom someday."

She looked a little emotional at his words. "I hope so," she whispered, putting her phone away.

Their shoulders bumped as they continued walking. "You and Farhan are close, too," she said—not a question but a statement.

"Yeah, luckily," he replied. "He can be annoying, but I love him to bits." She smiled. "Don't tell him that—he's already got a big head."

She laughed, and they continued talking, walking slowly. Eventually, they made it back along the path to where they had started.

"Are you hungry?" he asked. "I had planned for us to get dinner at a local spot, but since it's your birthday, we need to do something special."

"Oh, we don't have to," she said, cringing. He furrowed his brows, putting a finger to his lips.

"Don't argue," he said. "Answer the question." Her eyes widened a little at his bossy tone, but she didn't seem to mind it.

"Yes, I am hungry," she said.

"Good." He nodded. "I'll make you dinner."

Her mouth almost dropped open. "You can cook?"

"Don't act so surprised," he replied, and she shook her head.

"No, it's just that my brothers are useless in the kitchen, so I'm always surprised when men can cook," she explained. "Though I shouldn't be, since Aiden is great at it."

"Hopefully, you'll think I'm great at it, too," he said, "or dinner will be special in an entirely different way . . ."

She laughed. "I'm sure I will." Then, she called Torch, who appeared a few moments later. He pulled out his whistle to call Sharptooth when Emmeline seemed to get an idea. "Do you want to ride with me?"

"Oh." Torch looked at him curiously, and he looked between the dragon and Emmeline. "I've never been on a dragon before, but you know, I've always secretly wanted to," he admitted. She seemed pleased by that.

"Come on," she said, mounting. He looked up at her on Torch. Dragons were much bigger than chimeras, which was why they could carry more weight.

He climbed on, settling in behind Emmeline. She leaned back into him, and he wrapped his arms around her, both of them aligned perfectly.

"Ready?" she asked, and he nodded over her shoulder.

They took off, and his heart lurched. Dragons were faster

than chimeras, and his grip on Emmeline tightened. He heard the sound of her laugh, then it was lost in the wind as they zipped through the air.

Cold wind blew against his face, sharp as ice, but Torch was a furnace underneath them, keeping them warm. It took a moment for him to get used to it, but once he did, he grinned, feeling euphoric.

"This is incredible!" he told her, and she squeezed his hand on her waist.

They made it to his place, dismounting. He went and touched Torch's face. "Thank you," he told the dragon. Torch nudged against his hand, pleased. Emmeline beamed, then told Torch to go home, and the dragon took off.

Luke led Emmeline to the front door, unlocking it and taking her inside, where he turned on the lights. The house was quiet.

Emmeline looked around. "Is your mom asleep?" she asked. "I wanted to say hi."

"She's not home, actually," he said. "My parents went away for the weekend."

She nodded. "It's sweet you stayed home to take care of her," she said. "I know it's probably not the easiest thing in the world not to have your own place."

"Sometimes," he agreed. "But I'm just glad to spend as much time with her as I can."

They took off their shoes and he hung up their coats. Underneath, she was wearing an off-the-shoulder sweater dress that fitted down to her waist, then flared out. With her hair tossed behind her shoulders, every inch of her throat and collar were exposed, tantalizingly kissable.

He wanted to press his lips everywhere, to taste her skin. Desire burned through him at the thought, and he cleared his throat, heading for the kitchen.

She followed behind him, then went directly to the fridge. Before he could ask what she was doing, she opened the door, inspecting the contents.

"So what are we making?" she asked, searching for ingredients.

He gave her a funny look. "*We* are not making anything," he said, taking her hands off the fridge door. He led her to one of the island chairs. "Sit."

"I can help," she protested, still standing.

"I know you can, but I said *I* would be making *you* dinner," he replied.

She frowned. "But I can help."

He put his hands on her shoulders, reveling in the soft feel of her skin. He tried to get her to sit, but she didn't budge.

He narrowed his eyes. "Emmeline," he said, tone warning.

"But—" she started with a pout.

He put his index finger to his lips. "Sh." She opened her mouth again, but he gave her a stern glance, and she stopped fussing. "Sit."

She sat down.

"I know this feels weird, but I want to," he said. "Let me."

She blinked. "Okay." He could see she was thinking, and then she released a long breath, embarrassed. "I'm sorry," she said, hiding her face behind her hands. "You're trying to be nice and I'm being a control freak. It's just that no one's ever helped me . . ." She broke off, feeling shy. "I know most of that is because I never *let* anyone. I'm just not used to . . . I don't know what I'm trying to say."

Still, he understood.

"You're not exactly letting me, either," he said, rolling up his sleeves. He gave her a crooked grin. "Fortunately or unfortunately, I'm just as stubborn as you are."

Her lips twitched as she got comfortable in her chair. "I wouldn't take it that far—I'm still more stubborn."

He laughed. "Always has to be a competition with you, huh?"

"Yes," she replied with a bright smile, amused.

The truth was, he didn't mind. Not anymore. He'd gladly let her win as long as she was smiling.

It made him think of the coffee shop proposal, Anh's investment. He would try his best, but he realized at that moment that if he didn't win, it would surely be tough, but it wouldn't be the end of the world. And a part of him would be happy that Emmeline had won.

But he didn't want to think about that right now.

Instead, he pulled out the ingredients to make pizza. "Sorry," he said. "If I had known, I would have planned something fancier."

"I love pizza." She put her elbows up on the island, resting her face in her hands as she watched him.

"Good," he said. It was quick and easy and always hit the spot.

"I would have a go at tossing the dough in the air to try and impress you, but I'm afraid I'd only embarrass myself instead," he told her.

She laughed. "I can never toss dough either," she said. "My nails always get caught."

She showed him her hands with her long nails, and he wanted to kiss her fingertips, to feel her fingers in his mouth. Every moment felt like the prelude to a hundred other moments, as if the scene could play out in so many different ways, and he was keen to live each one. It felt like a present that held the promise of a future.

For now, he focused on feeding her, getting to work on the pizza dough, then letting it rest. Emmeline ambled over, sitting up on the counter beside his workspace. As the dough rested, he made a quick tomato sauce, and when the dough was ready, he assembled the pizzas. Once they were set on the pizza peel, she hopped off the counter.

"Should I preheat the oven?" she asked. He shook his head, smiling. This was part of the reason he wanted to make pizza.

"Nope." He grabbed the peel, then headed for the backdoor, slipping on some outdoor shoes. She slipped on the pair beside his and followed him outside, where he showed her the oven next to the barn.

"Um?" She looked confused. "Where does it turn on?"

He grinned at her.

"Sharptooth!" he called, and the chimera came out from the barn. When she saw Luke by the oven, she came over to the back, where Luke propped open the door.

Then, Luke took Emmeline's hand, stepping to the side. Once they were a safe distance away, Sharptooth fired into the oven, the heat of his flames cooking the pizza.

Emmeline's face brightened with delight, precisely the reaction he was hoping for. "That's so smart!" she said. "I love it."

Once the pizzas were ready, he took them inside, where they sat together and ate.

"Mmm, this is delicious," she said, digging into her pizza. It was perfectly gooey with a crunchy crust.

"I'm glad you like it," he replied.

They ate and talked for a long time, yet it didn't feel like enough. They had a lifetime's worth of memories and opinions and stories to share with one another, hopes and fears and everything in between.

They finished off the pizzas and baked cookies, which he let her take charge of, and when those were done, they moved from the dining table to the couch, sharing a blanket and getting comfortable.

He kept an eye on the clock, waiting, and whenever she got up to leave, he asked her another question, and she sat down again, the conversation starting down a new path.

Then, when it was almost time, she said, "I really should go, now."

He stood up, catching her hand to stop her. "Just a little longer," he asked, and she smiled.

"Thank you for a lovely night," she said. "Really."

"It's not over yet," he said. He glanced over at the clock just as it struck twelve, and he smiled. Bridging the space between them, he leaned forward to kiss her cheek. "Happy birthday, Em."

Her face lit up with surprise. She turned to look at the clock, noticing the time. "So *that's* why you were stalling me," she said, as if she had cracked the code.

He shrugged. "I wanted to be the first one to wish you a happy birthday," he said. "I hope this is your best year yet."

"I hope so, too," she said, voice soft.

Gently, he cupped her face in his hands. Everything else faded away. It was just the two of them. His heart pounded, his blood quickening in his veins like a river rushing towards a waterfall.

Her hands fell to his waist, holding him, and she closed her eyes. At long last, he brought her mouth to his, kissing her. It was a soft brush of his lips against her, achingly sweet.

His body hummed with desire, aching for more, but he pulled back, and she opened her eyes, gazing up into his.

"You won't break my heart, will you?" he asked, voice a whisper.

She smiled. "I can't make any promises."

He didn't care. He pulled her in for another kiss.

CHAPTER 26

Kissing him again after all these years felt like winter's first snowfall: the return of all that magic and wonder and awe.

It was even better than she remembered. She had wanted to kiss him all night. She had wanted to kiss him for weeks, if she was being honest, maybe even for years, ever since that first time when they were bright-eyed university students.

His hands moved down to her bare shoulders, skirting down her arms to hold onto her waist, pulling her closer. Everywhere he touched her felt lit with flames, and she moved her hands up his chest, to hold onto his shoulders as he kissed her slow and sweet.

It felt as if she had never been kissed before, not like this, like she was someone to be revered, someone to be savored. Her chest ached; her heart so full it felt like it would burst.

He pulled away, and they both caught their breath, foreheads pressed together.

"I've wanted to do that forever," he said, voice rough. He pulled back to gaze into her eyes, searching.

"Me too," she admitted.

He gave her a grin that was full of such simple joy that her heart swelled. She liked making him happy.

He pulled her in for another kiss and she slid a hand from his shoulder into his hair, twisting the tendrils around her fingers. He deepened the kiss, opening her mouth against his as the kiss went from slow and sweet to frenzied and passionate, as if the floodgates of their desire had opened.

They had both wanted this for so long, and they were making up for lost time. He kissed her harder, lips bruising against hers, but it wasn't enough, not nearly enough. She tugged his hair, holding him closer. He released a desperate groan deep in his throat, the sound vibrating through her, sending every single one of her nerves aflame.

She gasped, and he kissed her cheek, her jaw, his lips trailing lower. There was a slight stubble on his face late at night, and it scratched against her skin in a way that made her feel weak in the knees. She made a strangled sound as he kissed her throat.

Her pulse raced against his lips, and he clutched her closer, fingers pressing into her skin as their hips aligned. Heat pooled low in her belly, and he kissed her collar, sucking at her skin, every touch scorching.

She brought his mouth back to hers, kissing him hungrily. He slipped his hands under her dress, and even through the material of her stockings, she felt his large hands searing into her. She ached for more as his hands went higher, over the curve of her hips to her waistband, fingers skimming the bare skin of her stomach.

In a quick movement, he lifted her up, and she wrapped

her legs around his waist. She bit his lower lip, and he held her closer against him.

He walked them back until she was pressed against the wall. Her vision sparked. She clutched his hair tighter, their tongues clashing as they both lost themselves in a haze of desire.

Time slipped away—it could have been minutes, it could have been hours. She had no sense of anything except for him.

Until her phone rang.

Slowly, they broke apart, both of them breathing hard. He met her gaze, and at the same time, they both grinned, exuberant from the taste and feel of one another.

He let her down, and her phone continued to ring. She let it, instead looking up at him. She touched his cheek, her heart filled with such emotion that she felt at a loss for words. He held her hand, turning his cheek to kiss her palm. The phone began ringing again.

"You should get that," he said.

"I should."

But she couldn't tear herself away from him. He smiled as if he knew. With gentle hands, he tugged her dress down from where it had gathered over her hips. His hands lingered, and she went on her tiptoes, wrapping her arms around his neck.

She felt the way she had after her first dragon ride: exhilarated, and as if things would never be the same again. It was the beginning of something new and life-changing, and she couldn't wait to see all that would unfold.

Her phone rang again, and she disentangled herself for long enough to grab it, but by then, it had stopped ringing. She saw it had been Millie.

"She probably just wants to wish me a happy birthday," she said, texting Millie that she would call her soon. Millie sent a thumbs-up. Emmeline released a long breath, turning to Luke crooked over her shoulder as he hugged her from behind. "I should probably get back."

"Okay," he replied, but he turned her around, pulling her in for another kiss. She smiled against his mouth, kissing him back, little sparks of pleasure spreading through her and making her feel buoyant.

"I had a really great time," she said, pulling away. "Thank you, for everything."

"'Course," he replied easily, as if he hadn't done anything at all. But he had, and it meant so much to her. *He* meant so much to her, a fact that was impossible to ignore now, when her lips were still warm from the heat of his.

As he walked her to the door, she already wanted to see him again. Saphira had called earlier to invite her for brunch at the Baby Dragon Cafe to celebrate her birthday, and before Emmeline could think about it too much, she found herself inviting Luke to join her.

His face brightened. "I'd love that," he said. "I'll be there."

After a final kiss goodbye, Emmeline called Torch and headed home. Even after dismounting, she felt like she was flying, gliding through the air. She bounced through her house, heading for her bedroom, where she fell back on her bed with a sigh.

She couldn't believe that had happened, but at the same time, it had felt inevitable, and now, she was only relieved. Touching a finger to her lips, she smiled.

Then, she grabbed her phone, calling her sister.

"Happy birthday!" Millie said, picking up immediately. While her room was dark, her face lit up from the phone screen. Emmeline saw Eve feeding in Millie's lap.

She laughed. "You haven't wished me at midnight for years."

"Because my bedtime is ten p.m.," she said. "I'm awake because of Eve, otherwise I'd be passed out." She was cut off by a loud snore in the background, and her eyes twitched. "I'm two seconds away from smothering him in his sleep."

"Why don't we refrain from the murderous impulses today?" she said. "I've got news."

Millie gasped. "I saw you two days ago! You're hardly an hour into being thirty and you already have news? Tell me."

Emmeline gave a quick account of her date, ending with the kiss. Millie let out a squeal—well, more like a shriek. The snoring in the background promptly stopped.

"What-what is it?" Liam asked, panicked. Half of him came into view as he looked Millie over, searching for signs of injury.

"Emmy and Luke finally kissed!" she told him. He let out a long breath.

"That's great, sweetie," he said, relaxing. "Let's go back to sleep."

Millie gave him a dirty look. "Why don't you breastfeed your daughter and *I'll* go back to sleep?" There was no response from Liam. "That's what I thought. Now sh."

He flopped out of view, going back to sleep, Emmeline guessed, though luckily without such loud snoring. Millie focused back on her sister. "I need every single detail. Right now. You know, sometimes while feeding I listen to podcasts about how to be a better mother, but I realize now I should just call you for entertainment instead."

Emmeline laughed, then went into detail about the entire day. She got off her bed and took her phone to the bathroom, setting it by the sink as she washed her makeup off and did her skincare routine, easily chatting with her sister as she did so. She felt like they were in school again, sharing a bathroom and catching up on the day as they got ready for bed.

It was another hour before she hung up and got into bed and, even though she was tired, she felt too excited to fall asleep. She kept grinning to herself, feeling fizzy.

CHAPTER 27

The next morning, Emmeline woke feeling just as happy as she had last night, and her joy only increased as she realized it hadn't been a dream. It had been real. She could still taste him on her tongue, feel the way he'd held her flush against him.

Her heartbeat quickened, and she was dying to see him again. She had never felt this way before, and while it was kind of freaking her out, it was exciting all the same.

She got ready for brunch, humming to herself. Then, she flew over on Torch, who could sense her happiness and twirled through the air. Laughing, she petted Torch's scales and they dipped down in the air, the wind rushing against her cheeks.

They landed in front of the cafe, and she dismounted, touching Torch's face before heading in. She was excited to see her friends, but most of her excitement was to see Luke again.

When she entered, she saw the group sitting at the table in the back corner. Luke was there already, and the sight of him sent tiny sparks shooting across her skin. She felt ten years younger, like a teenager discovering the rush of infatuation for the first time.

"There she is!" Saphira said, waving. Emmeline walked over, and her friends all stood, welcoming her with birthday wishes. Aiden, Saphira, Lavinia, Theo, and Ginny. And Luke. Her gaze kept straying to him, even as she hugged her friends, and the girls absolutely noticed, giggling.

"Where's Motu?" Ginny asked. Fang was with her, and the baby dragon obediently sat by her black-booted feet.

"At my parents'," Emmeline replied, sitting down next to Ginny. "I'm going to pick him up later." She turned to Saphira, who was on her other side. "Where's Sparky?"

"Out in the garden," Saphira said, tucking an errant wave back into her braid. She was wearing an oversized pink sweater over a floral dress.

"How's riding going?" Emmeline asked.

"It was going well, but I'm taking a break now," Saphira replied. That made sense since she was pregnant.

Emmeline nodded, then turned her attention to the beautiful brunch spread Saphira had set up with vases of flowers and lit taper candles. Saphira had made a feast: chicken paratha rolls, cookie-butter French toast, along with karak chai and a gorgeous-looking cake that was topped with bright candied orange peels.

"Oooh, everything looks delicious," Emmeline said, taking everything in.

"It's an orange cake," Theo told her proudly. She noticed he had a scrunchie around his wrist; it must have been Lavinia's. Her straight hair was down at the moment.

"I think we should have cake first," Emmeline said, and he pushed it her way, along with a knife. They all clapped as she cut into it, then plated a slice for herself. She took a bite; it was sweet and zesty, with the perfect amount of citrus.

"How is it?" Theo asked, running a hand through his wavy hair.

"Oh my god, amazing," Emmeline told him. Theo beamed, pleased, and Lavinia hugged his arm, looking up at him with stars in her eyes. Saphira slid the cake her way to cut it for everyone else, but Aiden took the knife from her hands, doing it himself. He made sure to give her an extra-large piece, which Saphira happily took.

"Thank you all for wanting to celebrate my birthday with me," Emmeline said, raising her mug of chai. "I really appreciate it."

They dug into the brunch spread, chatting about random things. Luke was sitting across from Emmeline, between Theo and Aiden, and as she saw the boys talking, she felt her heart warming. She hadn't realized how special this could be, and the best birthday gift was seeing how seamlessly he fit in with the people important to her.

After they finished eating, Saphira turned to Aiden and said, "Why don't you take Fang outside to Spark with Theo and Luke."

Aiden looked confused for a second. "Why do I need to take Theo and Luke—"

Saphira seemed to silently communicate something with him, and he nodded. "Ah."

He got up, and Ginny sent Fang with him, the baby

dragon following the boys outside until only the girls were left. Luke glanced over his shoulder at her, and Emmeline's heart skipped a beat as he flashed her an easy smile.

"Finally, some girl time," Saphira said, once they were gone.

"Love the boys, but you're so right," Lavinia agreed, cutting herself another slice of cake, which was nearly finished.

"Now tell us *everything*," Ginny demanded. Emmeline smiled, then started from the beginning, explaining how the more time she spent with Luke, the harder it was to fight her growing feelings for him. How she had finally given in. Saphira and Lavinia squealed.

"I totally knew you liked him," Ginny said, pleased with herself.

"Right." Emmeline snorted. "How did you know that?"

Ginny shrugged. "Because I know everything." She smiled. "And I know you best."

"You got me there," Emmeline replied, pinching Ginny's cheek. Her younger cousin swatted her hand away.

"Now don't overthink it and ruin everything," Ginny said, her voice a warning. Emmeline's mouth dropped open at her cousin's blunt words. Ginny may have been the youngest, but she sure had a lot of opinions.

"What exactly is that supposed to mean?" she asked.

Ginny arched her brow, giving her a knowing look. "You're a control freak," she said. "But you can't micromanage your feelings for someone, or their feelings for you."

"Oh my god!" Emmeline protested. She looked to Saphira and Lavinia for defense, and they exchanged a glance.

"I wouldn't say you're a control *freak*," Saphira said gently.

"I would say you're meticulous—in a good way!—and like things to be in order."

"Emphasis on the '*in a good way*'," Lavinia affirmed.

Emmeline laughed. Ginny was her cousin, so she could get away with being a little monster, but Saphira and Lavinia were trying to be nice about it.

"It's okay," Emmeline said. "Maybe I *can* be a control freak. Sometimes."

She was self-aware enough to recognize the fact. But if she didn't manage things, who would? All she wanted was for her loved ones to be happy, and sometimes they needed a little help in accomplishing that successfully.

"Which is fine, except when it comes to love," Saphira said. She looked around, then spotted a hanging piece of artwork on one of the cafe walls. "Ishq soch ke kita te ki kita?" she read the line of poetry from the artwork aloud, and Emmeline covered her face with her hands.

"Oh god, don't quote Punjabi poetry at me." She laughed, but she knew Saphira was right.

"Translation, please," Ginny asked.

"It's hard to get exactly, but it basically asks: 'What type of love is a love carefully planned?'" Saphira said.

"So true," Lavinia affirmed, speaking from experience. "You really can't plan these things out."

Emmeline was so used to planning things out to the smallest detail, but what if she allowed herself to *not* overthink this? It felt reckless, in a way that frightened her, but she wanted to let go, to let things be as they were instead of analyzing everything. She wanted to keep feeling as good as she did.

It was freeing to give in to the way she felt about him, to trust him. To let him take care of her. She had never felt so . . . liberated.

"When's that big meeting with Anh?" Ginny asked, and Emmeline felt a dose of reality come crashing over her. She hadn't thought about the investment they were both competing for, how Luke was still technically her rival.

"Next Friday," Emmeline replied, nibbling on her bottom lip.

"Hey, don't worry," Saphira said, immediately noticing Emmeline's worry. "You guys are both adults; I'm sure that won't get between you two."

"Yeah, I'm sure you're right," Emmeline replied, feeling confident. She and Luke had agreed to no more fighting.

The girls hung out together for a little longer, discussing in depth every single pregnancy craving Saphira was having ("This baby is being built on bagels and cream cheese!") until it was time for everybody to go their separate ways.

They hugged and kissed goodbye. Emmeline had hardly made it a few feet down Main Street before she heard someone coming after her.

"Hey, wait up," Luke said. She turned to see him jogging to catch up with her, and she smiled, a bubbly feeling spreading through her chest.

"Hi," she said, as he stopped in front of her.

"Hi." He smiled. "You got out of there fast."

"Are you obsessed with me or something?" she teased.

He rolled his eyes, though she saw the amusement in his gaze. "I never got to give you your gift," he said. She grinned.

"So you're obsessed with me," she repeated, being obnoxious on purpose.

"Shut up," he said, laughing.

"Make me," she replied. His eyes darkened. He grabbed her waist, pulling her towards him, and her stomach lurched.

"You'd like that, wouldn't you?" he asked, voice low.

Honestly? She would. He smiled like he knew, a smug look coming across his face.

Taking the invitation, he pulled her in for a kiss, mouth pressing hotly against hers. She rested her hands against his chest, moving to play with the chains around his neck, twisting them around her fingers.

She tugged, pulling him closer, and he kissed her harder. His fingers pressed into her skin, and she broke away with a gasp, catching her breath. He pressed his lips to the tender space beneath her jaw, his teeth skimming across her bare skin in a way that sent sparks shooting through every one of her nerves.

She inhaled the sweet smell of him, cypress and spruce, winter on his skin. Pulling away, she met his dark gaze with an amused smile.

"So was that my gift?" she asked, his chains still wrapped around her fingers. "Not bad."

He laughed again, shaking his head. "No, but noted." He gave her cheek a quick kiss, then let go of her to pull something out of his pocket. Excitement spread through her, and she held out both of her hands. He deposited the gift into her palms. It was something small wrapped in one of his black pocket squares.

"I didn't have a box," he explained, looking nervous as she

undid the knot on top. "I just picked it up this morning. If you don't like it—"

She ignored him, pushing the fabric back to reveal a pair of gold chandbali earrings. She gasped, touching her finger to them. They were round with an intricate design, about two inches big; beautiful but understated, something she could wear all the time.

"Oh my god, I love them!" she said. They were so pretty, and she was touched he had gotten her something at all. "Where did you get them?" she asked. "I haven't seen a design like this at the gold store in town."

He looked sheepish. "Well, funny story . . ." He ran a hand through his hair. "I called my mom this morning to ask her for help, since I couldn't figure out what to get you so last-minute."

"You didn't need to get me anything," she reminded him.

He furrowed his brows. "Sh." She pressed her lips together. "So she told me to go to the drawer in her bedroom's dresser and take out this pair from her jewelry box."

Emmeline's mouth jutted open. "These are your mom's?" she asked. "I can't take these." She held them out for him to take back, and he frowned at her.

"Hush. Of course you can. I swear, she already likes you better than me, anyways." She didn't know what to say, and his face softened. "So you like them?"

"I love them," she said. "It's—They're . . . I . . ." She blinked. "Thank you, Luke. Really."

"'Course," he said easily, giving her a sweet smile.

"And tell your mom I said thank you, too," she said. "It really means a lot to me."

Emmeline owned a good deal of gold jewelry, but these earrings would be one of her most prized pieces, for sure.

Her heart swelled with emotion, and she put the earrings on. Pushing her hair behind her ear, she showed Luke.

"How do they look?" she asked.

He smiled. "Pretty." Leaning forward, he kissed her ear. Then, he cupped her face, turning her head to kiss her other ear. She smiled, throwing her arms around him in a hug.

"I love them," she told him again, hoping he could feel just how much the gift meant to her. He held her close, lifting her feet off the ground and spinning her around. She laughed, not caring as people walked past them on the sidewalk.

He breathed her in, and she felt anchored, like as long as she could hold onto him, she would never have to worry again.

Eventually, they pulled apart, but didn't let go of each other entirely. She played with the ends of his hair while he held onto her waist.

"So what are your plans for the rest of the day?" he asked.

"I was going to go to my parents'," she said. "My mom came back last night from Millie's." There were still a few hours until then, and she considered inviting him over.

But she paused. A part of her wanted to let him into her space, but a part of her was afraid it was too much, too soon. She very rarely invited men to her place.

"Will I see you tomorrow?" he asked. "At the bookshop?"

That reminded her again of their meeting with Anh, the investment they were both vying for. Before, she had been so focused, so determined, and a large part of that had been because she wanted to beat Luke—but now? She didn't want to beat him. A part of her wanted him to win, to see him happy and successful.

But where did that leave her? All her hard work? All her plans to expand Inferno?

"What are you thinking about?" he asked, brows furrowed.

She blinked. "Oh—the meeting with Anh," she replied quickly. "It's so soon."

"Are you worried?" He looked confused still. "I'm sure your proposal is going to be great."

But that wasn't what concerned her.

"How's yours coming along?" she asked. He paused, glancing away from her, then back.

"Maybe we shouldn't talk about it," he said, releasing a breath. "I don't want it to inadvertently come between us."

"Okay," she replied, though she didn't feel any better. She felt torn. She hadn't planned for this. She needed to think—to strategize. The girls' warnings rang in her head, about how she couldn't micromanage everything, but she ignored them. There had to be a solution that would lead to success; there always was. And she always found it.

"I'll see you tomorrow?" he asked. She nodded, giving him a smile. He leaned in to give her a final kiss goodbye, and she hummed against his mouth, perfectly content.

But as she flew home on Torch, she couldn't help but worry.

CHAPTER 28

Emmeline spent the rest of her birthday at her parents' place.

Samreen was back from Millie's and made Emmeline a special birthday dinner of mutton korma with homemade naans, and kheer for dessert. The rice pudding was one of Emmeline's favorite desserts, but it took hours to make, which was why Samreen refused to make it except for her birthday.

Emmeline was glad her mom was home; Samreen seemed more relaxed. Emmeline knew it was probably overwhelming for Samreen to be at Millie's with all the kids, which was why she had been a bit highly strung.

The next day, Emmeline had work at Inferno, and after, she went to the bookshop. She didn't really need to spend as much time at the bookshop anymore, since she had done most of the work for her proposal, but she still liked seeing Luke every day.

When she was apart from him, she spent her time thinking about when she would see him again, and when they were together, she was entirely present in the moment with him, not wanting it to slip away.

The week passed in bliss. She hardly got any work done as they distracted one another, stealing kisses when they should have been working, talking when they should have been focused.

They fell into an easy routine, one that made her feel as if it had always existed. After spending a few hours at the bookshop, they would get dinner someplace in town or in Bayview, a date for every night. After, they would walk around the lit streets or the lake, talking and kissing and laughing. They had so much to talk about, an entire lifetime's worth.

She hadn't had so much fun in a long time, and each day was just as good as the last, if not better.

On Friday, they didn't meet at the bookshop; instead, she went over to his place. Emmeline made sure to wear the earrings Luke had gifted her—she had been wearing them almost every day—and when he opened the door, his brown eyes lit up with warmth.

"Hi," she said, smiling. She loved making him happy. Closing the door behind her, he pulled her into a hug. She melted against him, utterly safe in his arms.

"Hi." He was wearing a casual outfit for once, a sweatshirt and sweatpants rather than his usual dress shirt and trousers, and she liked seeing this different side of him. He wasn't wearing any rings, either, and while she loved his ringed fingers, she liked his hands like this, too, completely bare. She twined their fingers together.

He kissed her cheek, then led her inside, and she held onto his hand, hugging his arm. It had been over a week, which wasn't a very long time, but Emmeline felt as if they had been together for ages.

At the same time, every moment also felt brand-new, like she was uncovering some hidden treasure. Being with him felt as comforting as reading her favorite book, and yet with every reread, there was something new to explore and discover.

She followed Luke to the living room, where Rhea was sitting with the baby chimeras at her feet.

"Emmy, hi," Rhea said, smiling brightly when she saw her.

"Hi." Emmeline went over to hug her hello, then tucked her hair behind her ears to show Rhea the earrings. Rhea beamed.

"Oh, they suit you so well!" she said, touching the end of the chandbali earrings. They made a little jingling sound.

"I adore them," Emmeline told her. "Thank you again."

Rhea looked at Luke. "See, I told you she'd like them."

He rolled his eyes fondly. "Yes, yes, as always, you are right."

"I finally finished their sweaters," Rhea told them. "Will you help me get the babies into them?"

She showed them the sweaters she had knitted; one was a buttery yellow while the other was a sky blue. "Adorable!" Emmeline affirmed. She picked up Butternut while Luke picked up Squash, and they both wrestled the bleating baby chimeras into the sweaters, which were perfect fits.

Rhea smiled, overjoyed, and Butternut leapt from Emmeline's arms to snuggle in Rhea's lap. Squash soon followed.

Then, Luke led Emmeline to his room, which was in a

separate section of the house. It was kind of like a studio apartment with a kitchenette, and after he closed the door behind her, it felt like they were completely separate, in their own private space.

Emmeline looked around, taking in every detail. She hadn't been in his room before, and he let her explore, making them chai on the little stove. His place was clean and simple, everything white and black.

There was a board with pinned photographs, and she looked over them. While they showed various ages and times, the characters were constant: Sharptooth, Farhan, his parents, and the Din siblings.

"This is so sweet," she said, pointing to a photo. It was Luke with the Din girls. He must have been about eight in the photo, and the girls were hanging off him, a toddler on his back and the other two on either side of him.

He came over, handing her a mug of chai. He took a sip from his own mug as he looked at the photo she was pointing at, smiling.

"Since I'm the oldest, I was always in charge," he said. "Basim and Farhan were probably off getting into trouble somewhere."

"Really?" she asked, surprised. "Basim seems so serious."

"He is a lot more serious now, but when we were kids, he was as bad as Farhan," Luke told her. "So it was always me looking after the girls. You don't want to know how many times I was forced into their games. They'd either be sticking butterfly clips in my hair or trying to paint my nails or who knows what else."

Emmeline laughed at the thought. "That is adorable,"

she said, sipping her chai, which was perfectly made. "You're good at taking care of people."

It was a quality she greatly admired. She was so used to taking care of things herself, but around Luke, it felt like she could trust him. He was competent.

"So are you," Luke told her. "I've seen the way you are with your friends and family—you do so much for everyone."

She shrugged. "It's nothing."

"It's not nothing," he said.

She ambled over to his bookshelf, looking through his collection.

"So many of these books look untouched," she said, running her hand along some of the spines.

"I haven't got the chance to read all of them, yet," he told her.

"How can you buy books you haven't read?" she asked, dumbfounded.

"Because I want to read them."

"What if you don't like it? Then it's just taking up space on your shelf."

He gave her a funny look. "Do you only buy books you've read and liked?"

"Yes! I only buy books that I would reread."

"Interesting." He made a thoughtful sound. "But then that takes half the fun out of perusing at bookshops."

"Mm, not really," she said. "It's still fun just to walk around, even if you aren't going to buy anything." It made her think of Tales & Tails. "I'm excited for the coffee shop at Tales & Tails—I hope it'll bring in new readers."

She paused. They hadn't spoken about the proposal since

they had agreed not to, but she wanted to talk to him about everything. This past week, they had talked about so many different things, big and small. It felt strange to hold back.

"Are you nervous for our meeting on Friday?" she asked. There was a week until then, and while she was almost done with her proposal and feeling confident about it, she had no idea what Luke was feeling.

"Not really," he replied easily. "I'm basically done."

"What were you thinking of doing with the investment if you won?" she asked. He hesitated. "I know we said we weren't going to talk about it," she added, but still, she waited for his response.

He laughed. "It's impossible not to talk to you about something," he admitted, and she smiled. "You tell me first."

She had been waiting to talk about her plans with him, to hear his insight. While she had talked about it before with her sister, she knew no one would truly get it, not like Luke would. He was in the same business, after all, and he was just as ambitious as she was.

"I want to expand my business's distributions outside of Starshine Valley," she said. "Since Inferno's doing well, I think I could take things to the next level."

He smiled. "I expected nothing less," he said, looking genuinely excited for her. "That would be amazing."

"What about you?" she asked. She was sure he had similar plans, but at her question, some of the brightness of his expression dimmed. He looked away. "Come on," she said. "Tell me. I won't steal your ideas, promise."

She was teasing, but he looked . . . embarrassed. She furrowed her brows, confused.

"I don't think you could, anyway. My plans are a bit different," he told her, meeting her gaze for a moment before looking away again. "Tempest hasn't been doing very well."

"What do you mean?" she asked with concern.

He sighed. "A variety of things piled up, and the business has been scraping by . . ." He ran a hand through his hair. "I can fix it—if I win the investment, that is."

"And if you don't?" Her heartbeat quickened. She had a feeling she already knew the answer, but she hoped it wasn't true.

"I'll probably close," he replied.

"But . . ." she started, frowning. But what?

All those years, all that energy, and all the money he had given to his business would go to waste. She knew how much his business meant to him—and she recalled what he had said, how he took care of his mother. She was sure those medical bills weren't cheap.

He couldn't afford not to have a job.

Dread ran through her like ice, and Luke shook his head, giving her an easy smile. "Hey, it's going to be okay," he said. "Don't worry about me."

But she did worry. She nibbled on her lower lip, looking away. She wanted him to win.

"Hey," he said, tilting her chin so she met his gaze. "Okay?"

She nodded. "Okay."

He kissed her forehead, then reached for a book from the bookshelf behind her. "Why don't I read to you?" he said, and her heart glowed.

They set down their empty chai mugs, and he led her to his bed, where she sat down snuggled against him, both of them leaning back against the pillows. She was still worried about him, about his business, and the investment, but as he began reading aloud, all those thoughts slowly went away.

She was hardly focused on the story; she was focused on him. She looked up at him as he read, watching him: the sweep of his hair, the line of his jaw, the brown of his eyes. His eyes were the color of her favorite coffee-roast.

And his voice—deep and a little rough. There was a particular cadence with which he spoke, and she touched a hand to his throat, wanting to feel the vibrations against her fingers, as if she could capture his voice in her palm.

Everything about him seemed entirely one of a kind, like there was no one else like him and there never would be. As if he was made specifically for her.

He continued reading until the passage finished, then took her hand from his throat. He lifted her hand to his lips, kissing her palm, his eyes questioning what she had been doing.

She felt shy, so she didn't respond. She loved his voice. She had just wanted to feel it against her skin.

He must have seen something in her eyes because he leaned over to kiss her cheek. She sat up, and he set the book aside, hands going to her waist. His eyes burned into hers, and she leaned in for a kiss.

Heat poured through her as his lips pressed against hers, her pulse quickening in response to his touch. She held onto his shoulders, and he pulled her onto his lap, bringing her closer. She slotted over him, her knees on either side of his hips as he deepened the kiss.

His movements turned frantic, his fingers digging into her hips. He slipped his tongue into her mouth and her stomach flipped, desire pooling low in her belly.

She reached for the edge of his sweatshirt, and he pulled it off, revealing his bare skin. She moved her hands across his chest, feeling every contour and dip, greedily exploring the solid feel of him. He made a desperate sound as her hands went lower.

Then, in a quick maneuver, he had them flipped until she was flat on her back, resting against the pillows, his body hovering above hers. His teeth scraped against her skin as he kissed her throat.

Her body was pulled taut, aching as he trailed kisses over her collar, down to her heart. She held onto his shoulders, nails digging into his bare skin. He lifted up her sweater, pressing a kiss to her stomach.

She made a soft whimper, and his hands went to the waist of her skirt. Her heart pounded against her chest. She brought her hand over his, urging him to continue. He lowered her skirt an inch, kissing her below her belly button, and desire pulsed through her, making her dizzy.

"Please," she whispered, throwing her head back.

He pulled her skirt and underwear down to her ankles. He kissed her between her legs, and she gasped, holding onto his hair. Heat poured through her, gathering in intensity as he continued to kiss her and kiss her until she was overcome with pleasure.

After, he lifted up, a smug smile on his face as he looked her over. He touched her cheek. "Em," he said, voice rough. "I really, really like you in pink."

She felt her cheeks growing warmer, her blush surely deepening, and he smiled.

Her chest tightened. And she knew.

She was falling in love with him. She suspected a part of herself had fallen in love with him all those years ago, but she had buried it so deeply, and now it was rushing to the surface, impossible to ignore.

CHAPTER 29

Talking about the proposal with Emmeline had been a little awkward for Luke.

She had plans to expand while his business was failing—it was embarrassing, almost, but he knew she wasn't looking down on him. He could see she was concerned for him.

Even though they were vying for the same investment, she was still worried about him.

Ridiculous woman. He was falling in love with her badly. A part of him had loved her since that very first night, but now the force of it was tenfold. He couldn't believe his luck. More than a week later, it still felt as if he was living a dream.

She was so loving and caring, with such a big heart. It was as if all of her defenses had stripped away, and he had been given the immense privilege of seeing the truth of her core.

He had seen her as a fierce and ruthless businesswoman, someone who was always in control, who was never fazed. But now he saw that beneath her armor, she was just as human as anyone else: she could be shy and nervous.

He loved her already, but with every new layer to her that he discovered, he loved her more and more. There was no one else in the world like her, and there never would be again.

Luke checked his phone; it was Sunday evening, and she was supposed to meet him at the Baby Dragon Cafe fifteen minutes ago. He was out on Main Street, looking up at the festive lights decorating the cafe's storefront. It was cold out, but he didn't mind waiting.

He had waited all these years, after all.

Then, his phone rang. His heartbeat quickened. He wondered if it would ever stop being exciting, being the object of her attention. He knew it wouldn't, at least not for a long time.

"Hey," he said, picking up.

"I'm sorry, I know I'm late, I . . ." she started, and his brows furrowed. She sounded frazzled.

"What's going on?" he asked.

"I'm sorry, I was heading out, when Motu created this huge mess," she explained. "I'm trying to clean up and—"

"Hey, take a deep breath," he said. "Do you want me to come over and help you clean up?"

She paused. "If you wouldn't mind . . ." She stopped herself. "No, it's okay. I can do it."

While she had been to his place, he had never been to hers. It felt as if she was guarding her home, afraid to let him in.

He wanted to take care of her. To be there for her.

"Emmy, can I please come over?" he asked.

She hesitated. Then, as if refusing to overthink, she quickly said, "Yes. I'll text the address."

Before he could respond, she hung up. A second later, the address came through. He pulled out his whistle to call Sharptooth, then flew over.

She lived in a little cottage up in the hills. It wasn't too far away from where he remembered her parents' estate was, and the memory of that night made him apprehensive. The last time he had gone to her place, she had broken his heart.

But things were different now. They were both different.

He knocked on the door, and a few moments later she opened. She was covered in—what was that? A smoothie? It was some thick liquid. He thought he saw chunks of banana in her hair.

"Hey," he said. "Nice look."

She didn't respond, and instead turned to walk into the house, muttering to herself. He closed the door behind him, following her to the kitchen, which was an absolute mess. He spotted a blender, which seemed to be the source: there was no lid on it, and all the liquid inside had splattered around like a smoothie had exploded. The cabinets under the sink were open, revealing cleaning supplies.

Motu sat guiltily on the side, half-hiding behind his wings. He was covered in the same thick liquid as Emmeline.

"I had a long day at work with the dragons," she explained, sitting on the floor, where it looked as if she had begun cleaning up the tiles. "And then Saphira said she wasn't feeling well, so I made and dropped off soup for her, and I didn't have time to eat lunch at work, so I was going to make a smoothie and Motu knocked into the blender—"

She broke off, releasing a long breath. "I'm just so tired."

It felt as if she was admitting that for the first time, and even that cost her. His heart squeezed painfully. He hated to see her in distress.

"Hey, it's okay," he said, going to her side. "You're allowed to be tired."

"And now I have to clean all of this up," she said, aggressively scrubbing the floor. "And Motu, too." She looked up at Luke with wide eyes. "I'm sorry. I know we were supposed to go to the cafe—once I get this all cleaned up, we can still go!" She tried to give him a smile, but he could see it was brittle.

He frowned at her. "Don't be sorry," he said, reaching for her hand. "Why don't you clean up Motu, and I'll clean up in here?"

She stopped scrubbing and blinked at him, confused. "What do you mean?"

"Exactly what I said," he replied, pulling her up to her feet. "Go clean Motu up. I'll handle the kitchen." He took off his coat, then his blazer, rolling up the sleeves of his shirt. She watched, stupefied.

"But . . ." she started.

"Motu," he called, and the baby dragon flew over to them. Emmeline scooped him up into her arms, and he nodded at her. She made for the exit, then hesitated by the doorway.

"Go," he said. "I'll clean up."

She nibbled on her lower lip, and he walked over, putting his hands on her shoulders, steering her out "Go."

"Okay, but make sure you don't miss anything, or it'll smell because of the milk," she said. "And make sure there aren't any streaks and—"

"Emmy, I know," he said, laughing a little. "Now go."

She went, and he watched as she made her way to the

stairs. He watched her go until she disappeared from sight. A few moments later, he heard the shower running.

Luke went back to the kitchen, cleaning up. The mess wasn't too horrible, but he was extra thorough just in case. After he'd finished cleaning everything up, he made Emmeline a fresh smoothie, since she said she hadn't eaten.

He was just pouring the smoothie into a glass when Emmeline came back down. Motu flew in behind her, squeaky clean, while she hadn't changed herself.

"For you," he said, handing her the glass. She looked dumbfounded as she looked around.

"It's so . . . clean," she said, impressed.

He snorted. "I'm not entirely useless, you know."

"It's not that—it's just, no one's ever done anything like this for me before," she replied.

He furrowed his brows. "But you're always talking about how you do things for your sister and family and friends," he said.

She looked away. "I like doing that." She frowned. "That makes it sound like no one ever wants to do things for me, which isn't true. I guess it's just hard for me to *let* other people do things for me. It makes me feel . . . bad. I don't know why."

"But it's how people express their love for you," he told her. "You should let them."

"Well, thank you for cleaning up in here. And for this." She held up the smoothie.

"Of course. After you finish, let's get you cleaned up, as well."

She glanced down, where there were dried splatters of smoothie all over her clothes and skin. "Right."

"I'll run you a bath," he said.

Before she could protest, he left the kitchen, looking around the rest of her place as he went for the stairs. Motu followed after him, going to a little bed in the living room.

Her home was so *her*. It was neat and orderly, which was to have been expected, with a sleek and modern design; but there were homey elements as well: framed pictures, toys for Motu, mementos and trinkets.

He wanted to dissect every inch, to ask her about everything, but there would be time for that later. Right now, he went up the stairs and found her bedroom. In the attached bathroom, he ran a hot bath, the space quickly filling with steam. There was a bottle of bath salts and soap on the tub; both looked hardly used.

He squeezed some of the soap in as Emmeline entered behind him. "I got those ages ago," she told him. "But I never have time for baths. And I love baths."

"Well, you've got time now," he said. "Come on."

Her lips twitched. "Now you're just trying to get my clothes off."

He laughed, holding his hands up. "My intentions are pure, promise."

Though he was surely having impure thoughts as she reached back to unzip her dress. He turned around, reaching for the door.

"Wait," she said, voice quiet. "Stay."

He stilled, his heart pounding. He didn't trust himself to turn, so he stood with his back to her, listening to the sound of her clothes hitting the floor. Then, he heard the water splash as she entered the bath.

"Luke," she said, just his name, and he couldn't bear it.

He turned. She was submerged in the water with her back to him, most of which was covered with her dark hair, which looked like a cloak of black silk. Her arms were wrapped around her knees, and she glanced over her shoulder, as if nervous.

He didn't know what to say, but he wanted to be there for her.

"Do you want . . . Can I wash your hair?" he asked, amending the statement. He had noticed that she rarely asked for anything, even when she wanted it.

She was so used to giving, but not used to receiving. So if he had asked "Do you want me to wash your hair?" she would never admit to wanting that. But if he asked, "Can I wash your hair?" it let her know that it wasn't any trouble, that he wanted to.

She bit her bottom lip, thinking. Then, she nodded.

She reached over for the shampoo, silently handing it back to him. His pulse quickened. He had never shared such intimacy with anyone.

Crouching down beside the bath, he lathered the shampoo onto his hands, then worked it into her hair. She tilted her head back, releasing a long breath. He washed the shampoo from her hair with a rinse cup.

She closed her eyes and he saw her cheeks shine with tears. His heart twisted painfully. He didn't know what to say; he didn't think there was anything to say. So he continued washing her hair, hands gentle.

When he finished, she wiped at her eyes, then noticed black on her fingertips from where all her kajal and mascara had smudged. "Can you give me a makeup wipe?" she asked. "They're in the drawer."

He did as requested, watching as she wiped around her eyes to get all the makeup off.

It was his first time seeing her bare-faced. She was always beautiful but there was something especially beautiful about her now. She looked so . . . young. He knew she *was* young, but it was the only word he could think of.

He was so used to her looking like someone who was perfectly in control and in charge, someone who didn't need anyone—but, like this, she looked like she could need him. Like he could take care of her.

"Thank you," she whispered. "I'll be out in a second."

Nodding, he rose to his feet. He left, closing the door behind him.

In her bedroom, he went to her bookshelf, looking at her collection. He spotted a worn copy of *Letters to Milena*, and he thought about one of his favorite passages, how Kafka wrote that—in his mind—he was dressing Milena with light, wrapping her in blankets of complete acceptance and giving himself to her.

Luke wished he could do the same with Emmeline, that he could make her feel safe, always.

The bathroom door opened, and he turned as Emmeline came out, all dried up. She was dressed in a silk pajama set, a camisole and shorts that were criminal.

She stood by the doorway, a little nervous, and he went over to her.

"Okay?" he asked, peering into her eyes.

CHAPTER 30

"Okay?" Luke asked, and Emmeline didn't know how to respond. She had never been more okay.

He had washed her hair. It was indescribable. She had never been more vulnerable or more afraid in her life, yet she couldn't bear to keep him away. So she had let him in, and it had been the most intimate moment she'd ever experienced, as if they had stopped being two separate people and had instead become one.

"Yes," she said. "Better than okay."

He cupped her face in his hands, and she turned her cheek to press a kiss into his palm. She stepped forward, wrapping her arms around his torso. He held her flush against him, the pair of them fused as they breathed together.

"Can I tell you something?" he whispered against her hair. She pulled back to gaze into his eyes.

He ran his thumbs over her cheeks. "I love you," he said, and the breath caught in her throat. "A part of me has loved you since the night we met. Loving you was inevitable. I mean, how can I not? Look at you!" He smiled. "Emmy, you're the most extraordinary person I've ever met. Knowing you feels like life's greatest privilege. You have the biggest heart of anyone I know—too big. And you're more beautiful than anyone has the right to be. It's like I dreamed you up."

"Luke, I love you, too," she said, heart squeezing. "I never thought that I would ever meet someone who could make me feel so safe and loved, so entirely accepted. It's difficult for me to ask for help, to be vulnerable around others, but you make it so easy. I love you without scruples or fear or restraint."

"Because the world is ending?" he asked, tone teasing.

She shook her head. "The world is only ending when I'm not with you," she said, and he pulled her in for a kiss, pressing his lips to hers.

She hummed against him, angling her mouth to deepen the kiss as heat swept through her. Then, in a swift movement, he lifted her up, princess style, carrying her. She laughed, holding onto his shoulders as he carried her to her bed, laying her down.

His eyes darkened as he looked at her, and she pulled him over her, bringing his mouth back to hers. Heat poured through her as they kissed, making her feel like she was burning from the inside out.

The heavy weight of his body came over hers fully, and her vision sparked at the feel of him, but it wasn't enough. She wanted him entirely.

She kissed him hungrily as his hands roamed over her skin. Desire beat through her, making her ache, and she undid the buttons of his shirt, pushing it off him.

He kissed her throat, his stubble scratching against her

skin as he trailed kisses lower, down to her heart. His hands skimmed the hem of her shirt, and she lifted the fabric off, cool air on her skin for a moment before his chest pressed against hers, both of their hearts beating together.

They undressed one another, and her skin burned, tension building inside of her as they continued to explore each other's bodies, until finally, he settled over her. She dug her nails into his back, desperate to have him closer as they moved together.

Everything else faded away except for the two of them, becoming one.

CHAPTER 31

Emmeline woke well before her alarm, not wanting it to disturb Luke.

It was Monday morning, and they both had work, but she turned her alarm off.

She turned back to face him, reveling in the sight of him in the quiet morning. He was lying on his stomach, his arms under the pillow. Her gaze trailed appreciatively over the muscles of his shoulders and back before turning to his face.

Sunlight slanted into the room, a rectangle of light right over his eyes. His brow was scrunched, and she realized the light was bothering him. She brought her hand out from under the comforter, holding it out over his head to block the sunlight. His face relaxed, and she smiled to herself.

After a few minutes, the muscles in her arm strained, but he was sleeping so peacefully.

She could hold her hand up a little longer.

He must have sensed she was awake. His eyes slowly blinked open, and he furrowed his brows, noticing her hand held above his head. But then he realized she was blocking the light, and his eyes softened.

"Good morning," he said, voice rough with sleep. He reached up and held her hand, kissing her wrist. He slid toward her, pulling her against him as he buried his nose against her neck, wrapping his arms around her.

"Good morning," she replied, turning until he was half on top of her, a heavy weight.

Neither of them had dressed again after last night, and it wasn't long until her skin grew hot from the feel of his. He lifted himself up, looking into her eyes, and she smiled, reaching for his face, pulling his mouth over hers.

He kissed her, body slotting over hers, and they slept together again, this time in the bright morning. Devastating pleasure spread through her, and after, she held onto him, beaming with love.

"We have to get to work, eventually," she said lazily, lying on her stomach. He traced circles on her bare back, sighing.

"Eventually," he agreed with a smile. He leaned over and kissed her temple. Her limbs felt as though they were made of liquid; she could hardly move, she felt so relaxed and sated. They lingered for as long as they could, until it really was time to get ready.

He made eggs and she made coffee, and they ate breakfast together in her quiet home. She felt utterly at peace.

Then, it was time to get to work, and he headed for the door first; he had to stop by his place to change into a fresh set of clothes. She walked him to the door, kissing him goodbye.

"I'll see you later?" he asked. She nodded. He kissed her cheek, then headed out.

Even after he had gone, she stood there for a minute, watching the shut door, the place he had been. She pressed a hand against her heart, taking in a shuddering breath.

She loved him. She loved him so much.

All day, that fact remained with her, unavoidable, unignorable. She had never felt this way about anyone before—she had never loved someone so deeply, as if he had taken root in her heart and spread through every one of her veins.

And with that love came a dilemma.

By the end of the work day, Emmeline knew what she had to do.

She headed for Main Street, then called Anh, asking if they could meet. "There's something I'd like to discuss with you," she said, walking down the street. Motu flew beside her. The sky was darkening with evening, turning a deep shade of navy blue. Cold wind pushed against her cheeks.

"Darling, we have our meeting in a few days," Anh replied into the phone. "Can we discuss it then?"

"I'd really prefer it if we discussed it now," Emmeline said, fiddling with the end of her hair. Motu gave her a curious glance, picking up on her unsettled energy. She gave the baby dragon a tight smile. "I'm on Main Street; I can meet you wherever you are."

Anh released a short breath. "Alright—I was going to pick up a coffee from the Baby Dragon. I can give you five minutes."

"That's all I need," Emmeline replied.

She made her way over to the Baby Dragon Cafe, arriving a few minutes before Anh came in through the front door.

Anh looked immaculate as usual, dressed in a tweed coat and skirt, though her expression was one of confusion.

Emmeline met her by the front of the cafe, where Anh kissed her hello, then petted Motu's scales. "What will you have?" Emmeline asked. "I'll order for you."

"Just an espresso shot, please," Anh replied. Emmeline nodded, going to order while Anh sat down with Motu. She didn't order anything for herself, too anxious to drink caffeine at the moment. She had a carefully laid-out plan in her mind; now, things just needed to go accordingly.

When Anh's order was ready, Emmeline brought it over, setting it down on the table before sitting across from Anh. Motu sat by Emmeline's feet, and the weight of him was a solid comfort.

In a quick movement, Anh downed the shot, then looked at Emmeline curiously. "Well?" she prompted, waiting.

Heart beating fast, Emmeline took a deep breath. "I want you to give the investment to Luke," she said. Anh's brows wrinkled.

"Pardon me?" she asked, as if she hadn't heard Emmeline properly.

Emmeline swallowed. She knew it would appear strange to Anh, but Emmeline had been considering this request for a few days, though for a time she hadn't been sure if it was the right move. But now, after spending the night with Luke—after understanding that she was irrevocably in love with him—she was confident it was the right thing to do. The only thing to do, really.

He needed the investment—much more than she did—and she wanted him to be happy. Emmeline could find someone else to invest in her business, or a group of people to do so. It might be more work, but she had never shied away from hard work before.

And if she wasn't able to find investors, then she didn't need to expand right now. Perhaps it wasn't the right time, and that would be fine, too. It wouldn't be the end of the world. Her business was still thriving—in a short time, she might even gather enough capital to launch the expansion project herself, if she was clever about her savings.

Luke, on the other hand, needed this investment. And he needed it right now. There were no other options for him. If he didn't win, he would have to close Tempest, and she couldn't bear that. Not now that she knew how much it meant to him. Not now she knew how hard he had worked.

"I want you to give the investment to Luke," Emmeline repeated. Anh continued to look confused. "He deserves it, and I know he'll do a great job with the Tales & Tails coffee shop addition. And I am sure you already know Tempest's roasts are excellent."

Anh blinked, dumbfounded by Emmeline's little speech. "This isn't what we decided," she eventually said, choosing her words carefully. "You were both supposed to propose your ideas to me. I was then to choose the better candidate. It was not a complicated arrangement, Emmeline."

Her words were stern, and Emmeline flushed, embarrassed. "I know, and I am sorry to change things at the last minute," she said, but still, she didn't back down. "But Luke is better. Trust me."

Anh sat back, digesting Emmeline's words. "This is out of character," she finally said. "What's gotten into you?"

I love him, she wanted to say. *I just want him to be happy*. It wasn't out of character at all; it was perfectly in character.

But how could she explain that to Anh without Anh thinking she was being ridiculous? Without making Luke look bad? Anh wouldn't respect him if she thought he'd driven Emmeline to lose reason.

But this was the most reasonable course of action, for all of them. Emmeline wouldn't be able to enjoy winning Anh's investment if she knew it had caused Luke's downfall. She couldn't bear it.

"Nothing has gotten into me," Emmeline replied with confidence. "It's simply the right decision, and I thought it would be best not to waste your time."

"That's for me to decide." Anh narrowed her eyes, guessing there was more at play; she was shrewd, after all. "What aren't you telling me?" Emmeline didn't respond, and Anh stood. "A few days won't kill me, Emmeline. The meeting is still set for Friday. Think about whether or not you will be there."

Her stomach plummeted. "I won't change my mind," she said, standing as well.

"Nonetheless." Anh stood. "Now, I must get going. Goodbye, dear." With a quick kiss to Emmeline's cheeks, Anh left.

Watching her go, Emmeline released a long breath. She needed to guarantee that the investment would go to Luke, and this was the only way to do that without him suspecting. If she showed up to the meeting and did a poor job on purpose, not only would she ruin her reputation in front of Anh, but Luke would suspect, and she didn't want that.

She knew he would be upset if he found out what she was

doing—but she wanted to do this for him. She didn't want to win, not if it meant him losing. She wouldn't be able to bear seeing his business close, all those years of hard work down the drain. She didn't want to imagine how worried he would be, how worried his family members would be.

No, it would all be too terrible. This was what was best.

Motu nudged his head against her legs, and she looked down at the baby dragon. His purple eyes were wide, confused, and she released a long breath.

"It's going to be okay," she told him, reaching down to scratch his chin. "It's all going to be okay."

She headed out of the cafe, turning down Main Street onto Elderberry Lane, going up to the bookshop. When she entered, the bookshop was busy with the usual stream of customers, but she spotted Luke chatting with Minh at the front table.

Her pulse quickened when she saw him, and he turned as the front door dinged, as if he had been waiting for her to enter. When he spotted her, a wide smile spread across his face, and she went over, Motu flying beside her.

"Hi," she said, and he pulled her in for a kiss.

"Hi," he replied. Motu knocked into him, as if offended he hadn't received any attention, and Luke smiled, petting him hello, as well.

Minh was watching them, smiling to himself. "I see you two have finally rekindled your flame from all those years ago."

Luke laughed, tucking a slightly embarrassed Emmeline into his side. "How do you even remember that?" she asked, surprised by the old man's memory.

Minh waved a hand. "Some of the very best stories are the ones that are real," he told them. "If you spend enough of your time reading like I do, then you'll start to recognize which ones those are as they play out in front of you."

Emmeline looked up at Luke, and he met her gaze. He leaned forward to kiss her cheek, and as he did, he whispered, "I love you," into her ear.

She loved him, too. Which was why she was even more resolved that the conversation she had had with Anh was necessary. It was the best course of action.

She would talk to Anh again in a day or two; she would convince her. It would all be okay.

They went to the office, pulling out their work. Motu lounged lazily on one of the chairs while Emmeline scrolled through her proposal, which was all but finished now. She expected to feel disappointed at all that work amounting to nothing—but she didn't.

She looked over her laptop to Luke sitting beside her, the focused expression on his face. Her heart squeezed. She had never minded doing things for the ones she loved, even if it didn't get her any credit.

"Hey, you okay?" Luke asked a little while later. "You've been staring off into space."

"Oh." She blinked. "Yeah, I think I'm just tired." She cleared her throat. She didn't want him to suspect, so she closed her laptop, standing. "I'm actually going to head up for the Baby Dragon Book Club."

Luke furrowed his brows. "Isn't it early?" he asked, while she gathered her things. "Are you sure you're okay? Do you need a painkiller or anything?"

She gave him a fond smile. "No, I think I just need some sleep. I recall not getting much last night."

He smiled at that, and she went over to kiss him. "I love you so much."

A crease appeared between his brows. He looked up at her carefully.

"Why are you saying it like that?" he asked.

Her heartbeat quickened. "Like what?"

"I don't know . . ." He trailed off. "What's going on?"

"Nothing." She shook her head, giving him an easy smile.

CHAPTER 32

Emmeline was acting weird on Monday evening, but Luke couldn't understand why. He didn't think it had anything to do with them sleeping together because she seemed perfectly content in that department, but there was *something*.

He felt it had to do with the proposal, because she didn't do any work on Monday evening and left for the Baby Dragon Book Club meeting a whole half-hour early. Before then, her focus had been frayed, as if she was anxious about something.

Then, on Tuesday, she didn't come to the bookshop. When he called her to ask, she said she was visiting her parents, that she would see him soon.

He thought it was strange. Their meeting was on Friday, and he expected her to be going over every last detail. He knew how clever she was, and he was certain her proposal was going to be an absolute knock-out. Even he was looking forward to seeing all her ideas, and he was sure Anh was just as eager.

While he'd worked hard on his own proposal, he was already kind of resigned to not winning, not when he was up against Emmeline—and that was okay. It was a bit disappointing and regrettable, but it wasn't the end of the world. Just the end of an era.

He could sell Tempest, then get another job working for a company rather than running his own business. It wasn't ideal, but he found nothing bothered him too much, these days. Not when he had Emmeline. He didn't care if all of his good luck had been used up in getting her. He could manage anything else, as long as he had her.

But then, on Wednesday, as he was heading to the bookshop, he received a call from Anh.

"Anh, hello," he said. "Is everything alright?"

"You tell me," she replied curtly. "Emmeline has called me again to insist there is no need for our meeting on Friday."

He stopped in the middle of Elderberry Lane, confusion washing over him. "I don't understand," he managed to say. *Why would she say such a thing?*

"Neither do I," Anh said. "She has gotten it into her mind that there's no need for the meeting—not when the investment should go to you, anyway."

He blinked, thinking he'd heard incorrectly. "I'm sorry, what?" His stomach twisted as the words sunk in. Emmeline wanted Anh to give him the investment?

Just like that?

Anh released a breath. "She's asked me to give you the investment, but I've told her the meeting will go forward as planned," she said, her voice carrying an edge. "But I do hope this idea hasn't somehow come from you. I would be deeply disappointed if so."

"No, of course not," he replied immediately, anger going through him at the accusation. "Absolutely not."

"Good," Anh said, voice softening slightly. "Still, I don't understand. It's out of character for Emmeline not to see something through until its end."

"I'll speak with her," Luke said. "We will both see you on Friday."

"Good," Anh said, then hung up.

It was freezing out, but his blood ran hot through his veins. Emmeline had asked Anh to simply *give* the investment to him? And it sounded like she hadn't only made this request once.

His thoughts raced as understanding dawned upon him.

And that only made him angrier. Anh was wrong; it wasn't out of character, what Emmeline was trying to do.

It was what she always did: thought of others before she thought of herself. She was going to let him win because she loved him, even if it meant she lost.

He stalked to the bookshop, utterly exasperated. When he entered, he spotted her browsing the bookshelves. No notebook, no notes, nothing.

The sight only further increased his ire. So that was why it had seemed like she hadn't done any work on Monday, why she hadn't shown up yesterday. She had already decided to give up—for him.

He stalked over to her. "Sterling," he snapped, and she glanced up, surprised by his tone. "Come with me."

Taking her hand, he walked her to the office. He shut the

door behind them, trying to catch his breath, but he could hardly think straight.

"Luke, what is it?" she asked, eyes concerned. "Is everything okay?"

"No," he said, voice hard. "Everything is not okay." He broke off, clenching his jaw, and Emmeline reached for him, but he held up a hand, stopping her.

"Luke—" she started.

"Why?" he asked, finally finding his voice again. "*Why* would you tell Anh to give me the investment?"

Her expression softened, the worry fading away. Stepping toward him, she touched a gentle hand to his cheek, but he shook his head.

"Because I want you to win," she said. Frustration beat through him. She was impossible.

"Even if it means you'll lose?"

"I can find another investor," she said. Of course she had an explanation; she would have gone through the entire reasoning to make it seem okay. She always thought she was so clever, the cleverest person in the room, but she wasn't always right.

He made an irritated sound, his temper flaring. "And I can't?"

Her brows wrinkled. "That's not what I'm saying—I'm just trying . . ." She broke off, sighing. "Please, let me do this for you. I want to."

"What about what I want?" He ran an agitated hand through his hair. "Em, how could you possibly think I would be okay with a situation like this? That I would just let you throw away all your hard work for my sake?"

Her eyes widened. He shook his head, chest burning. "You really think I'm that selfish—that self-centered? That I would just accept this?"

"No, that's not what . . ." She made a frustrated sound, stepping toward him. He stepped back, too upset with her. Hurt crossed her face. "I just want to help."

"I don't want your pity!" he cried. It wasn't fair, or right.

He knew she was coming from a good place, but he hated the thought of her giving up something she wanted for anyone, let alone for him. He couldn't bear it.

He didn't want her to do this, to give up something she wanted just for his sake. If he tried to say that, she would say it was fine—she was used to it.

But he didn't want that. Not between them.

He wanted them to be partners—equals.

"It's humiliating," he said through gritted teeth. Her eyes widened with despair. "And insulting. Anh thought that I had put the idea in your head."

"Luke, I'm sorry," she said. "I never meant for it to come across that way. I only wanted—"

Even though it killed him to do so, he needed her to understand he wouldn't let her sacrifice her happiness or success for him. He cared about her more than any stupid investment. And he wouldn't let her set this precedent in their relationship.

"I need some space," he said, holding up his hands. She shrank back, lip trembling. Every part of him wanted to reach for her, to hold her in his arms, but he knew that if she thought he was angry with her, then maybe she wouldn't do this.

He headed for the office door, barely looking at her. As he opened the door, he turned back, where she was standing completely still, watching him.

"I'm not going to speak to you until the meeting on Friday," he said, voice stern. "I'll see you there."

With that, he stalked away.

He left the bookshop, the frigid evening air helping to cool some of his anger. He wouldn't let Emmeline do this—he couldn't.

But he knew she was stubborn, more stubborn than he was. If she really wanted to, she would still go through with it, hoping he would just forgive her, afterwards. And she was right; a part of him knew that he would forgive her anything, no matter how much it hurt him—but he hated what she was doing, and he would try to stop her if he could.

He didn't want her selflessness. He wanted her to be selfish, to do whatever it took to guarantee her own happiness. *That* would make him happy.

But she would never think of herself first. Maybe it was him who needed to.

He pulled out his phone, dialing Anh as he paced down the street.

"Did you speak with Emmeline?" Anh asked, picking up.

"Yes," he said, out of breath. "And I agree that there's no need for the meeting. The investment should go to her. She—"

Just as he was about to put forth his case, Anh released a short breath. "You're both irritating me now," she said, sounding the closest to irked that he'd ever heard her. "I'll see the pair of you on Friday. We will discuss matters then."

She hung up before he could argue.

CHAPTER 33

Emmeline couldn't bear Luke being angry with her.

It had been an entire twenty-four hours since they'd spoken, and he'd held true to his word. Despite her messages and calls, he hadn't replied, and she knew that he wouldn't. Not until he saw her at the meeting with Anh tomorrow.

While she hated that he was angry with her, she knew she was doing the right thing. He needed this more than she did—why didn't he understand that? It cost her nothing to make this sacrifice for him. She would do it gladly!

She walked down Main Street, holding a to-go cup from the Baby Dragon Cafe, but even the karak chai wasn't enough to soften her mood. She was a tempest of emotions, the pressure building within her like clouds filling with water until they broke with rain.

She hadn't meant to hurt Luke—of course she didn't think he was selfish or self-centered. She was trying to do something for him, to do something for the man she loved.

What was so wrong with that?

She was determined for him to win. Which was why she

decided she would show up to the meeting, then leave out the key points of her proposal. She would make sure Luke's was better.

The situation would need to be handled with finesse. She couldn't be obvious about sabotaging herself or Luke would only be angrier; at the same time, she couldn't do a phenomenal job with her proposal and risk winning.

Emmeline paced down Main Street, finishing off her chai. As she passed one of the side streets, she spotted a familiar figure and paused.

She would recognize Ginny and Fang anywhere—but who was that guy she was talking to?

Emmeline stepped closer, recognizing the scar on his neck. It was Flint.

"For fuck's sake," she muttered, livid. Fierce protectiveness came over her. What was wrong with this guy? Emmeline didn't hesitate. She stalked over, rushing to Ginny's side. Fang made a sound of warning, and Ginny turned towards Emmeline, brows furrowing.

"Emmy, what—" Ginny started, but Emmeline ignored her, instead glaring at Flint.

"Whatever the hell is going on here is done," she said. "Stay away from my cousin."

Flint rolled his dark eyes.

"What are you doing?" Ginny seethed at Emmeline, annoyed. Emmeline ignored her, instead focusing her glare on Flint.

"Go on," she said, crossing her arms over her chest.

Flint gave Ginny a final glance. "Think about it," he said, and then he left. Staring daggers, Emmeline watched him go, making sure he didn't try and return. Once he was well and truly gone, Emmeline turned back to Ginny—only to find her cousin had already walked away.

Emmeline chased after her. "Hey!" She grabbed Ginny's arm, and Ginny threw her off. "Ginny!"

Her younger cousin whirled on her, and Emmeline was taken aback by the furious expression on her face. Even Fang hissed at her, clearly upset by Ginny's dark mood. Emmeline blinked, holding her hands up.

"I was only looking out for you," Emmeline said, trying to keep her voice gentle.

"I can take care of myself, thanks," Ginny said.

"Come on," Emmeline replied. "Do you even know who that is?"

"Yes. He works with the people in charge of the races."

Ginny had never kept it a secret that she was interested in dragon racing, but her dragon was much too young. Fang may have had accelerated growth and an early first flight at seven months, but he was still only a year old. The earliest a dragon could be saddled up was two, and even that was early. The youngest they could enter the championship was four.

Even then, Emmeline knew not a single person in the entire extended Sterling family would approve of Ginny racing, even if Danny used to. He had died only a few months after winning his first championship.

"He's dangerous," Emmeline said. "Luke knows him and he's a bad guy."

Ginny rolled her eyes, and her cavalier attitude made Emmeline's heart race with worry. She didn't know too much about the races or the gangs that ran them, but she didn't want to, either. It was an entirely different world, away from the cozy and comfortable hamlets of Starshine Valley.

"I can handle myself," Ginny said, crossing her arms over her chest. "I'm not as brittle as you all think."

"I'm only trying to protect you—" Emmeline started again.

"Well don't!" Ginny snapped, a nerve clearly struck. Her cheeks were flushed with anger. "You don't have to take care of everyone and everything!" She shook her head. "You just use it as an excuse to run away from your own problems."

They both paused, Ginny's words hanging between them. Ginny's eyes widened with regret, as if she had said too much.

"Oh my god?" Emmeline said, breaking the silence as she realized maybe Ginny was right. "I-I'm sorry," she said. Maybe she could get a little carried away. "I shouldn't have cut in. You are an adult."

"Yes, I am," Ginny replied. She released a long breath, looking up at the sky before turning back to Emmeline. "I'm sorry for being mean."

Emmeline's lips twitched as she looked at her cousin. "You don't really look sorry."

Ginny shrugged. "Well, what I said *was* true . . ."

"Yeah, but it was still brutal."

"You'll survive. You are *my* cousin, after all." Ginny cracked a smile, and Emmeline laughed. She suspected that Ginny might be the strongest of all of them. "Now come on; you owe me a treat."

Emmeline had no idea what for, but she looped her arm with her cousin's. Sensing they had made up, Fang relaxed, happily jumping into the air to fly behind them as the girls walked over to the Rolling Pin Bakery, picking up gooey cinnamon buns.

The bakery was small, with only a table or two, so they stood by the counter, eating inside in the warmth. Luckily, the place wasn't rushed, and Fang wasn't fully grown, so the baby dragon hung out by their feet.

"I know you guys only look out for me because you love me, but it can be overbearing, sometimes," Ginny said, picking apart her cinnamon roll. Her voice was smaller than before.

"When you love someone, you take care of them," Emmeline said.

"I know, but it shouldn't get to the point where you're making the other person afraid," Ginny said, still looking at her sweet treat. "Or overriding the other person's autonomy."

Emmeline nibbled on her lower lip. That was a valid point. "I guess sometimes things get out of hand," she admitted. "It's hard to realize when things have gone too far."

"You can take care of people, but you have to let them make their own decisions, even if you don't agree," Ginny said. "Even if it isn't what you think is best."

"Since when did you get so wise?" Emmeline asked, picking apart her cinnamon roll.

Ginny lifted her chin. "I've always been wise; you guys just insist on treating me like a baby all the time."

"Because you are *our* baby," Emmeline teased, and Ginny glared. Emmeline held up her frosting-covered hands. "You're right. I'll be better, promise."

Ginny smiled. "Good." Then she grumbled, "And while you're at it, tell Aiden, too."

Emmeline raised her brows. "Hey, I'm not a miracle worker, okay? I don't think Aiden is ever going to stop being protective of you. Especially since Danny—"

Ginny's eyes shone, and she hastily blinked. She stabbed her cinnamon roll. "I'll deal with him myself," she said, ending that conversation.

"Good luck," Emmeline replied. "To you and to him."

After finishing off their treat, Emmeline hugged her little cousin goodbye, and they went their separate ways. She stood and watched as Ginny walked down the street, Fang flying beside her.

Emmeline still worried for Ginny, but Ginny was right: Emmeline had to let her make her own decisions, even if she didn't agree or think it was best.

Calling Torch, Emmeline visited her parents' place, where she had left Motu yesterday. Haris's winter class was almost over, and while Samreen was back from Millie's, so she could have watched Motu now, Emmeline found she missed the little guy. It was only another week, anyway, then Haris would be watching Motu himself.

At her parents' place, Emmeline went to the kitchen, where Samreen was cooking a simple mutton curry for dinner.

"Hi, Ammi," Emmeline said, kissing her mother's cheek.

"Hello, jaani," Samreen replied, stirring the pot. "Can you cut those tomatoes up for me?"

"Sure," Emmeline said. Before she did, she went to kiss Motu hello; the baby dragon was playing with his toys in the living room.

She helped her mom cook dinner, the two of them chatting as they worked. It was nice. Emmeline asked her how it was being back at work after being away, and Samreen told her all about it.

It was a good distraction from worrying about Luke and the meeting with Anh tomorrow.

When dinner was ready, they set the table, then called everyone to eat together. Motu came to eat with them, sitting calmly on the side.

"He's so well behaved," Charles said. "Look how he's eating his food."

"He still has his moments," Emmeline said. Motu gave her an adorable look, and she shook her head at him. It was impossible to be angry with him, anyway.

"Well, Haris's class is almost over, so then he'll have to deal with him," Naveed said, tearing a piece off his roti.

"But if he's studying and needs a babysitter, then I'm sure Emmeline can still watch Motu," Samreen added.

Irritation flashed through Emmeline. She wasn't going to say anything, the way she never said anything, but then she thought of that day she had been overwhelmed, when Motu had made the smoothie explode all over her kitchen.

Being overwhelmed wasn't anything new, but what Luke had said had struck her. *You're allowed to be tired*.

And if she was allowed to be tired, she was also allowed to say no.

"I could, but I think Haris can look after Motu, now," Emmeline said.

Samreen frowned. "But—" she started, when Haris cut in.

"Yeah, I can look after him," he said. "He is my responsibility, after all."

"But medical school is so difficult," Samreen said.

"I know, and I appreciate Emmy helping me out these past few weeks, but I can do it," Haris restated, voice firm.

"Well, if you need help, and Emmeline doesn't want to, *I'll* help," Samreen said, an edge in her voice. Guilt rang through Emmeline. She considered amending her refusal, when Haris let out a sigh.

"I can do it, Ammi," Haris said. "If you let me."

Samreen was offended by his tone. "I'm only trying to help."

"I know, and I appreciate it," he replied. "But I can do it, too."

"Yeah, he'll be fine," Naveed piped in.

Samreen looked harassed. "I'm just looking out for you all," she protested, setting down her fork. "Is that such a crime? I am your mother. I just want you to be okay."

Naveed leaned back in his chair. "But then you drive yourself crazy, or drive Emmy crazy, and then she drives us crazy," Naveed said. "Just relax."

"Yeah," Haris agreed. "It's not the end of the world if the house is a little messy or we eat out sometimes. You don't have to tire yourself out doing all this work if it's just going to put you in a bad mood. Then we feel bad, and what's the point?"

Samreen and Emmeline exchanged a glance. It felt as if this was something the boys had discussed. She hadn't realized they were paying attention or noticing such things, but maybe she had never given them enough credit.

"You do drive me crazy," Emmeline admitted to Samreen, lips twitching.

"Well, I'm your mother," Samreen replied, unapologetic.

"It's my right." Her lips also twitched. The conversation changed, moving on, but her brothers' words stuck with her.

It made her think about Luke, the situation with the investment. She was so adamant about doing this for him, but she hadn't thought about how upset he was with her.

She wanted him to win because she loved him, but what was the point if that made him angry with her?

CHAPTER 34

The day of the meeting arrived. It was right after work, at Anh's offices, and Emmeline still wasn't sure what to do.

As the time grew closer, her anxiety increased. She wanted what was best for Luke, but she also didn't want to upset him. As she gathered her things to head out, she was still deciding what to do.

Her phone rang, and her heart lurched when she saw who it was.

"Luke," she said, picking up.

"I'll see you soon," he said.

Before she could respond, he hung up. She had missed his voice. It had only been a few days, but she missed him terribly. All of him. She needed things to be okay again.

That was the simple truth.

And so, after work at Inferno, she made her way to Anh's office. She didn't want to upset Anh by not showing up, either. When she arrived, Luke was already there, waiting in the meeting room, and the sight of him made her catch her breath.

She hadn't seen him for the past few days, and the sight of him now was devastating. He was so handsome. He was hers.

He glanced up, meeting her gaze, and his expression softened. She didn't know what to say to him, so she went and sat down across from him, pulling out her laptop. His was already out in front of him, and Emmeline thought of all the hard work he'd done to establish his business, how this was the last chance to save it.

But then she thought about Luke, being there for her. Luke, washing her hair, his hands gentle. The way he held her in his arms, the way he kissed her and took care of her and loved her.

How angry he had been when he'd learned what she was trying to do. She loved him, but she couldn't do anything that would make him angry with her, even if she thought that was what was best. She couldn't risk losing him.

"Luke—" she started, but just then, the door to the meeting room opened.

Anh entered, done up perfectly as usual—though her expression was sterner than Emmeline had ever seen it.

Luke and Emmeline both stood, and Anh held up a hand, motioning for them to sit as she took the seat at the head of the table. She folded her hands over one another, looking at both of them sharply.

"What is wrong with both of you?" she asked, voice calm. Emmeline blinked. "I chose you as contenders for this project because I know you both to be intelligent and determined. Yet now both of you are trying to simply let the other win."

"What?" Emmeline asked, gaze snapping over to Luke. "You were trying to let me win?"

His mouth fell open at her angry tone. "It's the exact same thing you were trying to do to me!"

"That was different!" she argued.

"How?" he asked, eyes blazing. "Why is it so easy for you to be selfless but so hard to let others be selfless for you?"

She blinked, his words sinking in. Her heart softened. "But—"

"Enough!" Anh said, annoyed now. "There is a simple and obvious solution. Frankly, I cannot believe neither of you have realized it."

"What?" Luke asked, confused.

Anh rolled her eyes. "My idea from the very beginning," she said, impatient with them now. "I'm fond of you both, so I'll forgive how much you've irritated me this past week."

"What idea?" Emmeline asked, not catching on to what Anh was saying.

Anh released a long breath. "The two of you should consolidate your businesses into one," she said. "Your products are similar enough, and such a step would surely increase profit margins."

Emmeline blinked, struck by the realization. They could work together. Nobody had to lose; they could both win.

"Why didn't I think of that?" she asked, mouth hanging open.

Anh's lips quirked. "Because love makes you stupid."

Emmeline looked over at Luke. "What do you think?" she asked, standing up. She walked around the meeting table. "Think we can be partners instead of rivals?"

He smiled, meeting her halfway. "I'd love to be your partner."

Anh clapped her hands. "Wonderful!" She stood, smoothing out her skirt. "That's settled then. You'll both work on the coffee shop, and I'll invest in your joint venture."

"Wait," Emmeline said, confused. "Don't you want to see our plans first?"

Anh released a breath, heading for the door. "No," she said. "We can discuss details in another meeting. I've had enough of you two for this week." Emmeline's cheeks warmed, and Anh gave them a final glance over her shoulder, her expression stern. "Now make up already and kiss. You'll be much more bearable afterwards."

With that final order, Anh left. Emmeline's heartbeat quickened as she turned to Luke.

"You heard her," she said.

He grinned and pulled her into his arms.

EPILOGUE

It was the beginning of December, and Luke was waiting.

He had planned everything out, but there was one thing he couldn't plan. So he checked the weather and waited, holding onto the secret. He wanted to tell Emmeline about his plans almost every day—it was impossible keeping anything from her—but he knew the surprise would be worth it.

And then, on the seventh, the thing he was waiting for arrived.

The season's first snow.

Today was the day.

He looked out the window from his office at the new roasting plant, where dragons and chimeras both roasted different blends of coffee for Inferno after the acquisition of Tempest and a hefty investment from Anh. It had all worked out in the end. Inferno was flourishing; Tempest had been saved from ruin; and Emmeline had been able to realize her plans of expanding the company's distribution across Starshine Valley and beyond.

Outside, the sky was marbled gray and white with clouds. The weather forecast predicted a one hundred percent chance of snow later that evening, and the sky seemed to confirm it. He'd been watching the weather all day.

Around five o'clock, when the work day was ending, Luke pulled out his phone, calling Minh. His gaze strayed to the door of his office, hoping his boss wouldn't come in and interrupt. While he loved working with Emmeline, it was decidedly difficult to keep anything from her when they worked in the same building and lived in the same cottage.

He had been carrying around a little box every day for the past week in his inside pocket for that same reason. Her hands were always exploring his body, and he knew she'd spot the box if it was in any of his pant pockets.

"Luke, hello," Minh said, picking up. "Is today finally the day?"

"Yes," he replied, voice a whisper. He kept his gaze trained on the door. "Is around six thirty okay?"

"For this, anything," Minh replied, and he heard the smile in his voice.

He released a breath. "Wish me luck."

"You won't need it," Minh replied jovially, hanging up just as his office door opened. Emmeline entered, her hair twisted up in a clip.

"Hey," he said, getting up from his seat.

"Hi," she replied. "Who was that?"

"Farhan," he said, the excuse ready. He met her halfway, pulling her into his arms so she couldn't tell that he was lying. "I was going to pop by my parents' for a bit to check in on Mama, but after that, I'm taking you out."

She pulled away, meeting his gaze with a smile.

"Really?" she asked, twining her arms around his neck. "What for?"

"Do I need a reason?" he asked, then he pretended to think about it. "How about because I love you?"

"That suffices," she replied, pleased.

"Perfect. Meet me at the bookshop around seven, and we can head out from there."

"Mmkay," she said. "Where are we going?"

"You'll see." He squeezed her waist, and she narrowed her eyes at him.

"You've been acting very suspiciously lately," she said.

His heartbeat quickened. "Gotta keep you on your toes," he replied with a laugh.

He could see she was about to interrogate him, so he pulled her in for a kiss, and that promptly shut her up. He spun them around, then broke away. She had a dazed look in her eyes, and he quickly kissed her cheek.

"I'll see you later!"

Before she could protest, he grabbed his coat and went straight for the door.

He flew on Sharptooth to his parents' place; he'd left everything he would need at theirs. There, he got ready, then grabbed his things, giving his mom a kiss goodbye before heading out.

"Wish me luck," he said, nervous now that the time was here.

Rhea laughed, touching his cheek. "You won't need it."

Minh had said the same thing, and from a logical standpoint, maybe he wouldn't, but still . . . It was only natural to worry when it came to one of the most important moments of his life.

He headed out, and Sharptooth bumped her head against Luke's chest. "No, you're right," he agreed. "I need to stay calm. Everything will be fine."

Still, his palms were sweating.

He mounted, and they set off, stopping to pick up flowers—red roses—then going to the Tales & Tails Bookshop. It was a minute before six thirty, and Luke saw Ola heading for the door, turning the OPEN sign to CLOSED.

As she came out, she didn't lock the door. Instead, she handed the keys to Luke. She patted his shoulder, then quietly left, and he took a deep breath, heading in. The shop was empty, all his for the night, just like he'd asked Minh.

Getting to work, he created a path of red flower petals and candles, leading from the front door to the shelves, where he set up the books he had brought. He glanced over to the coffeeshop extension in the middle of the first floor, the perfect union of both his and Emmeline's ideas. It served roasts from both her dragons and his chimeras and had been a roaring success ever since it opened, bringing a new layer of vibrancy to the already bustling bookshop.

Once everything was ready, he dimmed the lights, waiting.

He heard the front door ding as it opened.

"Hey!" Emmeline's voice called as she entered. His heartbeat quickened; a year later and it was still exciting being the object of her attention.

He heard her gasp; she must have seen the rose petals and

candles. "How come the front door said the shop is closed?" Her voice was getting closer. "What's going on?"

"Over here!" he called back, anticipation racing through him.

He took a deep breath as she rounded the corner towards him.

"Wha . . ." she started. Then, she stopped in her tracks, eyes wide.

Because right next to him, written across the spines of four books on the bookshelf were the words to the most important question he would ever ask anyone:

WILL YOU MARRY ME?

She clapped a hand over her open mouth.

"Emmeline," he said, going down on one knee. He pulled the little box out of his pocket, opening it to reveal a sparkling diamond ring. His hand shook. "Years ago, we met in this very bookshop, and then last year, it was this bookshop that brought us together again."

He took a deep breath, and her eyes shone with tears.

"No matter how many books I've read and loved over the years, our story is always going to be my favorite because it features you, my favorite person. You're better than anything anyone could have imagined or dreamed."

She stepped towards him, and he looked up at her, the beautiful woman he loved. His heart trembled.

"I've always found comfort in words, but since falling in love with you, it feels like there are no words adequate enough for me to express what I feel for you. No grand declaration will ever be enough to show just how much I love you, but I'm hoping a lifetime of devotion will suffice. Will you do me the honor of being my wife?"

Tears fell down her cheeks as she nodded. "Yes," she said. "Yes!"

Relief poured through him, so absolute that his own eyes filled with tears.

"Really?" he asked, as she held out her hand.

"Yes!"

He slid the ring onto her finger, holding onto her hand as he rose to his feet.

"Luke," she said, squeezing his hand. "You're everything—you're my partner in every way, and there's no one else I would rather spend my life with. I love you in a way that I only imagined possible in stories, but meeting you made me realize all stories get their inspiration from truth, and the love I feel for you could inspire books until the end of time."

His heart glowed, and he pulled her in for a kiss. She twined her hands in his hair, and he held onto her waist, savoring the taste of her, the warm press of her lips. She grinned against his mouth, and he pulled away, a stupid smile on his face.

"So that's why you were being so sneaky," she said. "But why today—"

He led her to the window, turning her to look. She gasped, eyes wide.

Outside, it was snowing.

"The season's first snow," he said, wrapping his arms around her from behind. She leaned against his chest.

Together, they watched the snow shimmering as brightly as the ring on her hand.

ACKNOWLEDGMENTS

Alhamdulillah; that's book eight, which feels a little unreal! Thank you for returning to Starshine Valley with me again!

This story would not exist without the tireless effort of everyone who worked with me behind the scenes, so thanks are in order. Thank you to my lovely agents, Victoria Marini and Sheyla Knigge. Thank you to my amazing editor, Amy Baxter: you make every book a true joy, and I adore working with you! Thank you to Penny Isaac for your ever thorough copy-edit. Thank you to Anne O'Brien for your wonderful proofread.

Thank you to the entire team at Avon UK for bringing this book to life. Thank you to Sarah Foster for the cover and interior design. Thank you to Alex Cabal for the cover illustration. Thank you to Emily Hall and Jessica Whitehead in Marketing for your work promoting my book. Thank you to Sara Eusebi and Emily Scorer, on the sales team, and the entire team at Harper 360 for getting this work out in the

US: Emily Gerbner, Sophia Wilhelm, Jean-Marie Kelly and Kamrun Nesa.

Thank you to my family: Mama, Baba, Sameer, Zaineb, and Ibraheem. Thank you to my best-friend-cousins, Hamnah, Umaymah, Noor, and Mahum. Thank you to my best friends: Arusa, Isra, Sara, Justine and Ifrah. I love, love, love you all!

Thank you to anyone who's read my work or spread the word; I appreciate it deeply.

Please pray for me. Until next time xx

Loved *The Baby Dragon Bookshop*? Don't miss this exclusive first look at *Rider of Dragons*!

CHAPTER 1

"Absolutely not," Edmund snapped at his daughter.

"Darling, no matter how many times you ask, the answer will still be no," Cecilia said, trying to be the good cop to her husband's bad, but Genevieve wasn't convinced by either performance.

She was in her father's office at their family estate, arguing with her parents about the same thing they had been arguing over for years. The problem was they never took her seriously, even though she was now twenty-four.

"Today is the only day to enrol," she said. It was May 1, two months before the Dragon Rider's Championship kicked off, with the first Grand Stake Duo on July 1. "I need to secure my spot."

She was doing them the courtesy of informing them now rather than telling them afterwards, but as they both huffed and puffed as if they did not know what to do with her, she came to the grim realization that she should have just told them after it was done. She genuinely loved and respected her parents; she didn't *want* to do things that would hurt them if it could be avoided.

"You're much too young," Cecilia said, standing beside Edmund. He was sitting down at the grand mahogany desk in his office, Genevieve across from them.

"I'm only a few months younger than Danny was when he raced his first championship," she protested. Mention of her dead brother sent a pang through her chest. God, she wished he was here. He would have supported her.

"That was different," Cecilia said, chin trembling. Clearing her throat, she fidgeted with the emerald drop earring hanging from her ear.

"Why?" Genevieve demanded. She already knew, but she was hoping if they said it out loud, they might finally see how ludicrous the argument was. Her father met her gaze head-on.

"He was a boy," Edmund replied.

She clenched her jaw, feeling like a kettle on the verge of shrieking. "So?" she asked.

Cecilia released a breath. "Oh, come now, it is different, you know it is," she said, trying to reason with her daughter. "Look at you! You've been raised in the utmost comfort and care. The races are brutal." She shuddered.

"But Danny—" Genevieve started.

"*Danny* shouldn't have gotten involved either, but he had experience with danger because of his rescue missions," Cecilia continued over her. "He started shadowing with the rescue team when he was sixteen. By the time he was twenty-five, he had been working in the field for three years, leading his own missions. Dear, you work at the library."

Genevieve clenched her hand into a fist at her side. She had wanted to work with the rescue teams, the same way Danny had, but she hadn't been allowed because, again, it was too dangerous. Now, that lack of experience was being used against her. The hypocrisy was staggering.

It was her parents who had encouraged her to work at the library because it would be safe, and she hadn't argued too much because she didn't care about her job for the first few years after graduating university. She was biding her time until her baby dragon, Fang, got bigger, old enough for her to saddle, then ride, and now, race.

All she wanted to do was race. For a variety of reasons, ranging from noble to sentimental to selfish. *Ask me why*, she wanted to entreat her parents. *Just ask me once.* But in all these years, they never did. To them, it didn't matter why.

"Danny should not have gotten involved in the races, either," Edmund added, agreeing with his wife. Her parents were always a united front; it was no use trying to appeal to one over the other. "But he was always adventurous."

And see where that got him. The words were not spoken, but they were implied. Danny hadn't died during a dragon race, but during a rescue mission, which was also dangerous, especially when the mission involved dealing with gangs trying to traffick stolen dragons or when the mission involved natural disasters.

His last mission had been to rescue a nest of chimeras from a forest fire. While most of the chimeras had been saved, Danny had perished with the remaining few. It had been just a few months after his win at the championship, and if talking about the races was off-limits while he was alive, it was impossible after his death.

Genevieve had always looked up to him even for the way he had died—the same way he had lived—being free and doing what he believed in. He had been boundless.

She wanted to be the same. Taking in a deep breath, she faced her parents. "I am giving you the courtesy of knowing that I am joining this year's Dragon Rider's Championship," she said, voice steady. "I wasn't asking for permission. You can't stop me."

Edmund laughed at that, and she clenched her jaw. "Sweetheart, of course we can stop you. How do you suppose you're going to pay the entry fee?"

"I have money," she replied, though she realized she was treading in deep waters as her father picked up his phone. He dialed a number, and on the other end, they picked up immediately.

"Yes," he said into the phone. "Freeze Genevieve's accounts until tomorrow. Actually, until the day after."

Her mouth jutted open. She wanted to shout, "You can't do that!" But he could, of course, he could. Most of the money in her account was his, anyway.

Since graduating, she had put her degree in Dragon History to use by working part-time at the university library in the archives, but that job hardly paid anything. Most of her time was spent training Fang as he grew from a baby dragon into a fully-grown one.

She had saddled him, getting him used to her weight before learning how to ride. They had spent every day since flying together, preparing for this year's championship season, when he was old enough to enter.

Well, nearly old enough. The recommended age was four years old, as dragons continued developing until age five, and Fang wouldn't be four until December. But he was a basalta breed—a bigger breed—and he had been well-trained since he was a baby, having his first flight a few months earlier than most baby dragons. He was ready, and so was she.

Genevieve had devoted all of her time to Fang, and riding him felt as natural as breathing; in the air, they became one, as if he was merely an extension of her limbs.

"Enough of this silliness, now," Cecilia said with a tired sigh.

"It's not silliness," Genevieve replied, on edge. Arguing with her parents made her feel like she was a teenager again, foolish and petulant.

But she wasn't a kid anymore, and while yes, she was incredibly privileged, she liked to think that she hadn't scorned those advantages. She had been a good daughter. She listened to her parents; she stayed out of trouble; she didn't cause scandal.

They rarely disagreed, except when it came to this. Dragon racing. But she was only doing the exact same things her brother had done. Why was it such an issue when she dared to follow his path, the path of so many Sterlings before him?

Ever since dragon racing began, there had been a Sterling on the track.

"Daddy," she said, imploring for one last time. Her father never refused her—except when it came to this.

He clenched his jaw, regret in his eyes. *I'm* your *daughter*,

And why not treat yourself to *The Baby Dragon Bakery*?